Dedication

To my wonderful family and wonderful readers.

By the same author

THE BOOKBINDER

The Woman and the Witch Series

THE WOMAN AND THE WITCH
AIRY CAGES AND OTHER STORIES
FRIEDA
FINDING FRIEDA

Finding Frieda

Amanda Larkman

This is a work of fiction. Names, characters, places, and incidents are the product of the author's imagination or are used fictitiously. Any resemblance to actual persons, living or dead, events, or locales is entirely coincidental.

Copyright © 2023 by Amanda Larkman

All rights reserved. No part of this book may be reproduced or used in any manner without written permission of the copyright owner except for the use of quotations in a book review.

First paperback edition April 2023
Cover design: Jem Butcher
ISBN: 9798390607374

CONTENTS

Chapter 1	3
Chapter 2	13
Chapter 3	23
Chapter 4	35
Chapter 5	48
Chapter 6	58
Chapter 7	72
Chapter 8	84
Chapter 9	100
Chapter 10	111
Chapter 11	125
Chapter 12	140
Chapter 13	154
Chapter 14	165
Chapter 15	179
Chapter 16	193
Chapter 17	205

Chapter 18	216
Chapter 19	229
Chapter 20	240
Chapter 21	252
Chapter 22	265
Chapter 23	276
Chapter 24	289
Chapter 25	305
Chapter 26	315
Acknowledgements	328
'The Woman and the Witch' series	330
About the Author	332

Chapter 1

I knew something was wrong the moment I woke up. The house was cold and seemed to turn in on itself, as if protecting a wound. Trevor wasn't lying across my feet and when I called there was no answering rustle of furry movement.

I sat up and looked across the room. The roof climbed above my head, a massive oak ribcage that creaked in the wind like an old ship.

'Trevor?' I called again.

It was still early, and I shivered, reaching for my thick dressing gown and wrapping the cord tightly round my waist. I looked under the bed. Sometimes, when Gary was home, Trevor would curl up under there - but the space was empty.

The silence was so loud it made my ears ring. The house was holding its breath. At the top of the stairs I leaned over the banister rail to look down at the hall three floors below. Sunlight was pouring across the chess board floor but there was no sign of Trevor.

I clicked my tongue, hoping to hear the scrabble of overlong claws across the tiles, picturing his brown and white fur and whiskered, now slightly greying, muzzle and curious brown eyes looking up at me, head on one side. For a second I could see him so vividly I breathed a sigh of relief, but then I blinked - and the vision was gone.

Unease stirred the hair on my arms. My little terrier always slept on the bed when Gary was away. I could ask Mrs B but there was no point in annoying her. She hated getting up early, preferring to read and drink endless cups of tea in bed until at least eleven. I looked at my watch, she wouldn't even be awake yet.

I muttered a quick seeking charm and cast the words on the air. They settled in glittering strands but told me nothing. Creaking down the stairs my breath frosted. The house hadn't felt this cold since I arrived, those chilly months I'd tolerated before persuading the old woman to put in some decent central heating.

I tiptoed down the corridor. God forbid I wake Madam up before 9.30, especially without a cup of tea and some toast in hand. Her bedroom door was closed - no Trevor curled up against the door. He'll be downstairs, I reassured myself. Looking for food perhaps. But there was a tightness in my chest. Trevor was getting old. He hated getting up early as much as Mrs B did; usually it took a lot of coaxing to get him out from under his blankets, especially if it was cold.

I wished I'd put my socks on as I skittered across the hall in my bare feet. The sun spread its honey-gold light over the floor, but it held no warmth. I poked my head into the library, sitting room, and even my old, long-neglected apartment at the back of the house, but there was still no response to my whistle.

I could feel the brush of cold air even before I got to the kitchen. The back door was wide open; I must have forgotten to lock it the night before and the wind had blown it open – or Mrs B had woken unusually early and decided to take Trevor out for a walk in the woods. My shoulders relaxed a fraction until I saw Trevor's lead, old and chewed into a thick twist of leather, hanging next to the door.

'Trevor!' The woods echoed my call. Clouds were beginning to scud across the sky, smothering the promise of the early sunshine. Dammit! He must have sneaked into the woods, rabbit season always brought out the puppy in him.

Cross now rather than anxious I climbed up the stairs back to my flat and changed into jeans and a jumper. Closing the back door behind me, I set off for the woods, a wodge of dog treats in my pocket.

The air was cold and crisp, and I took a deep breath, appreciating the drift of early summer that hung on the breeze. I was wheezing by the time I climbed to the top of the woods and reached the path that curved round to the top of the valley. My voice was hoarse from shouting.

I took a moment to savour the view, letting my thudding heart slow down. I scanned the valley looking for movement. Closing my eyes, I felt for the air and let the silk of it run through my fingers. I could feel birds and foxes, mice and rats, rabbits with their bobbing hops - but Trevor's energy wasn't there. Frowning I opened my eyes, I was sure I would sense him from up here; I could see for miles.

    I stretched my back, up to my wellies in the lush, long grass that swirled and rippled in the breeze like a deep, wide lake. Birds soared into the air above me and I looked down at Pagan's Reach with all its sleepy beauty and magical secrets. I loved its graceful proportions: its classical front and sly medieval back that was almost a thousand years old. It always looked its best as spring uncurled into summer.

    All was peaceful and lovely, the familiar view I'd fallen in love with the day I arrived. So why did I feel a pulse of anxiety as I looked at the house? Had my subconscious seen something my conscious self had passed over? A flame, or a thread of smoke. The wrong face in a window perhaps? I searched the front of the house again but there wasn't anything unusual to see. I'm getting old and paranoid, I thought.

    Periodically stopping to call for Trevor, I walked towards the house through the orchard. Dumpling, the old pony who was living out his days there came to greet me. He sniffed round, looking for the dog. I wished he was here, covered in mud and panting happily after a long walk in the wood. Where the bloody hell had he got to?

    A flash of colour caught my eye as I reached the front terrace. The thorny hedges planted either side of the wide steps had caught hold of something and held it up with spread, spiked fingers. It was a snatch of crimson material, long enough to flap back and forth in the wind. I caught hold of it and my blood froze.

    I recognised the pattern. Emerald green parrots strutting across a deep red background - the thorns had ripped fraying holes into the silk. This was from Mrs B's dressing gown; I knew it as well as my own. I'd seen it every morning for months.

The shock hammered a void into my brain, chasing away every coherent thought. I stared at the cloth, my heart pounding a tattoo in my ears. I spun round, searching the garden and trees beyond still holding the brightly coloured scrap in my hands.

I began to run. Straight up the steps, through the front door and into the hall, heedless of the mud slicking across the tiles. The squeak of my boots echoed in the hall changing to a muffled thump as I climbed the carpeted stairs.

She must be in her room, I thought as I got to the first landing and swung down the corridor. She must have taken Trevor out for an early walk and caught her dressing gown on the bushes. I bet I'd find her back in bed with a muddy Trevor lying at the end of it.

My body wasn't listening. Adrenaline was flooding into my throat and chest; I had to struggle for air and my hands were shaking. I paused for a moment in front of Mrs B's bedroom door picturing her sitting propped against a pile of pillows to support her crooked back, teacup in hand with a book on her knee, toast crumbs littering the sheets: a hundred-year-old prawn with tufts of white hair on her little pink head, and green eyes as sharp as glass.

I didn't wait to knock.

It was like opening the door onto a scream. My body recoiled. Every particle of air in the room seemed stained with a blood-red bruise, vibrating with a violence that hammered at my temples. Mrs B's bedclothes were thrown back and pillows had been hurled across the floor. I had to step back into the cool of the corridor as my skin flamed, burned by the fierce heat of what had happened in that room.

Only once before had I seen this. Years before when I was a young woman I'd visited the Tower of London torture rooms and had to run outside as the screams of the victims, their blood and pain, still choked the chambers despite hundreds of years having passed.

I forced myself to move forward. The charge in the air was so strong I felt the press of it against my eyes, my ears; it filled my sinuses. I pressed my hands to my head to ease the pressure as I searched the room.

Something terrible had happened here. My heart lurched and sickness rolled into my belly as I breathed the stench of fear and rage. There had been a fight, a deadly struggle so brutal it had changed the atoms of the room. I closed my eyes, placed my hand on the wall and tried to feel what had happened. I could see threads of different auras smashing against each other in the darkness behind my eyelids as I watched the essence of Mrs B take on an aggressive force.

The events played over and over on an endless loop, but I couldn't work out what had happened, no matter how hard I tried. I had to stop when my brain cried out in agony, the pressure of probing the air for its memories too difficult, too demanding to do for long. I realised I was still clutching the silk that was now damp and crumpled in my hand.

Using the last of the strength I had left, I stumbled to the door. I held onto the frame and gazed down the corridor, trying to follow the threads that still hung though they were fading fast. I could see nothing; they stopped abruptly at the entrance to the room.

Desperately I turned back looking for anything that could tell me what had happened. Already the charge was leaving the air and I could see the room with clear eyes.

Nothing had been touched except the bed. The books remained in their tottering piles and the jewels the old woman liked to paw through before she went to bed spilled in glittering heaps from her leather case. The curtains fluttered and I rushed to find the window open. Below, the terrace stretched, empty and cold, the thorned bushes standing guard.

*

Hours later, I limped into the house coated in mud, sweat running into my eyes. I'd searched and searched but could find no sign of the auras I'd seen in the old woman's bedroom. They had disappeared so fast I had no way of knowing which way Mrs B had gone.

For a second I'd found a splash of energy just under the window, but it had flared and evaporated just as I approached; whoever took Mrs B had fallen or jumped from the window and landed there. A sob wrenched at my chest. The old woman, my mentor and friend, despite the iron-hard strength of her character, was well over a hundred - and frail. I could pick her up like a bundle of twigs.

She was a powerful witch, but whatever had attacked her as she slept had been more than a match for her; the struggle I'd seen projected in a grotesque replay in Mrs B's room told me that. Powerful as her assailant must have been, I doubted he would have been as successful if she'd been awake when he found her.

I scraped my hands through my hair at the thought of this happening while I slept soundly in my bed up in the eyrie of my flat. Years ago, Pagan's Reach had been attacked by a wolf who had stalked Mrs B since the second world war. That night the house had woken me, warned me of the invasion; I couldn't understand how anyone could have got in without us knowing.

I'd walked from one end of the grounds to the other trying to find any trace – a tyre mark, footprints in the earth, a spiral in the air that told me a witch had passed by – anything to tell me which way Mrs B had been taken. There wasn't a single trace, not a single breadcrumb to follow.

I was exhausted but couldn't sit still. I kept walking from room to room, pacing out the thousands of square feet that made up Pagan's Reach, my sanctuary for the past four years. I was shocked to see night was already sealing the light from the windows.

The strange cold continued to steal through the house, numbing my face and hands. I couldn't face food, though I hadn't eaten anything all day, but was drawn to the kitchen. The place where Mrs B and I spent so much time bickering and chatting, drinking tea and experimenting with salves and ointments.

Rubbing my hands together for warmth, I looked round the kitchen for what felt like the millionth time. Mrs B and Trevor not being here had turned the house into a stranger; the colours had drained from the floors and walls. I longed for the comfort of a roaring fire but couldn't get it going, no matter how many charms I spoke or sparks I spilled into the waiting tinder. Why was the house so cold? Bloody boiler.

I needed to replenish, and soon, to continue looking for Mrs B. But I needed to hear what the house was trying to tell me. Dizziness made me stumble but I held onto the chair and stood. Carefully, I placed the palm of my hand against the chimney breast and leaned in, keeping my eyes closed.

I pulled away in shock. There was an emptiness I had never sensed before. Usually, there would be a swirling sense of life, like I'd plunged my head into the deepest of lakes, one that teemed with fish and plants and mysterious creatures. But not now. The heart of it was frozen.

Head reeling, I had to grab the chair to sit before I passed out. I rubbed my face, tried to muster up sparks. Eventually I tottered to the sink and splashed handfuls of the ice-cold spring water from the tap onto my face. But nothing could stop the darkness creeping from the corners of the room until I could see no more.

The fading echoes of a scream jerked me awake. The ache in my back told me I'd been on the cold flagstones for some time. I lurched to my feet, my mouth dry. It was still dark. There wasn't a sound. It was so quiet I wondered if I'd gone deaf.

I had to find Mrs B.

The thought of never finding her made me want to sink to my knees. The kindness she'd shown when I'd blown in on a storm of grief that had shaken me to my very core was something I'd never forgotten.

The day I met Mrs B I thought my life was over. Through her I'd learned of the magic I'd carried all my life, sleeping deep within my body. We'd been on so many adventures since then, but when I thought of her, I didn't think of the magnificent prophetess that could send fire from her fingers, but the impatient old woman who'd held my hand as I'd cried and shown me the strength of my power.

I was at a loss without her. Never had I understood the pain of those words. I was at a loss. I couldn't accept she was dead. I wouldn't accept it. The thought crippled, paralysed – rendered me useless.

I scrubbed at my tears until my face was dry. Mrs B's voice in my head was startling, and strong. 'Get up, Angie. You won't get anywhere snivelling on the floor.'

I stood. I'd replenish in the woods. Then I would use every single thing Mrs B had taught me to find her.

Chapter 2

Frost silvered the trees as I followed the path of the wood to the village. It was early, but I had to keep moving, and surely there would be someone up and about I could talk to.

Laurie Gray was just opening up the shop.

'Laurie!' I called out, then stopped to catch my breath.

'Angie? You shouldn't be going for jogs, not at your age.'

'I'm not going for a jog, Laurie. I've just been walking quickly.' I followed her into the shop breathing in the familiar mix of liquorice and instant noodles. 'Laurie, Mrs B is missing.'

She put down her pricing gun and brushed imaginary crumbs from her blue and white checked tunic. 'What do you mean, missing? She'll be off on one of her adventures, I'll bet - I wouldn't worry. Didn't she go to India last year?'

'Yes,' I said impatiently, 'she did. But obviously she wouldn't have gone anywhere without telling me. Have you seen anything unusual? Anyone hanging round you didn't recognise?'

Laurie's faded blue eyes lit up. 'Well, now you mention it …'

Hope leapfrogged into my mouth, and I leaned forward.

'There was something peculiar,' she said enjoying the drama, stretching out her words.

'What? What did you see? Did you see Mrs B?'

'Well, no,' she admitted, 'but there was a big van hanging about across the road. It was there a good while.'

'When was this?'

'Day before yesterday,'

'Oh,' I said, shoulders slumping. 'She went missing yesterday so that's probably not relevant.'

'It's been there on and off for weeks now. The Doc's wife was going to report it but they're off on their second honeymoon, aren't they. Not going to be bothered about reporting a loitering van.'

'Did you see who was driving it?'

'Nobody I recognised from round here. I thought it was a delivery guy – you know DPS or some such, but it didn't have any markings on the outside.'

'Laurie,' I said, looking up towards the front of the shop. 'Do you have CCTV?'

*

'I've never been in here before,' I said looking round the rather greasy little cubby hole tucked behind the tinned fruit. 'I didn't even know you had an office.'

'It's private, that's why.' Laurie opened a white cabinet which was crammed full of old video recorders and a couple of monitors. 'My son set this up for me, it's all recorded onto a disc thingummy. I'm not sure if it's any use. The camera only covers the front of the shop – stop them thieving kids from up the estate pinching stuff from the trays out there.' She continued rummaging. Impatience was making my skin itch.

'Have you found anything?' I said, desperate to get moving.

'Hang on a minute! Give me a chance, it's in one of these boxes …' Her head disappeared into the cupboard so her voice was muffled. 'You haven't been in for a while, Angie. You're not shopping at the big supermarket are you? I know you like your foreign food, you're a bit of a cook aren't you.' Laurie had a habit of making questions sound like statements; I never knew how to respond to them.

'I did go a few times last month,' I admitted, 'only because you didn't have the things I needed – I know it's difficult when you have to suit everyone … Any luck?'

Laurie reappeared, her grey hair frizzed into a dandelion cloud; there was a smudge of oil on her chin. 'He's taken it.'

'Who?'

'Damian, he keeps doing that even though I've told him a hundred times not to – he keeps pinching the discs to use in his camera. He's supposed to bring them back, but he never does.'

'Is he still living down by the old flower shop?'

'Yes, why? You going there now?'

'I am, I want to have a look at that van. Have you seen it today?'

'No – I've only just got here haven't I.'

There was a notepad pinned to the wall with a biro hanging from it on a grimy string. 'Look, here's my phone number. If you see anything, can you give me a call?'

'What am I going to see stuck behind this counter for twelve hours.' Laurie closed the cupboard with a snap.

'Right, well. I'd better be off.'

'I hope you find her. Mrs Beaudry. She's been a different woman since you moved into the house.' My mouth almost fell open at this show of uncharacteristic softness. 'You've been good for her.'

'Thanks, Laurie. That means a lot.' I was so tired I was tempted to rest my head on Laurie's blue-checked bosom and weep, not a feeling I had ever experienced before; usually I couldn't wait to get out of her shop because it was village gossip central, and Mrs B and I seemed to be a main point of interest. With a wave and a clang of the old bell over the door, I slipped out onto the street.

I suspected it was a dead end, but my pulse rate had rocketed. Glad I was wearing my trainers I bounced down the pavements as fast as I could, giving quick nods to the old boys and girls up early to fetch their newspapers and milk.

'All right, Angie!' a voice called.

Wanting to scream with frustration – Damian's flat was only feet away - I reluctantly stopped. It was Charlie Bosham. He'd been the village postman for years and had recently retired. The decades of walking up and down the hills in all weathers had taken their toll on his knees; they were swollen and red, hot with pain, and he came to me every week for easing.

'How are you, Charlie?' I said, bobbing from foot to foot.

'I'm in a bad way, love. It's the cold, gets right into my joints.'

'You need to lose some weight, Charlie,' I said, not for the first time as he hobbled towards me. 'And take the Doc's pills. I can't cure you – all I can do is ease it and that will work less and less well over time.'

'All right, all right,' he said good naturedly.

'Look, Charlie I can't stop. Mrs B's gone missing. I don't suppose you've seen her?'

His big red face creased with concern. 'I'm sorry to hear that, Ange. I haven't seen anything but I'll let you know if I hear any news. How long has she been gone?'

'Since yesterday,' I said with a gulp.

'You'd better get onto the police. You should have gone yesterday, she's a very old woman.'

'Yes, I know, Charlie. But you know what she's like. God forbid I get her mixed up with the police.'

He pulled off his woolly hat and rubbed his head. 'She wouldn't be happy, that's true. But you should still call them.'

'I will,' I said, thinking I really would have to, and soon. But how the hell would I explain some magical force had taken her? I'd sound like a mad woman – they'd never believe me.

'I'll see you later, Charlie. You take care of yourself.'

'You too,' he was off with a wave, and I grimaced to see the pain radiating in red waves from his knees and hands.

But I couldn't worry about that now. I needed to see that CCTV footage from outside Gray's. Maybe the van was nothing to do with Mrs B, but no creature could apparate inside the house, not with the shielding charms we'd set up. Any intruder would have to get in through a window or door, and they may have used that van to travel to the village.

I could smell the musk of ancient roses as I climbed the narrow stairs tucked behind the old flower shop. Lydia had retired to Marbella last year, but the trace of her wonderful blooms remained.

I checked my watch. It was still early. Chances were Laurie's feckless son would still be in bed. He worked nights at the local petrol station, so I was pretty sure he'd be in.

It took a few minutes of hammering before the door opened.

'For fuck's sake! What is it?' Damian was tall and thin with a shock of greying hair that hung in his eyes. He smelled of weed and petrol.

'Damian, remember me? Angie Tully from up on the hill. I'm a friend of your mum's. We're looking for the latest CCTV footage, your mum said you took the disc?'

He looked at me dumbly scratching at his hair until white flakes showered onto his shoulders.

'The disc, Damian. The one that records the footage from the camera outside the shop. Laurie said you borrowed them?'

Again, that blank stare. I wanted to punch him in the face.

'Damian? Oh, for God's sake.' I rubbed my fingers together and flicked some hot red sparks onto his arms.

'Ow! Fuck, man! What was that?'

As he patted at his arms, I pushed my way into the flat. Although it wasn't very clean it was very bare, so it was easy to spot the two cameras resting on the kitchen table.

'Are they in there? The discs?'

Seeing me reach for the cameras Damian sprung to life. 'Don't touch them!'

'I need to see those discs, Damian, my friend is missing, and that CCTV footage might help me find her.' I stood as tall as I could and forced fire into my eyes. 'Get them out and play them for me.'

A shifty look crossed his face.

'I don't care what you've taken pictures of,' I said. 'Just tell me. Have you already recorded over the footage from the last three or four days?'

'I don't think so, and it's a memory card not a disc. The one I took from mum is in the bigger camera.'

'Can you show me what's on it?' Urgency tightened my throat.

With slick movements he slid the back from the camera and plucked out a small chip of plastic. 'I'll have to put it into an old video camera for you to watch. I'll plug it into the TV.'

I wondered why he was being so amenable all of a sudden until he shot me a glance. 'What's this worth?' he said.

I was so infuriated I was moments away from firing a dazing charm at him, rendering him immobile for at least an hour.

That would be plenty of time to look at the video. But then I had no idea how to work the old camera, or how to plug it into the TV. I sighed. 'I've got £20 but that's it.'

He held out his hand and once he had the money safely tucked into his jeans, he flicked the TV on. I could hear the hum of the camera as he rewound it and then the view of the street from Laurie's shop jumped into view.

I took a shaky breath and squinted at the screen. It was poor quality, and I couldn't make out a great deal – it didn't help the film was in black and white – but I hoped it would be good enough to find some clue.

'Can you fast forward it?' I said. 'I'm looking for a white van.'

Damian grunted in reply and the view on the screen juddered as he whizzed it ahead. Villagers stalked past in super quick time. 'There!' I shouted. 'Stop!'

The van had sped into view and quickly left. I waited, jigging my foot, as Damian rewound the tape. He pressed play and I suffered an agony of waiting as the video moved in slow motion. Slowly, slowly, the van drove in. I couldn't make out the licence plate - something had been spattered across it.

In silence we watched the grainy image as the van door opened and a man poked out his head. Damian jumped as I hissed in shock.

I couldn't take my eyes from the screen, not even daring to blink as I watched the man drop out of the van door and walk away from the shop. Every hair on my body stood straight up. A ripple of horror took away my breath. Instinctively I covered my chest as if he was about to pull the life force from it. I pictured him turning, looking into the eye of the camera and meeting my eyes. A crazy thought – this video was from days ago – but my body was reacting as if he was in the room.

'Can you rewind more? See if he had been here any other time?'

Damian sighed and pressed the button.

The film went back five days and the van had been caught only twice. Both times the angle was such we could see nothing beyond that the driver was tall and solidly built with dark hair. He kept his head down, perhaps conscious of the camera, and quickly slipped away headed – I was sure of it – for Pagan's Reach.

'Was he there Monday? Or Sunday night?'

Damian shook his head.

I made him play the film of the van's appearances over and over again. My increasing agitation must have frightened him a little as he didn't protest. I watched until my eyes blurred, noting the size and shape of the van.

I could see nothing more of the man beyond the shadowy shape and flash of a white face. We paused on the frame but it just blurred into a fuzz of lines. I tutted with exasperation.

'Who is he anyway?'

'He's a wolf,' I said grimly.

Chapter 3

I tried not to think about what Mrs B would say if she saw me parking in front of the police station in town, ready to report her missing. In my pocket was Damian's memory card and a note on which I'd written everything I could remember about the dark-haired man.

The engine clicked as it cooled down. Restlessly my fingers picked at the fraying plastic of the steering wheel. Everything in me screamed to get out, get searching but I'd tried everything I could think of. My mind was scoured clean of ideas, and I felt light-headed with the emptiness. Someone or something magical had taken the old woman, I was certain of that fact. But the police could still help me find the van, and its driver. That would lead us somewhere, I was sure.

Every muscle in my body ached and my eyes were red-rimmed and swollen. After the sunshine of the day before, the morning was miserable. I was horribly conscious forty-eight hours had passed since I found Mrs B's empty bed and I was no closer to finding out what had happened.

I hadn't slept more than an hour. Last night I'd read into the small hours; going through the books Mrs B kept in her sitting room, away from her library, the special ones – the ones written by the hundreds of women who had lived in Pagan's Reach before us. I didn't know what I was looking for, but hoped I'd recognise anything that would help. Maybe there would be a charm that could seek out the van? Or something that could follow the wolf's trail?

Dawn was brightening the windows when my eyes began to fail. The cramped, sepia words jumped and twisted, and my head ached to try and make sense of them. I still couldn't get the house warm, and I missed Trevor. I kept glancing over at the fireplace expecting to see him, flat on his back, paws in the air, enjoying the warmth of the fire on his pink belly. I remembered how he would open one eye as I passed, not moving unless I had food or a lead in my hand.

My mind had been so consumed with worry about Mrs B I hadn't thought about Trevor. Perhaps whoever took Mrs B took the dog as well; or he'd been chased away to a place so far off he couldn't find his way home. Tears plugged the base of my throat at the thought. I pushed away the fear that something awful had happened to him.

Sheets of rain slid down the windscreen. Clouds raced thick as smoke bubbling from a cauldron, choking the light from the sun's face until it disappeared. Everything felt smothered and wretched as I got out of the car and locked it.

'I need to report someone missing,' I told the tired looking woman behind a Perspex screen.

I'd drunk three cups of revolting coffee and counted the number of cracks in the wall a thousand times before an officer finally entered the room they'd put me in. My skin itched to be trapped within these grubby four walls. The place had an institutional stink I couldn't bear. My gaze kept catching on the window as I longed to be outside, searching for Mrs B.

'Mrs Tully?'

I stood up, scraping the legs of my chair back so they screeched. A burly bear of a man was standing in the doorway a clipboard in hand. His thick blond beard was neatly clipped, and I was struck by the intensity of his unusual silvery-blue eyes. Behind him, a thin figure stood in the shadowed corridor; I couldn't tell if it was a man or a woman.

'My name is PC Mike Thurlow, thank you for waiting.' He held out his hand and I shook it. I picked up nothing from him; he was very guarded. I would have to work hard to lean into this one, I thought. 'This is PC Hawthorne.'

His companion took a seat at the table, laying out a pad of paper and placing a biro next to it.

'Aimee tells me you want to report a missing person?'

'Yes, Frieda Beaudry, my friend. She's very old and I'm very worried about her.' A wave of dizziness hit me as I said the words and I swallowed. My mouth was dry and bitter with the taste of old coffee.

Thurlow took a seat, running his thumb inside his collar where his neck bulged. He watched me as I lingered at the window before joining them at the table. Suddenly the room felt very small, and hot. I leant back a bit to create some space between me and the two of them.

'Start at the beginning,' he said.

As I spoke, Thurlow's companion took notes. Thurlow never took his eyes from my face, frowning slightly.

My fingernails rattled on the plastic surface of the table as I answered question after question. When had I last seen Mrs B? What was she wearing? Is there any reason why she would have left? Had we argued? Did she have a phone? Had she taken her cards with her?

'These questions are stupid!' I exploded. 'She hasn't run away like a rebellious teenager! She's an old woman – someone's taken her! I took out the memory card and laid it on the table. 'This is CCTV footage from the village shop. It shows a van parking there a few times in the week leading up to Mrs B's going missing. There's a man who gets out and I think …' my throat closed and I had to swallow hard. 'I think he may be the one who took her.'

The room stilled. Thurlow's chair creaked as he leaned back, rubbing the bristle on his chin so it rasped. 'What makes you think that, Mrs Tully?'

I paused. How could I explain what I knew? How I knew? I waved my hand in a useless gesture. 'I just have a feeling … she wouldn't leave me like that. And this man, he seems very … harmful.'

'I'll get this copied, if I may?' I nodded and Thurlow handed it to his companion who ducked out of the room. 'Could Mrs Beaudry have gone for a walk? Fallen and hurt herself?'

'No. I searched all round the house, in the gardens and out in the woods. If she'd fallen, I would have found her.'

'What exactly is your relationship to Mrs Beaudry?'

'I'm her …' I tried to find the right words. 'I'm her, sort of housekeeper.'

'Sort of housekeeper?'

'Yes. I looked after her when she fell and broke her hip, got her back on her feet. When she recovered, she asked me to stay. My husband and I moved in permanently and I do a bit of cooking and cleaning, make sure she's OK and the house is in a good state.'

'And where is your husband now, Mrs Tully?'

'He's away, working. He's with the army – got a consulting type role but it means he's often away for six or so weeks at a time. He used to be in charge of the domestics at the local school – that's where we met, I used to clean there, he's …'

'Have you been in touch with him recently?' Thurlow cut me off. I was so tired I couldn't help gabbling.

'No, he isn't allowed to take his phone.' I scratched my neck. The lack of air in the room was suffocating. 'Can we open a window?' It was a mistake to come here. I needed to be outside, snuffling up the air, finding the thread that would lead me to Mrs B.

'Mrs Tully?'

I forced myself to meet Thurlow's eyes.

'Can I just clarify a few points?' he said.

I nodded, despair striking me dumb.

'You're saying,' he went on with deliberate emphasis, 'that your friend, Mrs Beaudry, is … what were your words …' He leaned over his partner's pad and nodded at what he saw there. '… well over a hundred years old and she's been missing since day before yesterday?' His voice rose at the end, making me flinch.

'Yes, but she's not like an ordinary old woman.'

Thurlow slammed his meaty hand down on the desk and I jumped in shock. 'Have you any idea how important the first few hours are when a vulnerable person goes missing? Especially if, as you say, she's been abducted. Though I think that's unlikely. Chances are she's lying somewhere having got lost and fallen. Does she suffer with dementia?'

'No! No, not at all. She's sharper than me.'

Thurlow's look was speculative. His partner returned and leaned to whisper soundlessly in his ear. 'Here's your memory card back, we'll look at the footage you've got but in the meantime I think we'd better send some people over to the house. Leave your address with Hawthorne here and …' he pulled his cuff to check his watch, 'we should be there within an hour or so.'

I stood, stretching away the cramps in my legs. 'Can I go?'

Thurlow nodded and I didn't wait for him to move. Grabbing my bag, I squeezed behind his chair to reach the door. I heard him mutter something, but I was desperate to get out of there, so didn't wait to tune into what he was saying.

Wild thoughts chased me as I left the station and jogged across the road to my car. How many police would he send? I thought. Imagining Pagan's Reach swarming with police made me faint with horror. There were too many secrets hidden there. Mrs B would kill me.

*

The bitch fought like a hellcat. Gran had told me she was a little old woman. Well fuck that. She may have been small but you'd think I was wrestling a demon. At one point I nearly got out my knife. Silly really, when I can do what I can do without even touching skin, but I like my knife, like to feel blood slipping over my hands, the sink of flesh under the blade I keep nice and sharp. Not much the old witch could have done against a knife sliding into her heart.

Crawling into the belly of the house I'd dreamed about since I was a kid was something special. Gran had drawn me a map, but I didn't have a clue if it would be any good. 'It's your birth right, sonny,' she used to whisper while my ma made crazy gestures behind her back. They all thought she was nuts, but I thought she was great. And she gave me something special she never let on to Sam and Janey – even Ma didn't have a clue.

'Come look, Sonny,' she said one day when I was only a tiny thing. She was holding ma's dog by the scruff of its neck. Horrible little rat it was. Gran was holding it so hard the skin of its eyes stretched back. It was whimpering all terrified like. 'I want you to look at it really careful. Smell it. Can you smell how frightened it is? Feel the sort of buzzing?'

I looked at her. I didn't know what to think. She was always an odd one, dressed funny – not like my Dad's mum who was all aprons and smelled of cake - Gran smelled like cigarettes and gunpowder.

I held my hand out to the dog, trying to do what she wanted. Thought there might be a chocolate bar or a tenner in it if I did what she said. It took me a second but she told me what to do and I felt it. I really felt it. A sort of fizzing in my blood like I'd drunk a load of coke all in one go. I felt sick with it but powerful at the same time. She thought it was great, Gran did. Said she could see me get bigger with it.

She couldn't do it herself, you see. And when she saw what I could do she told me everything. About the house that belonged to her ma, my great gran, and by rights should be mine as I was her oldest grandson.

'Your ma can't have it,' she said. 'There's about as much magic in her as a carrot. I've got a little bit but you, Sonny. You're special. The house should be yours.'

I used to love it when she told me all the stories about the house. How it had magic rooms and was almost alive. 'It's filled with treasures,' she'd tell me when I was crying the day Dad left. 'They can make you invisible. There's weapons and shields and a library full of spells that could make you the most powerful man in the world.'

'How'd she lose the house Gran?'

'It was stolen from her wasn't it,' she spat. 'She told me all about it. Those sanctimonious bitches blamed her for an accident that wasn't her fault and they threw her out. You need to go and right that wrong. As soon as you're big enough.'

'I think I'm ready now,' I told her on my seventeenth birthday. A man already and big with it. I was well past using frightened dogs to feed my strength. Losers at school, girls who thought they could save me from my bad boy ways. Their terror gave me so much power my skin burned with it.

But she weren't sure I was ready. She'd taught me a few things she'd found in her ma's stuff, but she couldn't do it properly. I was bored with stupid scraps with local pricks, I wanted it all. The cars, the women, the money.

'You'll find everything you need to grow your powers in the house,' she said. 'But you've got to take it over, get rid of the witch it's loyal to. That won't be easy, Sonny.' She studied me for a moment, her grey eyes all cloudy. 'I don't know if it's true but she told me about something buried right in the depths of the house. Something so powerful it's protected by a thousand hexes and spells. Only the mistress witch knows how to release it so be careful. You won't be able to reach it without her.'

I'd watched the house for weeks – watching the old witches come and go. I daren't get too close, the house was wired top to bottom with defence spells. Wonder why that was? Trying to stop people like me. But I was different. I had a right. Through my great grandmother the house, and everything in it, belonged to me.

Gran handed over everything she'd got from her ma just before she died. God that hospital smelled bad. I'd gone in with a bunch of roses – I knew she loved them. They did a good job of masking the stink of death that hung about the beds. It made my nose twitch.

I was sad when she went. She was the only one in my family who thought I was worth anything. Everyone else thought I was an animal. She always understood me when everyone else pretended they couldn't work out what I was saying. It used to make me want to tear their fucking skin off.

Gran didn't care when I got chucked out of school or got caught up in fights. I was always the most vicious, the one who didn't know when to stop and it delighted her.

'Good to have someone in the family with some balls at last,' she'd say, stroking the fur on my shoulders. 'You remind me of my ma.'

Her eyes flamed the red of the hunter, and I knew mine were the same. 'It belongs to you, Sonny,' she said again. 'It's your birth right.'

I'd found the door easily enough; Gran still remembered every step of the trail her mother had described. The wood was rotten and sunk into wet fragments under my hands – soft as wet tissue paper. More digging where silt had filled the space until I cleared away an entrance to the tunnel. I followed it on my hands and knees, the stones scraping at my skin, tearing bloody holes. I licked them clean.

When I reckoned I was halfway under the house I sat still and reached into its innards, feeling it shrink with fear at my presence. The spells didn't reach down this far. The silly bitches couldn't have known about this tunnel - it hadn't been used for decades. My body swelled as the house tried to buzz an alarm and I yanked the energy into my bones and muscles, sucking the warmth from the rooms and walls above. The house stilled and began to freeze. It wouldn't be able to help anyone.

I crawled along the tunnel until it reached a passage big enough for me to stand. From the passage you couldn't see the little tunnel – its entrance was hidden by twisted tree roots and moss.

I scampered down that passage quick as a flash, the stones sparking under my feet. And then there I was, a jack in the box springing to my heels in the heart of the building.

I hadn't expected the dog.

I caught it as it leaped. Caught it by the muzzle. Smothering its roar of defiance before a sound could escape. I slammed its head against the wall and tossed the body behind me, closing the passage door behind it.

Gran told me to expect riches, but the house was like nothing I'd ever seen. It made my blood throb as I crept through the rooms in the dark, following the scent of the old witch. My nails were broken and bloody from digging through the earth, but exhilaration ripped through every nerve.

She slept deeply, flat on her back, blankets pulled up under her chin. I almost laughed, she was so tiny - she'd be no opposition to one such as I.

But Gran had been insistent.

'Whoever is the mistress of the house is the owner of the secret. She's the only one who knows where it's hidden and how to reach it. Control her and you'll find the prize. But whatever you do, don't underestimate her.'

The moment I touched the woman her eyes flared open, daggers of green, and she bucked into the air - throwing me back. She roared at me, loud as a lion. I had to throw myself onto the bed, holding my hand over her face. I reached for her fear but there was none. She was writhing furiously, clawing at my face. She was strong, and bolts of fire flew from her fingers, cinders fell on my face and eyes.

I slapped her, hard. She fell limp. That's when I dragged her from the bed, banging her head against the floor with a hollow thump. I picked her up and threw her over my shoulder with ease, opened the window, and sprang into the night.

Chapter 4

That afternoon I stood in the library shivering, watching the police walking round the front lawns. One woman in uniform stood at the end of the terrace holding a remote control in her hand. She was studying a monitor and I could hear the buzz and whine of the drone she was controlling as it flew out over the lawns towards the orchard.

Two officers had come into the house asking if they could take a look round, starting with Mrs B's bedroom. I hadn't gone in there since the day I found her gone. My skin was flayed raw by the awareness of them thumping and murmuring overhead.

I didn't dare lean into the house, knowing the pain and horror I would find there at this invasion. This was my fault, and I knew the house hated me for it – but what else could I do?

Feeling like I was fiddling while Rome burned, I moved to the fireplace to pick up the books the old woman had left there.

She was re-reading 'Captain Corelli's Mandolin' for the hundredth time and 'My Sister the Serial Killer', 'The Bloody Chamber' and 'Magpie Lane' were lying open and face down in a haphazard pile on the arm of the chair.

More thumps and crashes overhead made me jump. A few years before, Mrs B and I had almost died in a monumental battle with a wolf who'd chased the old woman for over eighty years. He'd brought a gang of bully boys with him, two of whom I'd killed – Mrs B had taken care of the others.

I was never quite sure what had happened to the bodies - the house had absorbed them somehow - I hadn't questioned it. I knew Mrs B had dragged one of them into an old priest hole tucked under the window seat in her bedroom. I'd dropped one through a hole that had appeared in the hall floor but there was no way the police could open these places without knowing the right charms. At least, I hoped so.

I slotted the books back into their place on the shelves and banged the cushions to fluff them up. I'd tried lighting a fire again, but it just wouldn't take. Looking at the empty grate I wondered if it was worth checking again the tunnel that lay hidden behind the fireplace.

I was tempted to reach and push the button tucked under the mantelpiece but was interrupted by Thurlow. He paused for a moment in the doorway taking in the beauty of the library. It was a special place. The ceiling soared two storeys above us, and every wall was lined with rows upon rows of books. Persian rugs rolled across the honey-gold floorboards and broad sofas, plumped with cushions, invited the viewer to come sit and read. Three sash windows gazed over the valley; I'd spent hours there, nestled in blankets, drinking in the view.

I was proud of how good the library looked - it had been a wreck when I first arrived. Mrs B had fired her housekeeper in the 1980s and let the house go to rack and ruin, spending the next forty years doing nothing but reading novels and drinking tea - her only companion an elderly black cat.

'Nice place you've got here, Mrs Tully. Must be worth a few quid.'

Thurlow stood waiting in the doorway. I'd forgotten the size of him and as I walked forward, my fingertips prickled. Something had changed; my body responded before I could work out what it was. The hairs on the back of my neck stirred. He was pale, the ruddiness of earlier had disappeared, a liverish smear now lay under his eyes.

'It's not my house,' I said, caution slowing my words. 'I told you.'

'Any chance of a cup of tea? My lot should be finished soon.'

My trainers squeaked as we crossed the chessboard floor of the hall, heading for the kitchen. Behind the grand staircase the frozen river of glass that stretched from floor to ceiling glittered, and my eyes were drawn to the woods beyond. I saw the trees standing, ancient and full of power. They sheltered the back of the house, the roots knotting deep beneath, keeping us safe, well that was what I'd always believed. I didn't feel safe anymore.

Thurlow's tread was heavy, he was moving with a strange, jerky movement as if he'd injured himself. 'How far do the grounds reach?' he threw over his shoulder as he walked in front of me down the corridor. His shoulders blocked the light. 'Mrs Tully?' he said when I didn't answer.

'Sorry?'

'I asked how far do the grounds reach?'

'Oh, I wasn't listening. Sorry. Miles away. They stretch from the front of the house to the line of oaks at the road and then back past the woods to the top of the hill before you get to the path leading down to the village. Is that where you're searching?'

My hands jittered. I couldn't stay still for long enough to make a proper cup of tea so dug out some instant coffee from the cupboard. Gary preferred it, and I felt a pang to see the familiar jar. I wished he were here to help. I'd try calling his CO again when the police had gone.

An alarm was clanging in my head and I couldn't work out whether it was my fear for Mrs B or the presence of Thurlow in my kitchen. He sat quietly enough; in fact his stillness struck me as odd. In the police station he seemed to vibrate with suppressed energy.

The mug was still boiling hot as I put it in front of him. I'd barely stirred it; I couldn't keep my mind on anything for long before it skittered away to obsessing about what had happened to Mrs B. I watched as he took a sip, winced, and put the mug down, wrapping his hands round it. I didn't blame him, our breath billowed ice. The house seemed to be getting even colder.

I took the chair across from Thurlow. He began to speak but a ripple of fear froze my blood as I met his eyes. They were blank. Flat grey discs. The clear, silvery blue I had noticed at the station was gone. Perhaps a trick of the light. But it was unsettling, nonetheless.

I blinked to focus on what he was saying.

'… I'm sure you'll be pleased to know there's nothing to suggest Mrs Beaudry was taken against her will.'

'That's not true!' Frustration drove away the troubling thoughts that Thurlow wasn't too be trusted. 'Didn't you go into her bedroom? It's obvious something dreadful had happened.'

Thurlow blew on his steaming coffee and took another cautious sip before putting it back down. 'A few pillows on the floor doesn't mean she's been abducted,' he said.

'But what about the …?' I stopped.

'What about the what?'

'The violence that's torn the air apart!' I wanted to shout at him. 'The struggle that's breathed its imprint onto every atom in the room!' My shoulders cramped and I rubbed them to loosen the fibres, the muscles felt like iron under my hand.

'The what, Mrs Tully?' Thurlow repeated. Again, that strange, blank stare; it was as if he was reading questions from a sheet of paper.

'Oh, well … I've got a bit of a psychic gift, you see. I sometimes can tell what's going to happen and I got a strong feeling …' I trailed off at the look on his face.

'OK,' he said slowly. 'I think I'm going to need a bit more than "a funny feeling."'

He smiled. I was repelled by its coldness and rubbed my arms. I shouldn't have said anything. Unease was continuing to creep along my skin. The loss of Mrs B, Thurlow's disfiguring presence, the continual sound of police crawling round, were all affecting my judgement. The house was sending me an urgent message, but its voice was muffled, dampened. Be careful, be careful it whispered.

'What about the CCTV film from the shop? Did you find anything about the van?'

'There's nothing to indicate that the van and the driver had anything to do with Mrs Beaudry's disappearance. It was quite a way from this house. It was just a delivery driver, that's all.'

I was tempted to explain the effect the driver had had on me but knew Thurlow would dismiss it as another "funny feeling".

'Is there anywhere she would go? Friends? Family?'

'They're all dead,' I said. 'Anyway, she wasn't much of a one for company. She liked to keep herself to herself.' As I spoke, a bell rung in my mind. There was someone I thought, my pulse quickening, but caution kept my mouth shut. I didn't like the way Thurlow was gazing at me so blankly. His hands lay on the table as if he wasn't sure what to do with them: the coffee cooling rapidly, his note pad empty.

'It's just you and Gary?'

I nodded, thinking hard. Mrs B had talked about a friend and her daughter. I pressed my forehead hard with the tips of my fingers. Think! I told myself.

'Has Mrs Beaudry left a will?'

His words wrenched me out of my trance. 'What's that got to do with anything?'

'Whoever is named in the will stands to inherit a great deal of money. This house must be worth millions.'

I looked at him, dumbfounded for a moment. My mind raced. 'I think …' I cleared my throat. 'I think I'm in the will. At least, Mrs B said she was going to leave everything to me. But that doesn't mean she did anything official about it. She always seemed pretty convinced she'd live forever. Things like deeds and wills bored her. I wouldn't put it past her to have never written one.'

'But she told you she'd leave you everything?'

'Yes … but that was ages ago. She could have changed her mind. Besides, even if I am in the will, I wouldn't kill her for it.' I stood up, almost knocking the chair over.

Thurlow raised his hands, roused for a moment from his immobility. 'I didn't say you did, Mrs Tully. We have to consider all possibilities.'

'Mrs B is the most precious thing in the world to me!' I stammered. 'As well as Gary and Trevor.'

'Trevor?'

'Our dog, he's a terrier, a dear little thing. He went missing the same time Mrs B did.'

'I see.' A man in uniform appeared at the back door and Thurlow got to his feet and went outside. I strained my ears to hear what they were saying but couldn't hear a thing.

'There's no sign of her in the garden or woods,' he said, bringing a breath of spring with him; it was an incongruous warmth that belied his newly sallow countenance, but being outside seemed to have blown away some of his strange inertia.

'I told you she wasn't there. I searched everywhere.'

'Probably not with infrared cameras the way we can,' he said. 'If she's alive and out there we would've seen her. Are you sure there's nobody she could have gone to visit? Perhaps you had a bit of a row?' His tone changed. 'It can't be easy looking after such an elderly woman. They can be difficult - say things they don't mean … caring can be challenging, can't it? Easy to lose your temper.'

'Stop putting words into my mouth!' I didn't want to tell him that Mrs B could be a cantankerous old cow who drove me mad, but the thought of hurting her wouldn't cross my mind in a million years. Besides, she wouldn't let me. She was still the most powerful being I'd ever met. 'Why would I report her missing if I'd done something to her?'

'People do.' Seeing anger flash across my face he made another placating gesture. 'I'm not accusing you of anything Mrs Tully. Do you have a photograph of Mrs Beaudry? I want to get this out across social media as soon as possible.'

I pulled my phone from my pocket and scrolled through the camera roll. Most of the photos were of Trevor and the woods but I finally found one of Mrs B. She was in the garden, glowering at me as I'd just stood on her newly planted spring bulbs. I handed it over to Thurlow who looked taken aback. 'Quite striking looking, isn't she? Fierce.'

'Yes, she is,' I said.

'Can you send it over? Here's my email and number.' He handed me a card. There was a hammering sound at the front door. 'Ah, that'll be the team.'

'What team?' I said.

'The forensic team. I want them to have a proper look at Mrs Beaudry's bedroom. I've assigned this as a grade 1 so don't worry, we'll find her. I've got a couple of officers going door to door in the village to see if anyone has seen anything. In the meantime …' he paused at the front door and turned to look at me. 'Let me know if you think of anything. I don't like such an elderly woman being out for so long. It's still cold and dark and she could be unwell or injured.'

He opened the door to let in two women who were putting on masks and rubber gloves. Behind them a man was opening a van door to release three police dogs. They disappeared round the back of the house. 'Just upstairs,' Thurlow directed the women. 'A few doors down – you can't miss it. PC Hawthorne's up there, he'll show you.'

'I better be off,' he said to me as they passed us and headed for the stairs. 'Don't go anywhere will you, Mrs Tully? I may need to ask you a few more questions.'

*

It was dark by the time the police left. Another day gone and I was no closer to finding Mrs B. I'd retreated to the shelter of my flat, lying on my bed wrapped in the duvet staring up at the sky as the clouds chased each other, blotting out the stars.

Instinct told me involving the police was a stupid decision. Exhaustion had robbed me of any sense – what good would it do them being in Pagan's Reach? At the very least it was a appalling intrusion into Mrs B and my privacy. It would also be difficult explaining why we had the bodies of thugs and criminals hidden about the place.

It didn't help that Thurlow seemed to think I'd bumped the old woman off to inherit the house. At the very least it took his attention away from whoever had really taken Mrs B. Why wasn't he following up on the van outside Laurie's shop? He'd dismissed it out of hand. I'd have to push that again, I thought. I can't access all the CCTV across the country, but Thurlow could.

Despite the cold I pushed off the duvet and began pacing. I couldn't think straight lying down – I needed to move. Mrs B had enemies, of course she did. Any woman that powerful was going to inspire rage and envy. She didn't suffer fools gladly and could be rude and graceless when she wanted to be.

She was rich beyond any imaginings. I suspected I didn't know the half of the wealth she had built up over the years. She owned two Picassos but didn't like them much so kept them locked up in a safe deposit box in London. Since he'd died, André Bartoque's work had soared in value, each painting worth at least four million and Mrs B owned five of them, including the stunning nude he'd done of her before the war – 'Madonna with Diamond and Green Shoes' it was called, and known round the world.

But nothing had been taken. Not a single piece from her jewellery box. No painting had been removed from the walls. Her purse and bag still lay beside her bed. Money wasn't the motive. So who had taken her, and why? The answer lay in her past, I was sure of it. Thurlow had talked of friends and family; I'd thought of myself and Gary as Mrs B's only family, albeit an adopted one, but she'd lived a very long time. There could be loads of others in her background who had reasons to seek revenge.

Mrs B didn't talk much about the past except to show off about the famous artists, writers and musicians she'd known. But there was one story she told that I'd found haunting. She'd described a village clinging to the tops of cliffs hanging over the sea. Something evil had flourished there, and a child nearly died.

As I walked down the stairs, I tried to remember the names of the woman she'd known there. In the kitchen I forced down a slice of bread and poured out a glass of apple juice. I could remember every detail of the magic comb Mrs B had described losing in the fight to save the child, but not the name of the village.

I banged my fists against my head to try and dislodge the memory. The mother had been a vicar's daughter. Very prim and proper – an unlikely friend for the heretical Mrs B.

The daughter had been something special, Mrs B had said. Clever. The old woman had helped her to get to university – she'd done very well … a scientist, I thought …

A surge of adrenalin pushed me to my feet, knocking the glass of juice flying. Physics. She was a physics professor. Mrs B had shown me her books – they were in the library.

I flew down the corridor and skidded across the hall floor, ignoring the mess the police had left behind.

I was panting by the time I reached the library, a stitch skewering my side. We'd been standing by one of the small tables in the corner of the room, I remembered. There'd been a picture. There it was.

It was a small, wooden framed painting of flowers, all blossoming with a riotous colour from an overgrown country garden. The energy of it sizzled against my hand as I picked it up – it was beautiful. I much preferred it to some of the large, self-important works of art hanging all over the house.

There were four books on the shelf behind the painting. I pulled one of them out. Penny! That was her name. Professor Penelope Howes.

Seeing it sparked a vivid memory so intense I looked over my shoulder to see Mrs B as I could hear her so strongly.

'It was such a shame,' I heard her say. 'I'd never met anyone so bright, so driven. But she never acknowledges her gift – she isn't interested in anything outside her obsession with Physics.'

Penny was important to Mrs B. She'd nominated herself as an unofficial godmother, I didn't think anyone had grown as close to the old woman until I'd arrived. I needed to talk to her. At the very least I needed someone who loved Mrs B as much as I did to help me search. I was sick of coping on my own.

The book I'd picked up was heavy and filled with equations and graphs with complicated looking diagrams. It might as well have been in hieroglyphics. I was more interested to see what she looked like and gazed at the author photo on the inside of the jacket. She was a good-looking, if bony, woman with thick, curly hair and an expression as sour as crab apples. There was something about her I found interesting, but I couldn't put my finger on what it was.

I read her brief and rather boring biography, but it didn't tell me much. There was something about the eyes … they were so full of life I expected her to turn her head and catch me with her gaze.

Stopping long enough only to shove a change of clothes and a toothbrush into a Sainsbury's bag, I grabbed my keys from the hall table and went out into the night. Sod Thurlow. He had my number; he could call me if he had more questions.

Pagan's Reach watched me as I got into the car. It was a wrench to leave, but I was out of options. The loss of the old woman had dragged a bloody weal across my heart, and I hadn't been able to breathe properly since she left.

I started the engine. It would take me four hours to get to the university – I should arrive just as Penny started work.

Chapter 5

Professor Penelope Howes woke to see the light dancing in her bedroom, mocking the cloud of gloom that pressed against her eyes. She checked her phone. Perhaps Martin had changed his mind - regretted the email he'd sent calling her in to 'discuss her role in the department.' Nothing. No change then.

She rolled over to the PC plugged in and whirring on the bedside table. The simulation had been running for over twenty-four hours but didn't seem any closer to finishing. She clicked her tongue and flopped back on the pillow.

Her wrists and forearms ached from yesterday's hours hunched over the keyboard trying to get a paper together. She rubbed them, noticing the liver spots on her hands were spreading, her long fingers just starting to bulge a little at the joints. Time was catching up with her. Penny reminded herself she lived well, ate with care, exercised regularly. She was in much better shape than many colleagues of her vintage.

She had done the research. Last week, on her sixty-third birthday, she'd created an algorithm that had estimated she had another twenty-five years. Penny was adopted, losing contact with her birth parents at thirteen, so she didn't have the comfort of long-lived ancestors to go by. But if she remained disease free and barring any unforeseen accidents, she thought twenty years of healthy existence wouldn't be beyond the realms of possibility. Would that be enough?

Penny watched the sunshine move its beam across the room. It was getting late; she should get up. She stared at the ceiling, pinned down by an unusual lethargy. She had a fight on her hands that morning and she wasn't sure she was ready for it.

Her alarm jangled for the fifth time and she slammed it silent, swinging her legs out of bed and sitting up. The sun slid across the most beautiful object Penny owned: a large oil painting.

Hung on the wall opposite Penny's bed it gazed at her with a patient eye. A garden, painted with a riot of colour. Roses and lavender, peonies and dahlias, they thronged to the front as if wanting to escape. If Penny looked at it for too long she began to smell their scent and hear the birds' liquid song.

With an impatient exclamation Penny pushed herself out of bed, crossing the room to retrieve her dressing gown. But the canvas pulled at her consciousness until she turned to face it head on. The picture radiated its colours until they painted the air: pinks and carmines, teals, and sapphires.

Penny reached her hand out to feel the bold strokes of paint beneath her fingertips. She touched the signature, 'Daphne', scrawled in violet across the bottom right corner; her adopted mother had painted with such passion and talent. She must be feeling vulnerable today, Penny thought as her eyes filled. For the first time in years, she allowed the electricity she usually kept so tightly bound into her bones and muscles to release. A charge crackled down her wrist into her hands and the painting sprung to life.

She closed her eyes: always too frightened to look. She stood, blind, and took a deep breath. A gust of warm, summer-scented air stirred the hair curling about her forehead bringing with it the memory of a childhood garden. But this was more than a memory. The painting lived under her hands; the birdsong rippled from it and Penny felt that if she strained her ears, she would hear her mother calling for her to come in for tea.

At last, the painting quieted like a spinning top losing its momentum. When Penny stepped back it hung passive, subdued. She flicked her hands to shake off the last prickling buzzes of electricity. Her mind was clear, her frightened heart quietened, she settled to get ready for work with a determined focus.

The usual roar of the Common Room dropped a notch as Penny entered to refill her water bottle. The word had got out already - colleagues were avoiding her eyes. Throwing aside caution she abandoned the water cooler and put an espresso pod in the machine, pushing up the caffeine content to its highest setting. Her third one of the day: she was risking palpitations but needed a jolt to prepare for her appointment with Martin.

After a dreary staff meeting Penny prepared to answer Martin's call to his office. In the bathroom she washed her hands. Her reflection showed none of the turmoil that seethed within. As ever, her thick, silver curls were beginning to escape their pins. Checking the door was locked she pulled out every grip and ran her fingers through her hair until each strand exploded upwards, uncoiling and writhing in glittering ropes.

Keeping her eyes lowered, Penny braided her hair tight flat with quick, neat fingers. Only then did she meet her reflected gaze, splashing cold water onto the pale oval of her face.

Dean Martin Fenwick was leaning back in his enormous, well-padded office chair, phone in hand as Penny entered. The room was packed with stacks of paper, journals and books. They slipped and slid from their piles and Penny wondered if this was why he managed his role with such inefficiency.

'Ah! Penny,' Martin jerked from his seat and pushed his phone into his pocket. He looked hot, and Penny wrinkled her nose at the faint thread of sweat scenting the air. 'Thank you for coming in, do take a seat – anywhere you like.'

Penny perched on a plastic chair feeling as if she were about to be scolded.

'Thank you for coming in,' Martin said again. Penny waited. 'It's always good to talk face to face.' His expression indicated he'd rather had this meeting online. It must be serious, she thought.

'I'll get to the point, shall I?' Martin said and patted his sweating forehead with a square of tissue.

Penny nodded. Impatient. She had better things to do.

'I wanted to talk to you about your ideas for retirement …'

'Retirement? What are you on about? I'm not planning to retire.' Her face reddened.

'We have an excellent package for you, including a generous settlement that I'm sure you will find most agreeable ...' Martin gazed down at the folder in front of him, avoiding Penny's gaze.

'Well, I won't be needing it,' Penny said, getting to her feet, swallowing hard. 'I'm not retiring, what a ridiculous notion.'

It wasn't until she had her hand on the door that she realised Martin was still speaking.

'... I'm afraid.'

'What did you say?'

'I'm afraid I've been given no choice, Penny. You haven't published in years ...'

'You know I won't publish until I have the mathematical proof that ...'

Martin waved his hand, 'Yes, yes, I know this, Penny. But that's the nature of theoretical physics. Others publish.'

'Idiots you mean.' Shock had made her brave.

'And you haven't brought any money into the department since before I took over as Dean of Faculty.'

'There aren't any grants that will recognise the work I'm doing, and Brexit hasn't helped.' Penny's heart began to race.

'And you refuse to diversify. You've been fixated on this one path despite not getting anywhere for decades.'

'But I'm so close!'

'The fact of the matter is I can't support your position in the department with an REF assessment coming up. You're sixty-two now, Penny …'

'Sixty-three, and my age is irrelevant. I'm sure my union rep would agree.'

'Of course, of course,' Martin's words tripped over themselves in their attempt to reassure. 'How old you are is, indeed, irrelevant, but as long-time colleagues surely I can suggest you start taking it easy? Travel a little? You've been bound to your desk for so long I wouldn't recognise you without it!' He gave a little chortle, but it died away at the look on Penny's face.

'I have no interest in taking it easy, nor travel. I am interested in my work…'

'An emeritus role would be available of course but we have to face facts, Penny. You have a responsibility as a professor to publish, take on PhD students and, most importantly, bring money into the university. You haven't done any of those things for the past ten years. You can't keep resting on your reputation at Cambridge – that was decades ago. I'm sorry, but this can't go on. I've defended you to the vice-chancellor's office for as long as I could but there's nothing more I can do.'

Only the tiny tremor in her clenched right hand gave away Penny's shock. 'You're firing me,' she said.

'No! No! Of course not. But, as I said, HR have put together a very attractive package, alongside a pension you can draw upon now.' Martin looked more and more uncomfortable seeing the blood drain from Penny's face. He rubbed at his balding head and sighed. 'Penny, take the package. Please.'

'You can't get rid of me because I'm over 60.'

'We're not. That's not the case at all. But we can't continue to pay your very generous salary when you aren't fulfilling any of the requirements of the role. Those are the facts, Penny. I'm sorry.'

'Is there anything I can do? Martin, you know how important my work is to me – it means everything.'

'Not really, not unless you have something extraordinary to publish in the near future?' He looked up at Penny who was moved to see genuine hope in his eyes.

'No. I have something… something special … but it's not ready.'

Martin's shoulders slumped. 'Look, take some time to think about it. But Penny the fact is, if you don't take the retirement offer then they will start discipline proceedings with the ultimate aim of …'

'Firing me,' Penny said.

'Take some leave,' Martin urged. 'You haven't been on holiday for as long as I can remember. Have a good think about what you want to do next. It's time for a change.'

'You're making a mistake, Martin. I think you'll regret not giving me a chance. When I've finished my paper you'll see it drop a bomb exploding today's thinking. Physicists all over the world will be referencing my findings for years.'

Martin gave a helpless shrug.

Penny raised her chin and strode out. She walked down the corridor to her office, collected her laptop and filled a bag with her things.

And then Professor Penelope Howes did something she had never done before. Not once. Not even when she was a young student. She cycled into town, locked her bike with care, went into an off licence and bought as many bottles of vodka as her bike could carry.

*

Penny wasn't sure how many days had passed when she woke, her head thumping. She couldn't remember the last time she'd eaten, but the thought of finding something to push down her throat and swallow was unbearable. She was desperate for water and grabbed at the glass by her bed, only to have to rush to the bathroom to vomit when she realised it was filled with neat vodka.

After rinsing her mouth out with pints of tap water, Penny ignored her reflection and staggered to the kitchen to make coffee. It seemed very dusty, and the air was burned by the stink of hard spirits. Her stomach gave a queasy roll. In the sitting room her books were piled over the coffee table next to open journals filled with incomprehensible scribbles.

Squinting through a paralysing headache, Penny tried to make out what she had written. She couldn't read a word of it. Getting painfully to her feet, Penny looked round her flat. At one point she must have thrown a folder of notes across her office as papers were everywhere. Drawers were pulled open, and her laptop was open on her desk when she could have sworn she'd left it in her bag.

Wincing at the early light streaming in through the bathroom window, Penny rummaged in the drawer until she found an old pack of paracetamol that was years out of date. She swallowed three, washing them down with handfuls of tap water.

She was lying on the sofa, staring up at the ceiling, waiting for the painkillers to kick in, when there was a knock on the door. Penny closed her eyes and pulled a cushion over her face with a groan. The knocking continued until it reached a hammering crescendo.

'All right!' Penny shouted, clutching at her head.

The hall was dark as she hadn't opened the curtains and there was no way she was turning on the light in this state. She wasn't even sure whether she was decent, but a quick check reassured she was clothed, if not particularly clean. She couldn't bear the noise for a moment longer; whoever was at the door wasn't going to give up.

Penny blinked in surprise to see a large woman in her fifties clutching a phone and looking desperate. For a moment they gazed at each other. Penny felt something, a strange kind of recognition, though she would swear she'd never seen this woman before. There seemed to be a sort of ... glow coming from her. Perhaps the results of the vodka? Penny had never drunk alcohol before, let alone copious amounts of strong spirits, so was unfamiliar with its effects.

'It's Penny isn't it? Please say you're Penny, I've knocked my way up and down this awful block of flats. You must be. You look like her, though I didn't expect the white hair.'

Bewildered, Penny took a step back to let the woman who'd introduced herself as Angie into her flat. She made it feel very small. Her large, colourful trainers and bright purple shirt dominated the little sitting room, and her voice was too loud. Penny felt peculiar, and a little faint.

Angie's face creased with concern. 'You better sit down, love. You look terribly pasty.' She leaped as Penny began to sway and helped her to the sofa, knocking books and papers to the floor to clear a space. 'Have a sit down, I'll get you some water.' But Penny couldn't hear. She was out cold.

Chapter 6

This wasn't at all what I was expecting. Mrs B had described her goddaughter as a world-renowned physicist. I'd pictured a stern-faced harridan glaring at me over her glasses, not this fragile child-woman with startling white hair that whirled round her head. I'd covered her with a blanket after she'd passed out on the sofa and her body was so small it barely lifted it.

I'd knocked for ages before she'd opened the door. Then suddenly it swung open so quickly the pull of air made me lean forwards. My first impressions were muddled. The stink was the first thing I noticed: stale air, rotten food, stagnant laundry, the smell of an unwashed body, and an unexpected reek of vodka.

Penny was so thin she bordered on emaciated. I recognised her from the book jacket, but she was much older now, her hair white with the lustre of pearl. Still beautiful - she always would be with that bone structure - but she looked ill. Really ill - yellowed skin and pouches under her eyes. Her black clothes bagged as if she'd been sleeping in them for days.

But there was something ... astonishing about her. Something that seemed to rip at the air. Her energy was so powerful I felt I could warm my hands on it as I would a roaring bonfire. My skin felt electrified. Even Mrs B had never held energy like this. It was extraordinary.

I lifted her sleeping hand and spread the long fingers to expose her palm but there was no mark to be found. I'd carried the sigil in the centre of my hand all my life. I'd dismissed it as an odd shaped mole, but meeting Mrs B and seeing the same sign in her hand, and the hands of many other witches over the years, I'd come to understand its significance. But Penny's hand was empty. What was this force she held that vibrated the atoms of the room with such power?

She startled awake at my touch. 'Who are you?' Her voice was deep but had a crack riven through it.

I waited until she sat up and rubbed her eyes, taking a long swallow of the water I'd brought her. I noticed the way she grabbed her hair that fell past her shoulders and quickly knotted it tight against the nape of her neck. She had all the wariness of a wild animal. I rushed to reassure her.

'My name's Angie, Angie Tully. You don't know me but I'm a very good friend of Frieda Beaudry – we live together.'

Penny's face changed. 'Frieda? I haven't seen her in years. Is she ...'

'She's not dead,' I said, laying my hand on hers, noting the pulse of energy. 'But she's been taken and I can't find her. I've searched and searched and got nowhere. I even had to go to the police.'

'What do you mean, taken?' Suddenly the child-woman has disappeared. Penny's face sharpened and her eyes focused; all vulnerability vanished as her strength returned and she studied me, her gaze direct and intent.

'That's the thing. I don't know. I can't sense her anywhere near the house. I've cast charms …' I hesitated 'Do you know? … About Frieda?'

Penny stood up, pulling on a long cardigan hanging on the back of the armchair. 'That she has powers? Yes. I've known since I was thirteen. I remember the first time I saw her help the dead to move on, the ones she said couldn't let go. I found it frightening …' she paused.

'She was good at that,' I said. 'Though she doesn't really enjoy it. She gets me to help them on their way when they come to Pagan's Reach. I've always called them the ones. I didn't know what they were or what they wanted until I met Mrs B.'

'I never knew Pagan's Reach. In fact, I haven't seen her for a long time, she did write …' Penny glanced round the room as if searching for the letter. She looked uncomfortable, wrapping her cardigan round herself tightly and picking up a bottle that had rolled onto the floor.

'I thought you were close?' I said, disappointment rising. I had invested everything in the hope that Penny would be able to help me. But judging by the state of the place she was in no position to help anyone.

'We were! We are … it's just she could be … difficult … She never really understood me. Always felt I should have gone another way.'

Impatient, I pushed myself up from the chair. 'Look, I'm sorry I barged in on you. I can see that this really isn't a good time. But I'm desperate. Mrs B has been missing since Monday morning and its already Thursday and I haven't got anywhere. I think she's in great danger if not already dead…' A sob clotted my throat, but I swallowed it back, hard. 'You and your mother are the only people she has ever talked about with any affection – you have to help me find her.'

Penny spread out her hands in defeat. 'How can I help? I haven't seen Frieda for years, she locked herself away a long time ago. She came to my mother's funeral and wrote, but that was years ago.'

'Penny, I've racked my brains over and over these past few days. She didn't leave, she was taken – that much I know. I need to find the reason why. The house is stuffed full of priceless things but they weren't touched – whoever took her wasn't interested in money. So why take Mrs B? She's a powerful witch, maybe they want to use her powers? Steal them from her?' Penny flinched so dramatically I stopped. 'What is it?'

'Nothing. Nothing. I … I just feel a bit sick, that's all.'

'I'm sure the secret lies in her past,' I went on. 'Someone or something knows about Mrs B and has managed to find her despite all the protective charms we wrapped round Pagan's

Reach. She was always so careful! Even when everything seemed safe she kept nagging me to replenish the protective mantle. She must have known someone would come for her. That's where you can help me, Penny. You've known her for so long – you're my only hope.'

Penny was shaking her head. 'I don't think I can, Angie. I'm sorry. I love Frieda, of course I do, but my life is such a mess right now I need to concentrate on getting back on track.'

'What could possibly be more important than finding Mrs B?'

'My work! They're trying to push me out, I have to stay and fight.' Penny turned away and started to try and restore order – gathering up papers and sorting them into piles. Her hands trembled.

'Penny, you're in no fit state to fight. Look at you. When was the last time you ate? It stinks of alcohol in here, and it's not normal to have all these bottles lying about …' I stopped. There was something shifting in the air. The astonishing energy she held within her amplified her feelings to such an extent I could almost taste them. 'You're scared,' I realised. 'And it's not about your work, is it?' I reached for her, tried to touch her skin, but she snatched her arm away.

'Stop it,' she said. 'I know what you're doing.'

I put my hands up, 'I'm not going to do anything.'

'I can see the sparks– the light in your hands. I'm not an idiot, or a child. Don't treat me like one.'

'Well, you'll need to be honest with me. I don't understand. I can tell it's more than your work – it's something to do with Mrs B isn't it? I know she's a dreadful snob, and can be dreadfully cruel sometimes, but she doesn't mean it. Most of the time it's just she's in pain and hates being old…'

Penny walked to the door. 'I think you'd better go. I'm sorry I can't help you. And don't try it!' Her voice rose. 'Don't use that … stuff to force me.'

I got up, my heart sinking. 'Penny, please. I won't force you, of course I won't.' Though I could, I thought to myself. Very easily. But I recognised that her life force was one I'd never come across before, so I wasn't sure how she would react to any charms I might use. 'You know, Mrs B used to talk about you a lot when I first met her. She told me the story of your village, and an artist who lived there. We have her paintings all over the house – they're beautiful, really beautiful. My favourites in fact.'

Tears sprung to Penny's eyes. 'Daphne, my mother. She loved her garden and she loved to paint. I miss her every day.'

'When did she die?'

'Oh, a long time ago now, but it doesn't seem to get any easier.'

I was moved by her grief and hated myself, but I had to use her pain to get her to help me. 'How did Mrs B end up being your godmother?'

'She wasn't really, well, not officially. When my parents disappeared she arranged for Daphne to adopt me. I stayed in the village until I went to university.'

'She was a vicar's daughter, your mother, wasn't she? I remember thinking it was an odd friendship – Mrs B wasn't very supportive of the church.'

'Yes. She was a wonderful woman, did a great deal for the village.'

'It's funny,' I said, putting on my coat, 'how you ended up at Cambridge coming as you did from a tiny village looked after by a vicar's daughter.'

She avoided my eyes.

'Did Daphne know a lot about university?'

'She never went. Too busy looking after her father. She should have gone to Art college.' She made an impatient noise. 'I know what you're getting at. Yes, Frieda was the one who encouraged me. I couldn't have gone without her support.'

I let a pause hang between us.

'It sounds like you owe her,' I said. Penny's expression softened, just for a second and I pressed my point. 'She's an old woman, Penny. She has her powers, yes, but that doesn't stop her being frail and vulnerable.' I was sorely tempted to roll a few encouraging sparks into her, but she never took her eyes from my hands. Any sign of my powers seemed to enrage her.

'But what can I do?' she said.

'You can talk to me about what you remember. Where she lived. People she knew. Anyone who hated her. That sort of thing. I haven't really known her that long, though she means everything to me now.'

I saw the compassion in Penny's eyes and my heart began to beat faster. 'Tell me what's happening with your job.'

'I'm too old, that's what's happening. I haven't published in years so they want me to retire. They've forced me to take some leave to think about it. There's a paper I'm working on that I think could save my career but it's not ready. I have a theory but …'

'Tell you what,' I said. 'You help me find Frieda and I'll find out a way to help you get your paper published. Mrs B and I, we have the power to show you how the world works, isn't that your field?'

'Sort of.' A tiny smile lifted the corner of her mouth. 'I'm a theoretical physicist. The Theory of Everything is something I've been studying all my career.'

'Never heard of it. What does it mean? Explain it to me like I'm a kid – I was never much good at school.'

Penny opened her mouth then stopped to think. 'I, and many other physicists of course, are trying to find a way to link together general relativity and quantum mechanics. At the moment they are incompatible. General relativity will explain some things and quantum mechanics explain others. We haven't yet found a way to explain everything in the universe with one theory, one thing that would explain all the phenomena of the universe.'

Her eyes brightened. Energy pulsed from her; she was mesmerising, though I didn't understand much of what she was saying.

'We may need to look at new dimensions, or discover the secrets of Dark Matter …'

'Dark matter? What's that?'

'Material we can't see, touch, hear or measure.'

'How do you know it's there?'

'Because of the way galaxies spin and the fact it can bend light which means there's mass - suggesting it holds a gravitation pull.'

'Oh.' For a moment I was stumped. Then an idea struck me. 'So if you could see this dark matter would you understand more of how things worked?'

'That's an interesting theory – but it's pointless. It's called dark matter for a reason. Nobody can see it.'

'What if you had our help?'

For a moment I thought I'd lost her. The idea of us helping her with her work seemed repugnant; I was surprised to see a kind of dreadful fear flicker across her face. Then something seemed to strike her, but she shook her head.

'I don't know,' she said at last. But I knew I was getting through to her, I could feel it.

'You're on leave already, there's nothing you can do now – it looks like you must get that paper published. I guarantee Mrs B and I can help you. All I need is your help for a few days. Please, Penny. I literally have nowhere else to turn.'

*

'I can't believe I'm doing this,' Penny said, gazing out of the car window.

'If it helps, I'm really grateful.' After an interminable journey round London, we were finally on the M11 and the roads were starting to clear. For the first time since I'd found Mrs B's empty bed, I felt hopeful. Penny had given me the lead I needed.

'Brokkton?' I'd said as Penny packed a few things into a bag.

'That's the village I grew up in, well from thirteen after Daphne took me on. It's in Norfolk, up on the coast. Frieda lived there for over a year, she told me once it was the longest she'd stayed in one place, apart from Pagan's Reach of course. She bought a house and when she left, she signed it over to me. I've never been back though. There didn't seem much point after Mum died.'

'So the house is as Mrs B left it?' I said now to Penny. We had an hour of driving until the next junction so I could relax for a bit.

'I assume so, though a large part of the village disappeared in the sixties when the cliffs fell into the sea.'

'I remember, Mrs B told me. It was a strange story. There was a missing child, and something awful happened.'

'It was awful,' Penny said. 'The community never really recovered. Many moved away because they'd lost their homes, or they couldn't bear the tourists who came to gawk at the village that had been broken in two.'

We fell back into silence, watching the road ahead. I knew we were on the right track. There must be something there, in Mrs B's past that would lead me to whoever had taken her. My heart thudded with anticipation, and I leaned forward over the steering wheel, urging the car forward.

'The house must be in a state if you haven't been there since you left.'

'There's someone in the village who goes in and checks it for me every so often. I don't think there's much there, Angie, so don't get your hopes up.'

I ignored her. I had to believe there was something that would help me understand what had happened to the old woman. To think anything else was unbearable. My heart throbbed with the ticking of the clock. How long had Mrs B been gone now? Nearly four days. I gripped the steering wheel hard and prayed Mrs B was still alive and unhurt, though the weight in my stomach reminded me how frail she was, how easy to harm. I had to squeeze my eyes tight shut for a second to stop the tears from falling.

It was getting dark by the time we arrived. Penny directed me through roads that grew more and more narrow until we drove past a tiny train station and turned left into a driveway covered in weeds. The front garden bristled with five feet high nettles and ahead the dark shadow of the house glowered over us. In the distance I could hear the rush and call of the sea.

Adrenalin jerked me to life as I stretched the ache from my hips and knees. There was something here. Already I could feel a charge in the air. While Penny took an infuriatingly long time to fish the keys from her bag, I let my palm rest on the bricks framing the front door.

I closed my eyes and concentrated, ignoring Penny's tut of disapproval. She'd grown up with Frieda in her life, why was she so funny at any hint of magic being used? Driving up in my little car with our bodies almost touching I was conscious more than ever of the power Penny carried. It was like sitting next to a frozen hurricane, as if a huge natural force like an earthquake, or a terrible storm had filled her top to toe with an energy that lodged deep within her and couldn't escape. I wondered what would happen if it was ever released.

The house told me nothing except that mice and spiders were all who had lived there for as long as it could remember. My shoulders fell. I knew it was a long shot that Frieda would be here; but faced with another reminder of her absence, I wanted to sit down and cry.

'Found them!' Penny held the keys aloft.

The door took a good shove to open. A slither of letters, hundreds of them, had jammed it shut and the wood had swollen over time. Immediately we were hit with a cold blast of air that carried the scent of mould and damp on its breath.

'It doesn't look like Tilly's checked on the house for a while,' Penny sounded irritated. 'There's dust everywhere and look at all this junk mail! Oh, the electricity's shut off I'm afraid,' she said as I clicked the light switch in vain, 'but there should be some wood by the fire.'

Flicking sparks into the air that hung as I moved, lighting my way, I went into the sitting room while Penny clanked about in the kitchen. It was freezing cold and unpleasantly damp; the walls reflected the glow of my lights with a watery sheen.

I headed for the fireplace, desperate to drive away the darkness with the cheerful flickering of a roaring fire. A pile of tinder framed by two big logs lay waiting in the grate – they were covered in dust. Rubbing my palms together until embers jumped from my fingers, I let them fall onto the wood until it began to steam. I breathed until the smoke jumped to a gleam and then a flame shyly licked its way round the brittle sticks and caught.

'We can't stay here for long, there's hardly any furniture and no food.'

'Are there beds?' I said, stretching my hands to the flames, letting the warmth ease the cold and damp that had sunk into my bones.

'There's one upstairs and we can use the sofa down here.'

'Right,' I said. 'Let's start looking.'

'For God's sake, Angie, there's absolutely no point in doing anything now. It's late, I'm exhausted, and you don't look like you've slept a wink in days. It's also pitch dark and no, you can't search the house with a few of your sparks, they never last long. My phone is close to dying and I want to save it - using the torch will flatten it almost immediately. Be sensible. You won't be able to do anything for Frieda until you rest.'

She was right. I was struck by how quickly she had recovered what I imagine was her customary vim and vigour. I felt like a child.

'All right, Penny. You take the sofa down here where it's warm. I'll have a look upstairs.' I threw another log on the now blazing fire and hoped it would spread a little of its heat into the rooms above. At the doorway I turned to Penny who was huddled on the sofa, gazing into the fire. 'Thank you, Penny. I can't tell you how grateful I am that you came with me.'

She glanced at me and there was a trace of mischief in her eyes, she looked positively girlish. 'I'm enjoying the adventure,' she said. 'That sounds bad doesn't it? When I should be worried about Frieda. But it's a relief, actually, to get away from my life for a bit. Besides, you've promised to show me how the Theory of Everything works. How can I turn that down?'

I returned her smile but inside felt hollow with worry. As I trudged up the stairs with the very last drops of energy I had left, I realised I had convinced myself that the minute I got to the house I'd know what had happened to Mrs B. That there would be some residue, some signal, some hint at her past that would help me find her. But there was nothing.

I felt my way through the dark until I found the bed that creaked under my weight. Tired and sore and in need of a bath and a change of clothes I stared at the outline of the window. Not a single star pricked the thick blanket of the clouded night sky.

Chapter 7

A crash ripped me from horrifying nightmares, and I almost screamed to open my eyes to a searing light that burned them raw. Sunlight was blazing in from a window across the room and I jerked upright trying to work out where I was. My head was empty, and dizziness made me reel. I couldn't gather my thoughts together. Blinking stupidly, I looked round the room. Mrs B's old bedroom! I remembered.

I rolled out of the bed and stood, regretting getting up so quickly as black spots danced across my vision and nausea rolled into my throat. I stumbled across the room and pulled on the jumper I'd thrown to the floor before getting into bed. It didn't smell too good.

Downstairs I could hear Penny in the kitchen. She must have gone out for supplies as I could smell coffee brewing. I rubbed my eyes to clear them as they were encrusted with a sticky rheum. My ears rang. The few hours of sleep I'd managed hadn't brought any refreshment.

The floorboards groaned beneath my feet as I walked round the room, adrenalin driving the last scraps of sleep from my brain. This was Mrs B's room. She'd stayed here for a long time. I had to get started.

Pulling the bare mattress from the bed took a great deal of effort as it was dense and heavy – it also revealed nothing except the ragged slats beneath. Nothing was on the floor. A heavy wardrobe was empty, but my senses flared as I opened the doors and caught the faintest drift of sandalwood. It faded within seconds, but it was enough to make my heart beat faster. Mrs B loved sandalwood, drenched herself in sandalwood perfumes and had statues carved from the wood she'd bought from India all round the house, so they scented the air beautifully. It brought a lump to my throat.

I ran my hands over the shelves and underneath the unit. Nothing but dust. The rest of the room was empty. There was another room across the landing, but it was completely bare, not a stick of furniture, not even a bed was left, and the floorboards looked brittle.

I gave up and went downstairs, preparing to tear apart the little house. Penny came out of the kitchen holding a mug of coffee. 'It's black, I hope that's OK. No point in buying milk. But there's some bread and cheese in the kitchen.'

I took a sip, relishing the warmth burning its way down to my stomach. 'Have you found anything?'

'I haven't really looked, I thought best to get some food first. It's a glorious day.'

For the first time I looked out of the kitchen across the overgrown back garden and up to the fields stretching to the edge of the land. The blue sky, full of scudding clouds, stretched overhead. It was wild and exhilarating, no wonder Mrs B had liked living here, she would have enjoyed the restless energy of the sea and wind.

Ignoring the food Penny had bought, I searched the kitchen. Two glass vases leaned against each other in one of the cupboards, but the drawers held nothing but dust. Old lino rimmed the floor in a faded yellow check. I tried to peel it back, but it wouldn't budge.

Penny irritated me by watching over the rim of her cup as I searched, making no attempt to help. She'd made it clear she thought this was a wild goose chase, but she could have at least pretended to help.

The room at the front of the house was in a bad way; damp rot flourished black and shining along the plaster wall and great cracks had split the surface of a big wooden dining table that stood at an angle across the middle of the room. An old-fashioned sideboard had been shoved into the corner and my heart leaped into my mouth when I spotted something wedged behind it, but it was just an old book about flowers – its pages spotted with blooming ink spots of mould.

I leafed through it, careful not to tear the damp pages, searching for a name, a note. Eventually I gave up and threw it aside in frustration.

I was getting increasingly frantic. I needed to find a link to Mrs B's past, one that would tell me my next step. I moved across the flagstone floor into the sitting room. The kettle hung, ready to whistle, above the fire and I had to resist the temptation to sit by it and rest for a moment.

I was staring round the four blank walls when Penny came in holding a roughly cut sandwich. 'You have to eat, Angie, you look dead on your feet.'

'No. I'm not hungry,' I said.

Penny stirred the fire with angry stabs, the end of the poker glowing red. 'Angie, you will collapse if you carry on not eating or sleeping. Then what good will you be? Eat this and we'll walk into the village for some fresh air. Then we'll search the house properly. You're stumbling about like a robot, look at you.'

I snatched the sandwich from her hand and choked it down, chewing hard. It tasted like cardboard.

'Now get your coat,' she said.

Nobody could have resisted gazing up at the great, glorious expanse of the sky that rolled above us as we walked towards the village that perched on the top of the cliffs. The wind rippled over us in bracing gusts, carrying with it the salt of the sea. I allowed myself to feel nothing but sensation, mindlessly putting one foot in front of the other.

The village was pretty with an odd collection of buildings from all different eras. They knelt and shuffled and leaned against each other but as the road began to climb, I stopped in utter shock.

'God! Mrs B told me about this, but I never imagined ...'

It was as if a giant child had reached for the village and simply snapped half of it away. The sea roared ahead, and I imagined it pacing back and forth at the base of the scar that seemed as fresh as the day the land fell into the ocean so many years ago.

I quickened my step, the sea pulling me towards it until Penny stopped me.

'I can't go any further,' she said, her face bone-white. 'I'm going to the churchyard, you go on ahead.'

Surprised, I started to object, but she had already turned away. 'I'll just have a quick look,' I called after her. 'Then I'll come and find you.' She waved her hand.

Mrs B had told me how she had saved this village, and the lost child, but in the fight the cliffs had split and shattered, toppling half the village into the sea. I gripped hold of the ugly metal fence that marked the end of the village and looked down. The edge of the cliff was inches away from the toes of my trainers and beyond the vertiginous drop to the boiling sea.

The drop tugged me forwards and suddenly I was back at Pagan's Reach standing at the window that led out onto the roof, shivering with fear, Mrs B holding my arm in her iron hard grip.

'Flying is the most terrifying and the most invigorating adventure you will ever experience,' her voice rang clear as a bell in my ears. 'I don't mean leaning into birds and travelling with them into the sky, I mean flying, glorious flying, shaping your body to float on the eddies you see in the air. Can you see them? Like whirlpools on a lake.' And she had pointed and yes, I could see them, and my heart yearned to leap into the vast expanse of blue.

But I couldn't do it. Too aware of the heft of my bones and muscles: the weight of my flesh that I couldn't cast off, no matter how hard I tried. She worked with me all that summer, but I never got anywhere. She hid it well, but I knew she was disappointed.

Feeling the ice-cold steel burning into my hands I saw the limitless expanse of sea and sky in front of me and the urge to take a leap was irresistible. Would it work this time? Would the charm be enough to lift my fat old body and fling it up to skim through the clouds?

I stepped back; frightened I'd fall. I could almost hear Mrs B's sigh of disapproval at my lack of confidence, it had held me back too long; I had to change, I'd never find her without it.

Penny stood, silent and still in the heart of the graveyard that fanned out from the village church. Her head was bowed, and I approached quietly, my mind soaring and my mouth tasting salt.

'My mother,' she said as I drew close. We stood before the tall slim gravestone as the seagulls circled on their strange cries. 'I thought you might like to see this.' She wound her way through the rows of stones towards a crooked one, more weather beaten than the others. It stood closest to the cliffs, so the wind and salt water had curled away the edges, adding a mellow softness. It carried a single name, 'Lilith'.

I gasped. 'Mrs B's grandmother?'

'Yes, she died here, helping Frieda to save me.' Penny's face was without expression, but her hands were rolled into fists, the knuckles standing white.

'She taught Mrs B everything about how to use her powers to do good, well she tried to. I suspect she didn't like the way Mrs B used them for more selfish reasons. Apparently she was an amazing woman.' I knelt and touched the stone, feeling a great reverence for this woman and the women who came before her. I'd read their recipes and diaries and notes going back centuries in my time at Pagan's Reach. All of them wanting to add to the great wealth of knowledge they'd gathered over lifetimes. 'I have a few of her things, Mrs B gave them to me for protection.'

I blinked as a sudden change in light made the stone shimmer and glow. Time moved slow as honey, and I watched as Penny paused, froze - caught for a moment in the action of pushing back a strand of hair. I clambered to my feet; I knew what was coming. My stomach contracted.

'Lilith,' I said.

As insubstantial as sea mist, drifting like a fall of the softest rain, and lit with the sheen of pearl, stood a tall woman with a silver braid over one shoulder. She smiled with infinite sweetness and reached out her hands. I couldn't speak.

She gazed at me for a moment with dark, dark eyes then moved to her gravestone, placing her fingers upon it and leaning towards the grass that climbed at the base. She met my eyes once more and nodded. Then was gone.

I dropped to the ground and began to tear up the grass.

'What are you doing?' Penny said, time had clicked back into place, and she moved again.

'I saw her,' I said, grunting with the effort of clearing the grass and weeds.

'You saw Lilith? That's imposs…' she sighed and sat on a nearby ancient tomb. 'What did she say?'

'She didn't say anything, she just showed me where to look.'

'You're not digging her up?' Penny said, horrified.

'God no! Don't be stupid. There's something … look! Here!'

I pulled out another handful of grass and there it was, rolled deep into the earth at the bottom of the gravestone. I pulled it out and rubbed at the solid shape with the sleeve of my jumper.

The light caught hold and there was a ravishing chime of clear light as pure as spring water. We had to cover our eyes to shield them from the dazzle. I covered it with my coat.

'What is it?' Penny said, leaning forward.

'It's a scrying crystal!' I said, my voice as bright and joyful as the light that danced in the depths of the luminous globe.

*

Watching the fat cow lumbering about looking for the old witch was good fun but wasn't getting me any closer to the heart of the house. The place was riddled with passages hidden in the walls and I prowled along them, discovering all the secrets I could.

The only problem I had was controlling the powers of the old witch. She hadn't stopped fighting from the minute I'd grabbed her and I was finding it fucking wearisome truth be told. Every squint of opportunity she grabbed with both her bony hands - I'd nearly lost her twice. Thank fuck for my mate Jez who's proved bloody useful. Not only did he have an old warehouse we could lock her up in, but he wasn't bothered about knocking an old woman about. In fact he seemed to love it.

I was tempted to just get it over with - slit her throat and throw her into the canal, but Gran was right. I needed the old hag to get to the magical thing my great-grandma had gone on about. Some kind of wand, Gran had said, but she wasn't sure. She said nobody knew as it had been hidden for so long. She reckoned centuries.

The house certainly smelled old as death, specially the back bit which was fucking creepy - like something out of an old horror film. Stone walls and flagstones, not my kind of thing. I'd rip it all out - build modern, all clean lines and lots of glass.

I was a bit put out by the police arriving, they swarmed all over the fucking place, poking about where they shouldn't. One of them, though. Easy as wax. I'd been practising and got pretty good – I could control any weak-willed twat – I was upping my game with this one.

When the fat cow left, racing away in her stupid little car, I could stop hiding. I'd smothered the house enough I could walk round without having to deal with its little tricks. I started to search, starting at the top and working my way down. I couldn't take too long, the police might be back any minute and I didn't want to have to explain what I was up to – even to the bloke I had wriggling in the palm of my hand.

I got through the top two floors no trouble. Nothing there. Except for the flat in the roof where the fat one lived, the rooms were empty. What a fucking waste. A hundred people could live in that house and not see each other for months.

My Gran's whole house could have fitted into the witch's kitchen. I thought of her, crumpled into her old brown armchair, living on the dreams passed down to her from my great-gran. What a shit life. And she could have been living in this place.

I thought I was doing all right for myself. My flat had all the mod cons, nice view over the river, kitchen that cost a fucking fortune. But it was nothing like this. Everywhere I looked was colour. Great big oil paintings were hung on every wall just like you'd see in a museum.

The old witch's room was packed full of jewellery and clothes with designer names – bright as a jar of boiled sweets. The lives of the rich are filled with colour. Clothes that hadn't faded by being washed a thousand times. Rugs and curtains made with cloth meant to last lifetimes. Food that was fresh and filled with vitamins, not like the deep-fried orange mess my ma threw on a plate at the end of the day.

Anger was making me reckless. I stalked through room after room, carelessly knocking over a violin here, ripping a hole in a silk dress there. Stupid. I didn't want to leave any trace. Not yet.

For now, the old witch was safely stashed away under Jez's watchful gaze, surrounded by nothing but concrete and metal so she couldn't draw on anything living. I wasn't sure how long I could keep her like that – I couldn't risk killing her – but beating and threats hadn't got me any closer to finding out where this bloody magic thing was or how to get to her. I needed something to threaten her with. Maybe I'd use that fat bitch who looked after her – they were obviously close.

The bedroom was how I'd left it. I'd checked the cupboards and now I searched the drawers by the bed. Pots of ointment looked dangerous, so I didn't touch them. On the far side a photograph had fallen face first. I propped it up. There she was, the old witch, looking a lot younger with some crazy looking woman with lots of curly hair dressed up in one of them student things – a gown and stupid hat. A graduation day. They looked close too. I pushed it into my pocket.

I left through the front door and pulled out the bottle Jez had got me. He'd drawn some blood off the old witch and managed to get a nasty scratch across his face for his trouble. He wasn't happy about that. Still, he'd got what I wanted.

I held it up. The smell of blood made my nose twitch, and I snuffed it up, making sure it was still fresh. Unscrewing the lid, I moved to the terrace steps. I poured gouts into my hands and threw them onto the stone. Dark patches appeared where the blood landed. Perfect. I'd tip the wink to my police guy to check the steps with one of them blue light things. Enough for suspicion to fall on the younger one. Enough to get her locked up maybe.

Time to go. One last thing still to do. I needed to keep fat woman out of the house as long as possible – didn't want her warming it up and taking it back from me. I stood at the bedroom window looking down over the valley and used the only spell I knew well. The only one Gran could remember properly. The one that summoned the dead.

I had to concentrate. I'd used it once before, but it didn't work out great. Opening the window, I enjoyed the rush of wind. I held my arms above my head. I stared into the dark, seeking out all the lost I could find, inviting them to come. Come rest. Get help. I told them.

Already there was movement in the garden. I was surprised how many there were already. And so close. They must be used to getting help here. Well now I'd let them in.

Chapter 8

'I can connect with Mrs B using this,' I said tucking the crystal under my arm and hurrying back towards the road, Penny almost running to keep up with me. 'Let's get back to the house.'

'You said you saw Lilith?' Penny said, breathing hard. 'Was it like the dead you see, what do you call them … the ones? Is she stuck?'

'No,' I said. 'It wasn't anything like that, it was more of a … I don't know how to describe it … like a visitation.' I couldn't find the right words. I was trying to remember everything Mrs B had taught me about scrying.

The house was too far away. If I could have got my thoughts together, I would have chanted the words and flown there. Penny kept talking but I couldn't take in what she was saying, I could only think about the feel of the crystal under my hands.

I burst into the house and tore my coat off. Penny closed the door behind me. In my heightened state I was conscious of a reluctance in her that bordered on fear. I didn't care. I was too focused on the weight of Lilith's crystal.

'I should do this by moonlight, but I can't waste time. Is there a candle anywhere? The fire would work but it's not ideal. I need a room I can make completely dark.' I walked blindly from one room to another - my brain a pane of glass that had been trodden into smithereens.

Penny moved silently into the kitchen and found a candle which she presented to me along with a box of matches. She then closed the mouldy curtains in the front room and dragged in a chair.

With veneration, I lit the candle and placed the globe in the middle of the old table. The door closed with a hush and click but I didn't turn round. I couldn't take my eyes from the pool of light gathered deep within the crystal. It held within it the radiance of the sea and sky. I'd never seen one so alive.

I had to sit for a long time before my pounding heart began to slow and my breaths lengthened enough for me to find the centre I needed. I'd only done this a few times before. Molly, a girl in the village had lost her head to a local boy and used to make me scry out if he was cheating. We didn't have a crystal, so I'd use a bowl of water. It never really worked, I'd see some things and speak a few vague phrases, but this time I had to get it right.

Lilith's crystal was heavy; I needed two hands to hold it. My jumper became an impromptu stand, and I took off Mrs B's bracelet and placed it close, so the light from the globe picked out the charms inscribed in the gold; I would use it to centre on the old woman.

I remembered the day she gave it to me, then let my mind drift to the look on her face, the way she smiled, the crooked hobble when she walked, and the sound of her voice. The room stilled as my eyes relaxed and lost focus. I had to bring her to me, I had to see her before I could look into the depths of the crystal.

The candle nodded and bobbed. Magnified by the lens of the clear stone, the room filled with the dance of the flame.

I didn't want to open my eyes. I couldn't bear the agony of finding nothing but my upside-down reflection.

Time ticked on and I sat, frozen, hating myself for being such a coward. It was only when I could imagine the old woman so clearly I could hear her complaining about the tea being too cold, that I found the courage to open my eyes.

I gasped.

Deep in the heart of the crystal was a fragment of green light. As I watched, it stretched and spread until I could see the tops of trees speeding fast, almost too fast to make out. I leaned forward, barely daring to take a breath.

The vision dived into the darkness of a wood, and I swayed as I followed the motion as it swirled in and out of trees. I tried desperately to slow it down and try to work out where the crystal was going but the movement grew dizzyingly fast and we were back up in the clouds. It was a struggle to stay calm and focused as I wanted to scream with frustration.

I had to guide the vision towards Mrs B. With delicate caution I willed it to show me where she was, ignoring the tension in my chest that felt like an elephant was sitting on it.

I felt it in my stomach first. Rage. And pain. Fear as well. I swallowed hard and stared into the depths of the crystal until my eyes burned. The flickering images steadied and swooped into a building, too fast for me to make out any details. Then it slowed and I could see space so large the end of it disappeared into shadows. It was modern, with a black rubber floor and harsh, strip lighting. Polished concrete walls shone with a wintry gleam.

I leaned closer, desperately searching for clues, anything that would tell me where this place was, then reared back in shock as a face loomed into view.

'Lilith?' it said in astonishment.

'Mrs B!' I cried. 'It's Angie.' Her cheekbone was split, closing one eye, and her mouth was bruised into a puffy mess. She heard me and leaned forward, twisting her neck. Her hands were tied behind her back. She was still wearing her torn dressing gown, I realised, with a sob of horror. 'Tell me where you are!'

I was concentrating so hard my head felt on the verge of cracking open. Exhilaration she was alive was tempered by fury at what had been done to her. I wanted to dive headfirst into the crystal and rip the heart out of whoever had done this. She felt close enough to touch but could be hundreds of miles away.

'How do I find you?' I said again, my fingers reaching for her face but meeting only the cold, dense walls of the crystal that separated and united us at the same time.

She was mouthing something and I held the sides of the crystal, willing it to sharpen the image. Her eyes darted to the left and she looked back at me with urgency. 'My room!' The whisper echoed in my head though no sound came from the globe. 'My room! Look. Look in my room! My …'

She was gone, disappearing under a monstrous shadow that obliterated her from view. I squinted, trying to work out what had happened until it shifted, and a pair of silver eyes pressed against the wall of the globe, distorted into something horrifying.

Instinctively I covered the crystal with my hands, trying to hide from this predatory gaze that peered directly into the room, seeking me out. I had to snatch my hands away as the crystal began to heat, burning my skin. The eyes met mine and for a moment the world held still.

Then, with an ear-splitting boom, the crystal exploded.

*

I screamed in shock as slithers of glass shattered into the air, cutting my face and hands with a thousand tiny slices. I began to bleed and got to my feet, staggering as I was so drained by the power I'd used to control the crystal I could barely put one foot in front of the other.

'Angie! What happened?' A square of light appeared as Penny opened the door and crunched across the carpet of a million crystal fragments to take my hand. 'You're bleeding!' she said. As our fingers touched, I cried out. The force she carried rocketed along my veins, replenishing me as quickly and strongly as if I'd plugged into the mains. The shock of it was electrifying.

She pulled her hand away and held it to her chest, cradling it with the other.

'What the hell was that?' I said.

'You drained me,' she said, hot with outrage.

'Well, I didn't mean to. I'm sorry.'

She turned and left the room. I didn't know what to think. Mrs B was alive, I had to hold onto that though I hated to see her bloodied and bruised. Someone was holding her, someone I now knew to be very powerful, powerful enough to react with me through the crystal and destroy it. And what was wrong with Penny? The house was filled with her inexplicable anger.

I needed to write down everything I'd seen of the space where Mrs B was being kept. I wanted to talk it over with Penny, see what she thought. And we had to go back to Pagan's Reach. 'My room,' Mrs B had said. 'My room.'

But I'd searched every corner of her bedroom and hadn't found anything. Hopelessness washed over me again. I had no idea where the old woman was being kept and I was frightened the monster that was holding her would do terrible things now he knew I'd made a connection.

Penny was standing in the garden staring towards the cliffs as I opened the back door and stepped outside.

'Over there is where a beast made of shadows would have killed me if Frieda hadn't used her powers to stop it.' She sounded so flat it made me shiver. I was desperate to talk to her about what had just happened, but her posture was so frozen, so full of grief and pain it stopped my tongue.

I remembered what she said about Lilith dying to save her, and the pieces fell into place. 'You were the lost child,' I said, realisation dawning.

Penny looked at me over her shoulder; her face was cold and set as marble and her hair, loosened from its grips by the wind, flew into a wild tangle.

'My great-aunt's house was just over there,' she went on, her gaze fixed on the horizon again. 'Long gone now, fell into the sea. It was the first to go. Frieda was the only one who knew what was happening. She understood the darkness in that house well before my mother did. She wouldn't believe it.'

I eased myself onto the garden bench, almost holding my breath as Penny spoke into the wind that rattled and blew from across the ocean.

'I still dream about it, every so often, Them. Dragging me from my cell of a bedroom and forcing me into that room. It stank of sickness, and death.' She rubbed her arms. 'I could feel it, you know? The pull of it as they connected me to the dying woman. It was like my veins were being peeled away. I felt it a little just now when our fingers touched.'

'I'm sorry,' I said again, but she shook her head.

'You couldn't know. But that's what happened, here in this dark little village. A wicked, wicked monster lived in that house and knew what I had and how to use it. I was so little I had no idea what was going on. They almost killed me. That's why I'm here. It's not just because Frieda supported me the way she did, it's because she saved my life. She killed the monster and found me a home, and a mother who loved me as her own.' Penny's words were slow and precise, as if they were being unwillingly tugged from her very core.

'Oh, Penny I don't know what to say. Mrs B told me she had to find and rescue a village child, but I didn't know any more than that. She didn't really like to talk about it. I'd no idea you were so dreadfully abused in that way.' I wanted to stand and reach for her, but her ramrod figure repelled any gesture of comfort.

'The beasts were the worst,' Penny continued. Her hand shook as she pushed her hair away from her face. 'They'd swallow you up, cloak you in darkness so you couldn't see or breathe. Frieda used her light to blast one of them into harmless black shreds. I remember thinking she was some kind of superhero sent to save me.'

At last, she turned to face me.

'That's why I think I'm going to have to go home, Angie. I can't get mixed up any more in this world of monsters and witches. It's why I love science so much. It has its own magic, but there's no evil to it and no good. It's just … neutral - impassive.'

'You can't go home, Penny! I don't think I can find Mrs B alone. I promise I won't touch you again. I didn't realise that would happen and I totally get how horrible that must have been, what with all those dreadful memories of what happened to you here. But Mrs B needs us now, she needs you. Just as she rescued you from those beasts you need to help me rescue her.'

'But I can't, Angie!' she cried. 'Can't you see? When they drained me of this life force I have it nearly killed me. Frieda said my body was desiccated - every organ sucked dry. You can't guarantee that won't happen again. You can't guarantee you won't do that to me if you need … what did Frieda call it … replenishing?

'I won't! I promise!'

'I can't risk it. It's a part of my life I've put behind me. You can't tell me there's no danger ahead, Angie. I thought I wanted an adventure but the minute I felt you draining me I came to my senses.'

'I wasn't draining you! It was an accident!'

'Nevertheless, the effects were the same and I can assure you they weren't pleasant. We need to go. I'd like you to drop me off at the station, please. I'll find my own way home.'

'Please, Penny. I saw Mrs B. I know she's alive. I just need to find where she's being kept. I don't think I can do this alone.'

'Well, you'll have to I'm afraid. I need to protect myself. This is all too dangerous.'

I kept up my pleading, but it was a lost cause. Penny was resolute. She stared straight ahead as I drove her to the station and kept herself as far away from me as she could, clearly not trusting me not to use my powers to manipulate her into changing her mind. I was devastated. I'd go on to Pagan's Reach but as she got out with nothing but a terse 'goodbye', I realised what a comfort it had been to have her by my side.

I drove away, leaving her standing alone. I tried to swallow down the ache of sadness, but it stuck in my throat; I could barely breathe.

*

Penny settled into the carriage and pressed her forehead against the window, watching the darkening countryside slide by. She breathed deeply in a vain attempt to calm her thoughts. Heavy, mossy anchors of guilt she'd buried deep in the ocean of her mind began to rock and loosen. Guilt about not spending enough time with her mother before she died, guilt about Frieda and Lilith, and, most of all, guilt about sending Angie on alone when she knew danger was in her path.

But that moment when they touched! Penny leaned back in her seat, closing her eyes remembering the snap of connection and the immediate sensation of draining. It made her feel sick to think of it: the pull on her nerve and sinews, the sense her blood was being drawn from her at a terrifying speed. The dizzying horror of falling into the vacuum of darkness and death was shockingly familiar, despite fifty years having passed since it last happened.

The night Frieda destroyed the monster she had brought the girl Penny home and the child had understood for the first time what it was she had that others wanted to plunder.

'I noticed it the day I met you,' Frieda had said, the firelight flickering across her face. 'It's extraordinary. I haven't been round children much and at first thought it was just your youth. But now I can see there's something very special about you. Your body harnesses a life force that is so powerful it can be used to help others. No. Not in the crude way that monster used you, but in an amazing way – once you learn how to use it.'

But Penny had never learned how to use it. She didn't know how and wasn't interested enough to try once science had caught her under its spell. She wondered now whether that was a waste.

She dismissed the thought. This energy, whatever it was, had brought her nothing but pain and horror. Even now her sleep would be cracked open by nightmares that she was back in that house, chained down and teetering on the brink of death.

The reflection in the glass reminded Penny she was no longer a frightened child but a successful and respected woman in her sixties. She had to hang onto that. She didn't owe Angie anything.

Reaching for her phone she remembered the battery was low. She wanted to make some notes for her paper, but there wasn't enough charge, she mustn't waste it. She'd make notes in her head instead, she thought, watching the sun disappear behind the horizon.

But no matter how hard she tried to ignore it, she couldn't stop thinking about Angie's words, and remembering what Frieda had sacrificed to save her. Penny shifted in her seat as the memories she'd kept buried for so long swam remorselessly to the surface.

She remembered standing, hidden in the stairwell of the house in Brokkton, fifty years ago, listening to Frieda talking about how her grandmother, Lilith, had died.

'Saving Penny killed Lilith,' she said. 'Lilith knew the only way I could get the child out of the house was to hold the monster back, she did this long enough, so we managed to escape. But when we got back here the life drained from her. It was hopeless.'

Penny wiped her eyes as she recalled the devastation on Frieda's face. The guilt she'd felt that had driven her to race out into the night, forcing Frieda to come after her to rescue her again, but this time causing the village to fall into the sea.

How had she repressed these memories for so long? How could she have allowed her relationship with Frieda to fade into the odd exchange of Christmas cards after all her sacrifices?

Angie's words circled Penny's head. 'It sounds like you owe her,' she'd said. And she didn't know the half of it, Penny thought. Angie had been wretched with worry from the moment she'd knocked on Penny's door. She hadn't slept and barely eaten since the moment she found Frieda missing.

Penny wondered if there was anyone in her life who would fight to find her with the same desperation Angie had shown. Maybe a couple of PhD students? She thought with a grim smile.

No. There was no one. And whose fault was that? She asked herself.

There was two percent left on her phone. She picked it up.

'Angie? I'm just coming into Colchester. Can you come and get me?'

*

The journey to Pagan's Reach was interminable. I thanked God Penny had changed her mind, but she'd barely spoken since I collected her from the station. I daren't talk to her as her decision to stay seemed so fragile.

'What are you doing when you put your hand on the walls?' We had been driving in silence for so long Penny's words made me jump. 'You did it at the house. Frieda used to do it too.'

'Do you mean leaning in?'

'Is that what you call it?'

'It's what Mrs B called it – I don't know if it's the official term.'

'What is it?'

'It's one of the first things Mrs B taught me, it's a way of, like, checking in on someone, or something.'

'You can lean into people? What does it feel like?'

'It's like putting your head under water,' I said. 'You open your eyes and you're inside the essence of someone. You can see what's knotting them up, what's blocking them, or sometimes it's a good way of finding out secrets.'

We stared at the black road rolling ahead, lit by the twin beams of my headlights. One of them kept flickering.

'But I can't do it with you,' I said thoughtfully. 'You send out a kind of wall that blocks everything off. It's like trying to push against a pane of glass. Actually,' I frowned as I tried to find the right words. 'It's not like glass, it's more like pushing against something that no matter how hard you push, it pushes you straight back.'

'Like a magnet,' Penny said.

'Exactly!' I smiled. 'I used to love those at school, especially when you put the bits together that didn't want to go together. It was like something was living between them. A little giant that's stopped the ends meeting.'

'Has anyone else "pushed back"?'

'Yes. Once,' I said with a little shiver.

'Tell me.'

'Not now. That's a story that doesn't need retelling.'

'How do I stop pushing?' she said.

'I don't think you can,' I said. 'It's probably something you aren't even aware of. But after feeling what I felt today,' I shook my head, 'I think that energy of yours could be very dangerous indeed.'

Penny nodded, her eyes drifting back to the road ahead.

'I am sorry, you know,' I said, looking over at her, seeing her profile, a curve of light against the passing night.

'For what?'

'For draining you the way I did. I didn't mean to. I was just completely empty of energy and my body just … sort of sucked it from you. It wasn't something I consciously did.'

'I understand. It's fine.' She yawned, making me yawn in sympathy. 'So what happened? Back at the house? Did you find something? What happened to the crystal?'

'It showed me Mrs B,' I said. 'She's being held in some weird room – like a big cellar. She looked …' my voice clogged, and I had to clear my throat. 'She looked as if someone had beaten her.'

'Oh, Christ,' Penny muttered.

'But she knew I was there,' I said. 'She thought I was Lilith at first, there must be something of Lilith at the heart of the globe that Mrs B recognised.'

'How did it break?'

'While I was trying to hear what Mrs B was saying someone came between us. They knew I was there and reached through the crystal. I think it smashed into pieces to protect me.'

Penny rubbed her face, she looked as tired as I felt. I had to run a handful of energising sparks into my face to keep my eyes from closing.

'Is it much further?'

I glanced at the map on my phone. 'Another hour, I think. I need to search Mrs B's room again. She told me to look there. I don't understand what I missed the first time. Then I'm going to work out where she's being kept and who's taken her. And why.'

It wasn't until I drove through the gates and up the drive of Pagan's Reach that I realised how much I had missed the place - though it hadn't felt the same since Mrs B had been taken.

'Let's get something to eat and I need a shower,' I said to Penny as she got out of the car. 'Then we can start looking again.'

'That sounds good,' Penny stretched her back before tugging at the neck of her jersey. 'I'd like to wash my clothes as well.' She looked up as I dropped my bag to the ground. 'What's wrong?' she said.

I tore my eyes from the ground floor windows ahead to look at her. 'It's the house,' I said. 'It's full of the dead.'

Chapter 9

I began to run towards the front door, rummaging in my coat pocket for the keys.

'Do you mean the ones you talked about?' Penny was close behind, her face creased with concern and fear in her eyes.

'They never come into the house,' I said. 'They wait outside for us to help them. I don't understand how they got inside.'

'Can they hurt us?'

'I don't think so,' I said, hoping to reassure her, but I'd never seen so many ones together in one place.

I reached the front door and stopped. Penny banged into me.

'Penny, you must wait outside, OK? I've never seen so many all at once in one place and I don't know how your energy will affect them. Can you stay in the car? Promise not to come in.'

'Will you be all right?'

'I'll be fine.'

I waited until she was safely locked into my little car before turning back to the house. I couldn't understand how this had happened. Mrs B and I had left Pagan's Reach in the past and no ones had dared to enter – they wouldn't have been able to, the charms we regularly cast would have made sure of that.

I could sense the buzz as I got close to the door; ones never impacted the atoms this way unless they hadn't apparated. I shuddered to think how many must be in the house to charge the atmosphere so powerfully I could almost touch it.

I didn't want to face too many at once in the main hall so walked round to the back of the house, taking comfort from the familiar scent of nicotiana and sweet peas drifting from the borders.

At the back door I took a moment to lean into the house. Something was very wrong. The house retreated beneath my touch. It had been stifled, numbed. Resting my forehead against the wood of the door I reached as far as I could into each room, counting the number of ones congregating. Most of them were still - resting quietly, waiting to be released. But a few were filled with rage and splattered the air like flame throwers. I'd have to be very careful with those.

My energy levels were low - exhausted by worry and the endless chase from one move to another in my hunt for Mrs B. It seemed incredible now that I had reached fifty without understanding who the strange people were who drifted after me since I was a very small child. Nobody but my mother could see them as I could, and when she died, I just pretended they weren't there.

It had been in a pub. Mrs B wanted wine and had dragged me into the village local where I'd been horrified to see a one whose eyes bulged with the pressure of the rope he'd hung himself with. I'd avoided looking at him until Mrs B bustled over and I watched in amazement as she held his hand and listened to his story. It took a long time, but as he whispered to her, he faded and faded until disappearing altogether.

It took a lot of focus and strength to help a one move on. I'd have to absorb their stories, bear the weight of their grief and pain before encouraging them to let go of their earthly life and move on. I couldn't begin to work out how the hell I was going to be able to move on so many. There were hundreds in the house.

I couldn't listen to all of them, I decided. I simply couldn't do it on my own. I'd have to deal with the strongest and try and use some other way to get the rest to leave, promising I'd help them later.

I stepped into the kitchen. Shocked again by the numbing cold. Ignoring two ones standing quietly by the window, I walked through past the grate and Trevor's basket and on towards the sitting room. The ones began to follow, congregating and circling as I walked, not daring to reach for me – not yet.

Mrs B had taught me not to fear the ones. Especially those who had apparated so I could see them. They had used all their energy clinging onto their physical presence, she said, so had nothing left to do any harm. The ones to worry about were those who'd given up their bodies but clung onto their rage and pain, manifesting as something that could affect the outside world; they were dangerous.

My powers attracted them, they could sniff them out so I quietly spoke words to create a shield that would hide me from the weaker ones. I needed to get to Mrs B's big old cabinet in the sitting room. There was something there that I hoped would help. The ones were thronging closer, I was reluctant to use my power to push them away for fear of attracting more, so kept walking as quickly as I could.

The cabinet gleamed darkly as I entered. More ones waited there, attracted by the magic it emanated. What I was looking for was on the top shelf and I struggled to reach it. I wasn't sure it would work; I'd only seen Mrs B use it on unwanted visitors – her physiotherapist usually.

With a grunt of effort, I tugged it loose until it dropped into my hands. A soundless bell. Mrs B had been given it by an Indian witch she'd met in Jaipur, one of the few witches she'd got on with.

Ignoring the ones who pushed ever closer, I examined the heavy brass chamber. It was decorated with engravings of elephants and tigers. The artist's skill had been such that the animals seemed to move, crouching and leaping as I turned the bell in my hands.

I reached into the back of the cabinet again to find the special brass clapper. It fitted into my hand as if made for it and I held up the bell and prepared to strike. I hoped it would work.

A one was very close to me now, staring into my face. If it had breath, I would have smelled it. His shoulder and half his chest had been ripped away. War got this one, I thought. Taking a breath, I slammed the clapper against the bell.

The effect was immediate. I couldn't hear anything, but all the ones in the room stirred, putting their hands over their ears. I struck again and they took a step back. I could see the sound waves rippling like I'd dropped a pebble in a lake, and when they reached the ones, they jerked and twisted away.

I kept hitting the bell, feeling the vibrations shudder up to my wrist, but everything was eerily silent.

I moved into the hall and then up the stairs, pleased to see the effect the bell was having. All the ones I could see reacted, disappearing back through the walls and out of the house. Eventually, I could see no more, and knew all that was left were the ones who hadn't apparated but lingered in the house, powering up their pain to destroy everything they could see.

Sure enough, once I put down the bell and stood still, I could hear crashing. It was coming from Mrs B's room. I thought of Penny sitting in the car outside, wondering what was going on. I worried she would come after me, so I had to sort it out quickly.

A smash of glass made me jump and I rubbed my fingers together until the sparks flared, I needed to be ready. I waited for a moment outside the door before pushing it open.

The scene was chaotic. This one had poured none of its energy into externalisation, so there was no physical presence – just a vibration in the air in the centre of the room. Another judder and the atoms flexed, pushing over a tall bookcase. I recoiled at the violence.

I placed my hand on my chest and took a breath. As objects continued to fly round, I closed my eyes and considered what charms would work best. The words fell from my lips, round and golden. I lifted my voice and let them float into the air. They spun and fluttered like sycamore leaves as they hit the turbulence surging from one wall to another.

They spread like little parachutes and rode the waves until I saw the colours change and the golden warmth began to do its job, soothing and calming the angry charge that made my hair stand on end with static. Glass crunched under my feet as I stepped carefully through the rubbish strewn across the floor. A strange wind whistled in my ears, deafening me; for a moment I was disorientated. I kept walking, waiting for it to drop, and when it did a woman appeared. She was sitting in the middle of the rug; her head buried in her hands.

I was just about to bend to talk to her when I heard a creak behind me. Keeping my body stock still so as not to frighten the woman, I looked over my shoulder furious to see Penny standing in the doorway. Her face was impassive but the fast rise and fall of her chest told me she was badly affected by what she had seen. She stared at the wreck of the room and her fingers rippled, unconsciously picking up the electric charge as it billowed past her.

'Get back!' I hissed already feeling the jolt of her presence and the effect it was having upon the dead woman. I glared at her until Penny stepped away, disappearing into the shadows of the corridor.

It took all of my energy to get the woman to acknowledge me. She was so caught up in her rage and pain she couldn't see past it. My words had robbed her of her aggression and power, but I couldn't force her to connect with me. I waited patiently, though my knees ached with pain as splinters of glass pressed into my skin.

'Let me listen,' I said in a whisper. With infinite caution I stretched out my hand and reached for her shoulder with the lightest breath of a touch. I was almost thrown backwards by a massive bolt of electricity. I had to grit my teeth and steel myself to keep up the contact. I heard Penny gasp and I threw her a fierce look of warning. 'Keep back!' I thought, hoping she would understand.

It was hard. Terribly hard to hear this one's story. She screamed and gibbered with rage at the injustices she had suffered. The fine, tall son she had lost. The wasted life of drudgery and boredom that had ended before she was ready. She raged against age, the theft of her early beauty. She pointed to her thinning hair, her slack skin, her crone hands.

I tried to absorb some of her anger into my body, but it was too much. It was like trying to contain lava. It wouldn't stay and erupted from me in waves of heat.

She wasn't ready or able to let me help. I wasn't going to be able to soothe her enough to make her let go. She held onto her rage with both hands, blind to anything else. This was rare. If I didn't do something she would stay trapped in the house – not something I could allow to happen. The thought of this furious woman crashing round damaging everything was horrifying.

I sighed. The last time I'd had one this bad it had ruined Mrs B's little study on the ground floor. That was a nasty experience. In the end the house had swollen the front and back door shut until we'd dealt with it. Mrs B was forced to turn to her oldest books to find the right words. It had been a struggle and I suspected moving this woman on would be equally difficult.

Conscious of Penny standing outside, I tried to stay calm and think. I needed to drain the energy from this broken woman's sprit so she couldn't do any harm, at least for a while, until I worked out what to do with her. I held up my hands and spread my fingers. Concentrating so hard my head began to throb, I tried to find the core of charged matter that electrified the room. It was such a dense cloud it was difficult to identify the source but finally I located the heart that burned, tiny and searingly bright.

Quickly, as I could see the woman beginning to fade so I knew she was moving her energy away from apparating, I moved my fingers to push into the heat of the core before spreading it into filaments, winding them onto my hands, electric strands that glowed and burned like copper wires. As I pulled, I felt the tug of her resistance as she gathered her power close, but she lacked my strength.

My hands burned but I kept pulling, breathing cool, ice-blue words that fell and sizzled. When I held as much as I could, I let go - shaking my hands vigorously until the static crackle fell harmlessly to the floor.

The room was silent and still. The house breathed a sigh of relief. She wasn't gone; a tiny vibration remained that I knew would eventually grow and cause trouble again, but that would do for now. The temptation to lie down among the broken glass and smashed furniture and close my eyes was irresistible. My knees were bleeding, and my body cried out for rest. I would have to replenish, and soon.

I stumbled to the edge of the bed just as another great sweep of energy flew into the room. Another one. A man this time. Old and just as angry as the woman. I couldn't believe it. What was going on? How had this happened?

Wearily, I got to my feet ready to face him but his force was so strong he slammed into me, knocking me to the floor.

'Angie!'

Dazed, I looked round, Penny was running into the room.

'Don't!' I cried weakly but it was too late. She was grabbing me, pulling me up to my feet and the second we touched a blast of light, as bright as nuclear explosions I'd seen on film, zipped through the air sending us both flying. A high-pitched noise screamed in my ears and I was completely blinded. It was as if we'd released the sun from a bag, like Odysseus releasing the wind.

My mind raced as I searched for Penny with my hands. Just as I thought, the presence of the one – who hadn't apparated and existed entirely in a cloud of energy – had connected with my powers, amplified by Penny's and caused an explosion. I expected my skin to feel flayed, burned to a crisp, but it was cool and whole.

'Penny! Can you hear me? Are you OK?'

'I … I think so, but I can't see anything. Whatever that was completely blinded me.'

'Keep blinking,' I said, rubbing my eyes. The good thing was I couldn't sense the one anymore. I suspected that explosion of energy had torn him into nothingness. I felt for the edge of the bed and pulled myself up, pulling Penny – careful to hold her by her jumpered arm so our skin didn't touch – with me. 'Can you stand?' I said.

'I think so.'

I could still see nothing but a blinding dazzle. I held my hands over my eyes but it bought no comfort; still nothing but white. Had that explosion blinded us permanently? Fear threatened to overwhelm me, and I struggled to swallow the hysteria down.

'I think … I think I can see something.' Penny said.

'Really? Thank God,' I said. I kept blinking and slowly, slowly, the dazzle began to break into pieces and dissolve. I slumped on the bed, which I could feel was covered with debris, and tried to make out anything.

'Angie! Look!' Penny said in such shock my stomach turned over.

'What is it? I still can't see!'

'On the walls! And the ceiling! Everywhere …'

Frustrated, I found the strength to muster up a few darkening sparks and rubbed them into my eyes. My vision finally began to clear.

'Oh my God…' I breathed.

Penny was right. All over the walls, the doors, the floorboards, even the ceiling, words were appearing as if written in an ink drawn from the sun. They blazed.

Over and over and over again. *Joshua… Joshua P…. Joshua Pettigr…Joshua Pettigrew* – the writing becoming more confident. *Joshua PettigrewJoshuaPettigrewJoshua PettigrewJoshua Pettigrew Joshua PettigrewJoshua Pettigrew Joshua Pettigrew Joshua Pettigrew Joshua Pettigrew Joshua Pettigrew Joshua Pettigrew Joshua Pettigrew…*

Chapter 10

Sunday morning found Penny and me in the kitchen dressed in layers of jumpers and scarves we'd scavenged from the house. I couldn't light a fire and Penny was getting frustrated with the boiler.

'I don't understand it,' she said. 'The pilot light is on, I can hear the pump, the radiators are warm, but the air is frozen. Something is causing a highly accelerated entropy. It doesn't make sense.'

'It's warmer outside,' I said staring dully out the window. Everything was grey. Muggy clouds pressed damp and warm against the windows turning icy as they met the glass. Penny placed a mug of tea on the table.

'At least we have a name,' she said. 'It's a step forward. And you've seen Frieda, so you know she's still alive.'

'I should have seen the words days ago!' I burst out. 'What if I hadn't come to find you? Why wasn't my power enough? She trusted me to follow her message and I didn't even see it!' I pushed the tea away. 'And who's Joshua Pettigrew?'

Penny sat down at the table and sipped her tea. 'I tried Googling the name last night when you were getting rid of the last of the ones,' she said. 'But I couldn't get a signal. The Wi-Fi doesn't connect and even up on the hill it kept dropping out. Not that I think I could have read much, my eyes are still blurry.'

'We'd have to go into town to get a decent connection,' I said. 'But it's pointless. Whoever took Mrs B isn't going to show up on bloody Google.'

'You'd be surprised what you can find there.'

'I know, Penny, I have used it before – even people who didn't go to fancy universities can use Google, you know.' I rubbed my eyes. 'I'm going for a walk,' I said.

Mrs B's words had blazed right through to the outside walls of the house, I saw as I closed the back door. The name Joshua Pettigrew glowed faintly from the roughened bricks; I felt the burn of their reproach as I walked the familiar path into the woods.

I hated myself. Tomorrow Mrs B would have been gone for a week and despite my best efforts she was still alone and wounded - God knows where - and Pagan's Reach was dying. What has Penny called it? Accelerated Entropy.

Penny was right, I thought as I tramped through the crumbling earth, already sweating in my coat. I took my jumper off and hung it on the crumbling gate post, along with my scarf. I should focus on the positive, Mrs B was alive, and I had a name.

For the thousandth time I wanted to find a wall and smash my head against it. Why had it taken Penny's presence for the old woman's message to show? I'd cast countless reveal charms and found nothing. The thought of how badly I'd let her down made me feel sick. I'd felt sick for days, a hollow nausea that turned food as tasteless as rubber.

The influx of the dead had held us back. It had taken most of the night to move on the ones closest to the house, the ones who threatened to slide in through the walls. Penny couldn't see them, but I know they made her uneasy – she could sense the vibrations of their presence, and they were attracted to the power she held.

I rubbed my eyes again. Both of us still couldn't see properly after the blinding explosion of the night before. Every time I blinked white pools of light would bloom, making reading impossible. They were starting to recede, but I suspected it would be a while before either of us would be back to normal.

But at least the massive surge of power had fuelled Mrs B's desperate message so her words flamed to life. She must have cast a powerful charm to carve the words on every surface of the house. It would have taken a lot of energy, I thought with a sharp pang, energy she needed to fight her attacker.

And I missed it, I thought in despair. Carrying that guilt was a heavy kind of agony; I felt saturated with its weight.

I walked and walked, and every step reminded me of the hundreds of times I'd walked by Mrs B's side - Trevor bounding into the undergrowth ahead, wagging his stumpy tail so fast it was a blur. All those years of safety I'd taken completely for granted, safe under the sheltering arm of Mrs B. And now she was frightened and alone and I wasn't even a good enough witch to read her message without someone holding my hand.

The woods were beginning to work their magic. The birdsong and hushing sigh of the canopy of trees began to ease the ache of tiredness from behind my eyes. The richness of the soil beneath my boots refreshed my blood and my muddled thoughts began to clear.

Penny and I would find Joshua Pettigrew. I knew he had silvery eyes and the power of a wolf. The CCTV footage showed me the man who had taken the old woman, I was sure of it. At the very least he was in league with this Joshua Pettigrew.

So I knew he was tall and bulky with dark hair. Also, that Mrs B was being held somewhere that looked recently built and was alive. That put me a step closer to finding her, though it wasn't much to go on. As I turned to walk back to the house, I saw another group of ones threading their way across the orchard. There had been so many, more than I had ever seen. Why were they there?

My brain, jump-started by the energy of the woods, began to piece together the jumbled mess of impressions that filled my head until it felt it would burst: The chill of the house. I first noticed it the day Mrs B was taken. It had gotten worse and worse until ice now formed on the inside of the windows, despite the boiler going full blast. The crowd of ones, some very dangerous, who filled the house in a way they would have never dared to attempt when Mrs B was in charge.

Penny looked up in shock as I threw the door open and bustled into the library, boots smearing mud and my coat still on.

'He's in the house,' I said, my breath coming in gasps.

'What?' she said, standing so quickly the book she was reading fell to the floor.

'It explains everything. Why the house is so cold, how all those ones managed to get in …'

'Do you mean Joshua Pettigrew?'

'Of course – or one of his henchmen, wolves always go round in packs.'

'But wouldn't you sense him?'

'I thought so, but after I missed Mrs B's message, I reckon I'm not as powerful as I thought I was. That or he's just very good at cloaking. I've done it myself, it's easy – but you can't keep it up for long.'

'So what do we do?'

'I've been thinking about that. There's nothing you can do to help me in the house – in fact to get rid of that last one that's knocking about on the top floor it's probably better if you and your energy are as far away as possible.' I walked up and down, my breathing still ragged. 'I need you to use all your contacts. You must have log ons to all the libraries in the world. Could you search for Joshua Pettigrew? I can't think what else to do.'

'Of course,' she said. 'I'll do all I can, but it will have to wait until tomorrow, my eyes are still playing up – everything still goes white whenever I blink.'

'I'll make us something to eat,' I said. 'And then I'll get rid of the last one that's crashing about in the top nursery. We should get an early night. I'll need all my strength to find what's trying to take over the house.'

*

Penny left early, regretting she couldn't use the powerful PC she had at home. Her flat felt a million miles away, she realised with a small shock. Though with no internet access in the house and the temperature inside below freezing, it was a relief to drive Angie's car out into the weak sunshine that was struggling to break through the morning clouds.

She was worried about Angie who seemed driven mad by guilt. She refused to sleep, despite making Penny go to bed early, setting her up in a spacious guest room and making sure she ate properly.

Penny had heard her pacing up and down the corridors of the house through the night. Over tea that morning her eyes were rimmed with red and a hectic energy jangled from her – she couldn't sit still. Her bulk was melting away, leaving her gaunt - her startlingly green eyes sinking into hollows.

Penny hadn't driven for years and winced as the gears clunked and growled. She hopped her way down narrow country lanes before turning onto the main road heading into town.

The library wasn't big, but Penny only needed to connect to the internet. She hoped everything they needed would be online. She didn't fancy scrolling through hundreds of documents on the microfilm readers she remembered from her days as a student.

After an interminable period of form filling and explanations, Penny was finally allowed into the 'hub' where four computers sat. Two of them were occupied. One by a cross looking man in his 70's who was peering over his glasses and swearing under his breath. The other, a young woman wearing headphones watching a film.

Penny couldn't wait to get started. She was desperate to help Angie and find Frieda. Research was something in which she excelled of course, and she was far more comfortable using her mental skills rather than causing magical explosions to discover the next step.

Thank God her eyes were back to normal. She still hadn't processed what happened that night. The light had been extraordinary, as if they'd split an atom. It had been enough to affect their vision for a few days, but it would seem it hadn't been permanent.

Penny began by typing in the name 'Joshua Pettigrew', an obvious place to start. But unless he was a computer analyst from Philadelphia or a seven-year-old maths challenge winner from Bedford, the initial results weren't promising.

Angie was right. She wasn't going to find this man through LinkedIn or Facebook. But he must have some connection with Frieda. Otherwise why would he take her? Penny started to try different search terms. Pettigrew and Beaudry, Pettigrew France

Beaudry– she knew Frieda had loved France and often visited … nothing.

Penny sighed. She needed something to take back to Angie, she was relying on her. She closed her eyes trying to remember what she'd been told about Frieda growing up. She used to spend summers in Margate when she was little. Pettigrew Beaudry Margate. Nothing. Then Penny tutted with irritation - Beaudry was Frieda's married name.

Her fingers dancing over the keyboard, a smile lifting the corner of her mouth, she typed in Frieda's maiden name. Pratt. Pettigrew Pratt. Pettigrew Pratt Margate. Pettigrew Pratt Lilith. A stream of results appeared but nothing relevant.

Penny scratched at the roots of her hair. Think! she told herself fiercely. Minutes ticked by as she stared into the distance, not seeing how unnerving her head-phoned companion was finding her thoughtful scowl. Penny gazed up at the dusty ceiling and stretched her arms above her head, her back cracking.

She got to her feet to walk about a bit and clear her head when she bumped into a low circular table upon which was spread a display of books on architecture. Her face cleared and she grabbed her chair to sit down again. This time. This time she'd find something she was certain – why hadn't she thought of it before?

Pagan's Reach Pettigrew she tapped. The screen refilled. Penny smiled. 'Bingo,' she said.

*

'Pettigrew used to live here,' Penny said, barely waiting until she had got out of the car. Angie was sitting on the terrace steps, driven outside by the cold of the house. The sun had finally come out in force and the garden stirred under its beams.

She was chewing on her nails and her hair stuck out at the top of her head where she'd been running her fingers through it. It was dark with grease. It worried Penny how little Angie was looking after herself.

At Penny's words she jumped to her feet. 'What do you mean? He can't have done, only women have lived here.'

'Ada Pettigrew,' Penny said in triumph, handing over the papers she has printed out. Angie snatched at them and shook her head.

'I can't make sense of this,' she said. 'Tell me.'

'Let's go and sit down, I'm gasping for a cup of tea.'

'Don't you dare,' Angie said, her eyes snapping. 'Tell me now.'

'OK, OK!' Penny took the papers back and perched on the top step. The stone was warm. 'She was born around 1890 …'

'Well she can't be anything to do with this! She'd be well over a hundred.'

'So is Frieda,' Penny pointed out. 'But I found Ada's death certificate. I couldn't find anything yet about her family, but what I did find is this.' Penny unfolded one of the pages. 'It's a census, from 1921. Look at the address.'

'Pagan's Reach,' Angie gasped.

'And look under "relationship to head of house"'.

'It says head.'

Penny nodded. 'It means there weren't any men in the house – she owned it. And she was single.'

Angie jumped up and started walking up and down. 'That's it! That's the link! Of course it is. Oh, Penny you're a superstar. If she's dead it must be a relative of hers. Someone who found out about Pagan's Reach from this Ada Pettigrew.' She turned to Penny, colour high and hectic in her cheeks. 'They're not after Mrs B, they're after the house! That's why they haven't killed her. She's its mistress. They can't take it over without knowing how to unlock all the charms. Even I don't know how. She told me she would pass them onto me when she knew it was time. But we thought that wouldn't be for years.'

Penny raised an eyebrow. 'She is well over a hundred, Angie. You have to face that.'

'Yes, but she's not an ordinary woman. She's a powerful witch. Besides, I'm really not ready to become the mistress of Pagan's Reach, I've got so much more to learn.'

'I would imagine any details about the women who lived in this house would be kept here, not out on public record. It was a surprise to see Ada Pettigrew on the census. I can't imagine they were the kind of women who'd register on the electoral roll.'

'Absolutely not, they like their privacy, well Mrs B certainly did.'

'Well, what are we waiting for?'

I followed Penny as she bounded up the steps, as limber as a teenager. I wondered where she got the energy from, I seemed to be living on my nerves. Worry was driving me on, but it wasn't sustainable, exhaustion was always at my side, step for step. I could feel it trying to pull me into oblivion; it was a constant struggle and I dreaded to think what would happen when I couldn't hold it back any longer.

'Where are you going?' I said as we went through the open front door and Penny headed for the library.

'I thought we were going to look at the house records. You said the women wrote everything down and they went back years.'

'Yes I did, but they aren't kept in the main library, they're all through here.'

The sitting room contained the old woman's special things. The giant cabinet she'd had made contained a jumble sale of objects: pieces of blown glass, blue crystal bowls, golden figurines, some faded photographs, a clutter of walnuts. Every single thing in there carried with it a powerful memory of the old woman; I could barely bring myself to look at them.

Instead, I focused on the end wall of the room that was filled with books, folders, papers and journals. Some were properly bound in leather with gold writing, others just folios of paper tied with ribbon or in thick cardboard folders. My heart sank to look at them. There were thousands of books there; the top shelves disappeared into shadows of the roof.

'This is hopeless,' I said, slumping onto a Liberty print armchair. The books and shelves swam before my eyes, and I blinked to steady them. 'I don't know where to start. And it may not even lead us to Mrs B.' I dropped my head into my hands with a groan; I couldn't think straight anymore. My heart was jumping uncomfortably in my chest, and I rubbed it to ease the tension.

'We have to try,' Penny said. 'It's the only real lead we have. Somewhere there is the story of Ada Pettigrew, and once we find that I'm sure we will find Joshua. That's what Frieda wanted us to do isn't it?'

I nodded but felt so wiped out, so lost, I could do nothing but sit and watch as Penny began to move along the shelves.

'She was here in 1920, we know that.' She perched a pair of thick-framed black glasses on the end of her nose. 'I'm sure these books are in some sort of order.' She tilted her head back to look into the shadows of the roof. 'Those ones at the very top look positively medieval,' she said. She stretched on the tips of her toes and pulled down a sheaf of papers pinned together by a gold button, sneezing as a cloud of dust rose from a thin pamphlet decorated with a primitive woodcut. Part of me was mortified to see the dust, but I was beyond caring.

'It should all be in a museum – look,' she reached for a yellowing page. 'This is a bill for… "hosiery, hats and gloves."' Her face shone and I tried to smile but my face was frozen. 'I was expecting it all to be magic recipes and spells.'

Her voice was drifting in and out. I closed my eyes to ease the dryness. Penny's steps back and forth were as monotonous as a clock. My head began to nod, and I pulled it up with a jerk.

'The further we go back the more organised it looks,' Penny said. 'It looks like someone sorted it all out about eighty years ago. Maybe they had to move everything during the war …'

Her voice droned on and turned into the buzzing of bees round the hives. I thought of honey and bread and cups of tea. I felt the warmth of sun on my face and turned to it, frowning as it began to darken and cold, ran its fingers over my skin, making me shiver. The ringing in my ears became a call, muffled but urgent and I wondered idly what it was.

Mrs B? I said, but no sound left my lips. I turned to look into the darkness, and it reached for me, pulling me down and I tried to push it away. But I kept falling and before me a pinprick of light began to hover. Mrs B I said again thickly, my tongue grossly swollen in my mouth. I heard a chattering in my head, as if I was in a crowd of people.

'Angie …'

I'm coming, Mrs B. Where are you? I was galloping forward, wind blowing hard in my face. Something was carrying me, I felt with my hands, but they fell through the shadows.

'Angie …'

With a crash I fell, flagstones were cold under my hands and knees. Mrs B, curled into a ball with her back to me. I could see the white tufts on her head. I crawled across the floor towards her, pulling at her shoulder. She rolled over to face me, her toothless mouth agape and her eyes black holes.

Horror tore my breath away. She was cold. So cold. My hands turned blue touching her. I screamed.

'Angie!'

Chapter 11

Shocked, I opened my eyes. Penny was shaking me, hard, her face panicked. 'Angie! Are you all right? You were screaming.'

I wiped my mouth with a shaky hand. My heart pumped thick and hard, shaking my ribcage with its force. 'Sorry,' I said. 'I must have fallen asleep.'

'I'm not surprised. You can't have had more than a couple of hours in the last week. You're exhausted, Angie – you can't go on like this.'

'I saw Mrs B,' I said, my blood sounding the remembered horror. 'She was … she was …'

'It was a nightmare, Angie. Whatever you saw. You're driving yourself mad by not eating and sleeping, no wonder you're dreaming awful things.'

I nodded, feeling my heart begin to slow down. Dizziness receded and I drunk greedily from the glass of water Penny put in my hand.

'Better?' she said, concern hollowing her face.

'So what did you find?'

'Angie I think you need to go to bed. It's really late and you're dead on your feet, we …'

'Tell me what you've found! There's something. I can see it in your eyes.'

I looked over at the shelves. Books and papers were lying on the floor in neat piles. Great gaps loomed where Penny had pulled books and folders like teeth.

Using the arms of the chair I pushed myself up and tottered forward, my head spinning.

'Careful, Angie!'

'I'm OK, I'm OK. Tell me. What you found.'

Penny drew herself up and regarded me with flashing eyes. I pictured her students quailing under the force of that gaze. 'I'm not going to tell you anything, Angie, until you promise me that afterwards, you'll go straight to bed.' She held up her hand. 'I'm not arguing with you. There's nothing we can do now it's …' she turned her watch to check the time, 'well past midnight. Agreed?'

The image of Mrs B on the floor, her eyes black, flashed up like a movie reel and I started to argue, but my body wouldn't obey. I sat down before I fell. 'Agreed,' I said wearily.

'Well. I've found the records about Ada Pettigrew.'

Adrenalin jerked me fully awake. 'You have? Where? Show me!'

Penny studied me for a moment before moving to the side table and picking up a large book with thick, coarse cut pages.

'This is some sort of punishment record,' she said. 'Ages ago it looked like there was quite a community of women here drifting in and out. They would hold courts if someone broke the rules.'

I shifted in my seat. 'What kind of rules?'

'Telling secrets, bringing in men, using their powers to wound rather than heal, betraying the sisterhood – that sort of thing. But what Ada Pettigrew did was one of the most terrible of crimes.' Penny opened the book and laid it flat on her lap. She ran her finger along the page.

'It was somewhere around 1926,' she said. 'There are many women's names here that weren't on the census, they must have hidden when the Enumerators came round.'

'OK, get on with it, Penny for God's sake.' She glared at me before turning back to the book.

She read aloud, following the handwriting with her fingertip. 'Ada Pettigrew is banished from Pagan's Reach and condemned to live in the outside world for the rest of her life: never again to practice as a witch; be a part of any witch community; there shall be no return to Pagan's Reach – on pain of death.'

'Christ! What did she do?'

'It's bad, Angie.'

'What? What did she do?' I said again.

Penny found her place and pushed her glasses up her nose. 'For the summoning of the dead, not to ease them into the next world, but to conquer and control. For plotting the destruction of Rebekah Andrews, Dorothy Curlew, Agnes Simmonds, and Ruth Beattie - and the wounding almost to the death of Grace Wilson.' Penny looked up at me, her eyes wide.

I shivered. 'She sounds terrifying,' I said.

'From these records I worked out when she'd joined the community in the house and, here …' She heaved another book from the table and placed it on top of the other. 'I found all the details of who she was and where she came from. It says …' She began to read again. '1915 Ada Pettigrew of the parish of Hurstbridge …'

'That's only about fifty miles from here!'

'… of the parish of Hurstbridge,' Penny continued. 'Home of the Pettigrew family for centuries. A highly skilled and learned witch.'

'And ten years later she was banished. I wonder what happened to her?'

'They stripped her of her powers it says,' Penny said, resting her hand on the book. 'It sounds a painful process.' Both of us winced at the thought.

'That's where we need to go, Hurstbridge.'

'I knew you were going to say that,' Penny said. 'That's why I made you promise. We're not doing anything until you've had a proper night's sleep. We can leave in the morning.'

There was no point in arguing. I could barely stand; Penny had to push me up the stairs. She helped me change, careful not to touch my skin, and watched me button up clean pyjamas that smelled of fresh air and laundry powder. I toppled into bed, asleep before Penny pulled the covers over my shoulders.

*

Wrapped in jumpers with thick socks and my heaviest jeans I waited impatiently in the frozen kitchen as Penny took an age to finish her coffee. I jangled my keys in the pocket of my coat until she shot me such a look I thought it would be better to wait in the garden.

I felt so much better for a night's sleep, but I couldn't dislodge the feeling I had betrayed Mrs B by sleeping in my comfortable bed as she lay beaten and broken on the floor. It made my chest fill with grief to think of it.

The day was bright and cold, the purity of the sky had the clarity of glass and birds soared into the bowl of blue. Summer was stretching its arms as it woke; flowers and trees bloomed under its touch. But it was as if I was looking through a cold fog - nothing could warm me. I looked back, wondering when Penny would come. Mrs B's words had faded from the walls.

She'd been gone a week and a day. Penny had convinced me the nightmare I'd had was just stress and exhaustion, but I couldn't help the awful fear that it was a message. Mrs B was beginning to fade; just like the words she'd engraved in the house. She couldn't stay trapped with no access to the natural world without rapidly diminishing. We had to get to her. And soon.

'Come on, Penny! What's taking you so long? I want to get to Hurstbridge before everyone goes to work.'

Penny appeared at the back door, her face white.

'What is it?'

'The police. They've just driven up to the front door.'

'Oh, bloody hell, probably to ask more questions. Can't we just go?'

'They'd have seen your car is here.'

I strode across the kitchen and through the house to the front hall. It didn't seem possible, but the house was even colder – my feet slipped on the crust of ice skimming across on the floor. Was it wise to leave Pagan's Reach? Whoever was affecting the house could do even more damage if we weren't here. But I had no choice. I had to find Mrs B. We'd deal with the house later.

The police were already hammering on the door as I approached.

'All right! All right!' I called and wrenched it open – it seemed stiffer than ever. The wood always swelled until the weather warmed up. That's why everyone always came round the back.

Thurlow marched forward. Three or four officers waited outside.

'What's this all about?' I said. 'I've already told you everything'.

Thurlow's face reddened as the cold of the house struck his skin. I saw his eyes flicker, the colour draining from them, and fear dragged at my chest.

'Angela Tully, we have reason to suspect you of being involved in the murder and unlawful disposal of Frieda Beaudry. '

'What are you talking about?' I said. Penny's face was stunned into immobility. Shock wiped my brain blank.

'Therefore, I am arresting you on suspicion of murder…'

One of the officers stepped forward and took my arm. I wrenched it away, gathering sparks in my hands, ready to let them fly.

'Angie! No!' Penny cried. She met my gaze and shook her head. 'We'll sort this out, Angie, don't worry. Don't do anything stupid.' She looked meaningfully at my hands that fizzed with heat.

Like a robot, Thurlow continued. 'You do not have to say anything, but it may harm your defence if you do not mention when questioned something which you later rely on in court. Anything you do say may be given in evidence.' He looked down at his notebook for a moment and stilled for so long I thought he'd fallen asleep. What was wrong with him? Then his head snapped back, and he continued in a drone. 'The necessity for your arrest is to prevent further injury, allow a prompt and effective investigation in order for you to be interviewed, and to prevent your disappearance due to the severity of the allegation.' He nodded at the officer who took hold of my arm again. He began to move me towards the front door, followed by a lumbering Thurlow who didn't seem to know where he was.

'What have you found?' Penny called. 'What possible evidence do you have that Angie has anything to do with this? You don't even have any proof that she'd dead!'

Thurlow paused. 'We found blood on the front steps,' he said. 'And forensics have just confirmed its Frieda Beaudry's.'

*

Blood! They'd found her blood! How could that be possible? I'd not seen any sign of blood anywhere, and I'd searched every square inch of the house and garden, including the terrace and steps. My seeking charms would have shown up any trace of violence, certainly something as resonant as blood.

I remembered what Penny had found, how close we were to tracking down Joshua Pettigrew and slammed my fists against my forehead. A police officer sat impassively by my side in the back of the car, Thurlow in the passenger seat ahead.

Desperately I gazed at the countryside as it flicked past, gradually fading to grey as we got to the edge of town and the roads began to fill with traffic. Rain spattered the windows, drops of water liquifying and running into each other stretching the light caught within them into stars.

I imagined touching my fingers to the glass, melting it into water so I could clamber out and fly into the damp air, not stopping until I found Mrs B.

Thurlow seemed reluctant to question me straight away. An unsmiling custody officer signed me in and, in a surreal parody of a hotel check-in, signalled to an officer to take me to my room. It was small with a bench, toilet, and letterbox sized window, way out of my reach, that let in a slice of light.

With the door slammed shut, I was alone with my thoughts. The worry about Mrs B was now a constant, gnawing ache in my stomach. Food, something that had been a comfort throughout my life, now seemed nothing but dead matter; my body convulsed a violent rejection just at the thought of it.

Panic was beating its wings about my head - without the ability to replenish my powers would be badly affected, reducing my ability to escape this little room. Thurlow had told me they would be requesting to extend how long they could hold me to forty-eight hours.

Forty-eight hours! Time I couldn't afford to waste. I had to get out, get back to Penny. Getting to my feet I walked from one corner to the other. It didn't take me very long. The walls were painted a shiny cream marked with angry scratches and phrases written by those who'd been trapped here before me. They reminded me of Mrs B's blazing words – Joshua Pettigrew, Joshua Pettigrew – and sorrow filled my heart afresh: I had so let her down so badly.

Scrubbing away tears I thought through my options. Without being able to replenish, I had to conserve the energy I had left. I had an idea, but I needed to lean in to the building to see if it would work.

But not for long, I reminded myself.

Concentrating hard, I laid the palms of my hands against the cool of the walls. Rapidly I scanned the building. Would I find what I was looking for? I tilted my head. There. He'd do.

There were quite a few ones tethered to the place. Criminals, mostly, but also a few old police officers who hadn't been able to let go. I wanted one that hadn't used all its energy to apparate completely – I needed as much energy as I could get my hands on.

I'd never done this before. I didn't know if it would work but I couldn't see any other way. Staying imprisoned was untenable. Mrs B needed me, and every cell in my body told me we were running out of time. I needed to get out without Thurlow knowing for at least a few hours, enough time for me to get as far away as possible.

Keeping my voice soft, I began to whisper. I had to be careful not to attract the other ones who stalked the rooms and corridors, driven mad by their anger and grief. The one I wanted was gentle, held by a love for his job rather than frustration and raging regret.

I'd caught his attention. He was close. I risked a charm, a small one – a hithering that glowed, just for a moment, before drifting through the walls.

As the old boy moved forward, the others – gibbering and vengeful – turned their heads.

*

Penny put down her phone and sighed. She didn't like to rely on the kindness of others, but she couldn't think what else to do. Sally had been a good friend at university and an extremely successful criminal lawyer. She'd been surprised to hear from Penny, but her response had been warm, warmer than Penny deserved, she thought. She resolved to make more of an effort to connect with old friends once all this was over.

Sally promised to contact the station that afternoon. In the meantime, there was nothing for Penny to do except wait. She put the kettle on for yet another coffee. Waiting for it to boil she rubbed her arms, cold despite two jumpers and a jacket.

Penny had tried and failed to get a fire going. In the library she found a blanket hanging over the back of an armchair and wrapped it round herself. Through the great sash windows she could see warmth stealing across the valley, yet inside it was still winter. She remembered Angie's words about a wolf stalking the house, draining the life from the building, and she shivered. She tried not to think about something hidden in the walls watching her every move.

In the kitchen she heard the kettle whistle but suddenly the thought of more coffee made her feel sick. She hurried in to lift the kettle from the oven and set it aside. Back in the main hall, she noticed for the first time a wall of paintings.

One of them, smaller than the others and overshadowed by huge, modernist landscapes, caught her eye. She took a step forward and smiled at the same time tears sprang to her eyes. It was a gorgeous picture: a girl with wild dark hair in a crimson dress caught mid-spin as she circled to make her skirts billow.

Penny had seen so many of her mother's pictures but this one held within it a tenderness she hadn't seen in the others. The child's face, Penny's face, had been given an angelic radiance that belied the devilish mischief in her blue eyes.

Penny laid a finger on the cheek of the painted girl. It was so full of energy she almost expected her younger self to spin out of the frame. She could still taste the toffee she'd stuffed into her cheeks when Daphne used all her powers of persuasion to get her to pose in her new red dress. She sighed. How is it she could remember the smell of the sea that day - the faint drift of her mother's lily of the valley perfume, but events over the past few years had disappeared into a blur? It made her feel old.

Beneath the chill of the air in the house Penny could smell woodsmoke and roses. A spicy undernote of sandalwood brought another rush of memories. Frieda had brought Penny a sandalwood carving of an elephant from Mysore and its heady perfume had enchanted her. She'd kept it by her bed for years. She wondered where it was now.

The scent seemed to be growing stronger. Curious, Penny tried to work out where it was coming from. She'd got so used to smelling the dead, cold air of the house this warm perfume was a striking change.

Penny checked her phone was in her pocket and fully charged with the sound on. She didn't want to miss Sally's call. The sun shining across the floor from the library drew her in, though the room was as cold as all the others. Here the richness of the rugs, the brightly coloured books and windows looking over the green valley gave an illusion of life. Penny checked her phone again. She couldn't stop thinking about the look on Angie's face as she was driven away.

Penny shared her frustration but was glad Angie hadn't fired off any thunderbolts at the police. She had every faith that Sally would be able to get Angie out. Why hadn't Angie called? Aren't arrestees allowed a phone call? Penny recognised she knew little of how the law worked. Spending time with Angie was forcing Penny into the realisation that, outside of her work at the university, she knew and understood little of the world in which she lived.

She had been moved by Angie's passion, her agony at the loss of her beloved mentor. The bond between them was stronger than anything Penny had known, though perhaps she'd felt something like it in her relationship with Daphne.

That scent again! It was strong in the library. Penny wondered if it came from another sandalwood statue, or perhaps a candle. She looked round, taking slow breaths to trace the fragrance. She felt like the Bisto kids she remembered from her childhood.

The drift of sandalwood was growing stronger, it pulled her towards the centre of the room, and she turned away from the windows to face the fireplace. Framed by two comfortable looking armchairs the grate and mantelpiece above it were enormous. Penny longed to build a roaring fire, letting its crackling flames fill the room with their merry glow, driving away once and for all the ghastly chill that hung on every surface.

But any match struck sizzled out immediately. Even Angie's sparks, fired in electric streams, couldn't get the tinder to catch. Perhaps it was the basket of logs that was sending out the delicate fragrance? Penny bent over and shook her head; all she could smell was damp wood.

As she stepped back, she caught another current of sandalwood. What was going on? The hairs on the back of her neck stirred. Something strange was happening. The scent was too beautiful and too nostalgic for her to believe it was malevolent. Was the house trying to tell her something?

Angie was always talking about how Pagan's Reach communicated with Frieda and her: warning them in times of danger, celebrating at times of joy, revealing secrets at times of great need. Was that what this scent was?

Penny concentrated hard, allowing the fragrance to fill her senses. She closed her eyes and took a step, measuring how it billowed when she turned one way, waning when she turned another.

Allowing her senses to guide her, Penny followed the call of the sandalwood until she was standing right in front of the mantelpiece. She stared blankly at the empty grate. What did the house want her to do?

Frustrated, she ran her hands over and under the mantelpiece, the marble as cold as a gravestone. But the scent was warm, she was sure of it. Maybe something up the chimney? Hitching up her trousers Penny squatted inside the void and looked up – far, far above she could see the chimney opening showing a tiny wink of blue sky. Nothing else.

But as she carefully pulled her head out, gripping onto the walls for balance, her fingers brushed over a metal hook wedged into the stone. It was well hidden, set deep in the fireplace in the shadows of the chimney.

A kind of excited fear rippled through Penny as she ran her hands over what she thought was a solid stone wall against which was pressed the huge metal basket of a grate. Her fingertips sought out the very finest of cracks.

It was a door, she realised.

Without giving herself a chance to think it through, she pulled out the clasp and pushed at the stone. It moved beneath her hand and, with a gravelly crunch, sank into the ground beneath to reveal a dark passage behind. The smell of sandalwood was overpowering.

Penny stepped over the grate and stared into the passage beyond.

Chapter 12

The light from the letterbox window was fading by the time I got the one to come close enough for me to catch hold of him. I was frightened that the others would follow, drawn by my whisper, so tried to use as little energy as possible.

I'd made sure I'd shaped the blankets on the bench so, at a cursory glance, it would look like I was sleeping. To add to the effect, I cast a masking charm. It wasn't one that would last long, but hopefully would convince anyone peering through the observation slot that I was safely asleep in my cell for a few hours at least.

I wasn't even sure what I was planning next was possible. I'd never seen it done, though Mrs B had boasted about doing it to escape a persistent admirer during her time in New Orleans.

The one was very faint, like a charcoal drawing sketched with hasty strokes. I guessed he'd been drifting about the station for a long time. He didn't have any rage, which made things much easier. I had to fight hard to control my impatience - rushing things wouldn't work. When he drew close enough, I encouraged him to tell me his story, holding his big square hand in mine, but I didn't want him to disappear; if he moved on too quickly there was no way I could get myself out of the station.

His uniform was old fashioned, but I hoped was similar enough not to draw attention. I'd have a better chance at night, I thought. I took a deep breath and concentrated. Using a one in this way wouldn't cause it any pain or suffering, but I still felt very uncomfortable about what I was going to do. I thought of Ada Pettigrew, stripped of her powers and banished for using the dead to destroy rather than moving them on, and vowed I would make sure this kindly old policeman found the courage to let go of the world that was so dear to him, but where he no longer belonged.

He was standing by the bench and I got up, still holding his hand, and took a step closer. My stomach fluttered with nerves until I thought of Mrs B and my resolve returned. I had to be careful to enmesh our energies. My life force was so much more powerful I was in danger of smothering his, so I breathed in, pulling my vitality deep into my heart and belly, leaving my skin cold.

I stepped into the one. Immediately my vision dimmed. I felt him rock with shock, and I held onto him tight with my mind, like calming a startled horse. I felt the beat of him flutter, a thrumming of wings. I strained every nerve to keep him still; if he panicked his energy would vaporise, blown to the four winds, and he'd be lost.

Breathing a cautious sigh of relief as he steadied, I felt my way round the shape of his being. As I grew in confidence I stretched my arms, pushing my hands into the sleeves of him, drawing him across my back. The moment he relaxed I knew it was going to work.

I felt heavy, the press of him weighed me down so I struggled to keep upright. I couldn't understand where the weight was coming from and worried he was trying to press into me, steal under my skin the way I was stealing into his.

I lifted our hands and banged on the door. I needed to replenish soon; I couldn't keep this connection with the one for long.

After what felt like an age someone came to the door and with a jangling of keys unlocked it. When it swung open, I was ready, words already falling from my lips. I needed to daze the officer, and quickly.

He was young with a thick black hair that fell into startled blue eyes as he caught sight of us. We must have made a strange sight. My presence inside the one was enough for him to apparate into a solid, physical existence, and the young lad must have wondered what a Victorian policeman was doing in the cell.

He opened his mouth to call out and I flung my dazing words at him. They settled on his eyes and mouth and the expression of surprise was wiped clean - a TV screen unplugged from the wall. I hustled him back the way he came and laid my hand on his forehead, pulling the last few moments from the river of his memory.

Now to get out of the station without being seen. When I came in I'd seen the eye of CCTV cameras at the end of every corridor and in the reception area, as well as outside the main door.

I needed to get past them without causing alarm. I hoped the one's uniform, from a distance and viewed on the grainy screen of their cheap monitors, would pass for a live police officer. I was out of ideas; this would have to do.

I locked the door with the boy's keys and put them back in his pocket, turning him so he faced away from the door to my cell. He remained frozen, but I only had a few minutes before he'd come round. He would remember nothing and continue walking past my cell, forgetting what he had come down to do. By that time, hopefully I would be out of the station and on my way to Pagan's Reach and Penny.

The one and I lumbered down the sleeping corridor and softly climbed the stairs up towards the reception. I'd rather hoped nobody would be able to see us. Mrs B, my mother, and I were the only people I knew who could see the ones.

But I hadn't anticipated the effect of sliding a living, breathing body inside the energy field of the lost. Suddenly my one had all the physical presence he'd had when he was alive. Before we reached the top of the stairs, I tried to wrench off his weird, rounded hat and voluminous tunic top but he wouldn't let me, they stayed fixed on our body.

I would have to get across the reception area and out the door before anyone could get a good look at us. I could feel my powers draining with the effort of holding the two of us together; I didn't have much time – I had to get outside.

The same woman sat behind the plastic screen as she did the day I reported Mrs B missing. It seemed like a hundred years ago. She had her head down and the reception area was thankfully empty except for a scattering of worn chairs and a scuffed vinyl floor.

With a burst of effort we shuffled across the floor. I could already smell the welcome chill of night floating through the double glass doors that didn't quite meet. They were only ten steps away, but the distance loomed and stretched like a fun fair mirror, making my head spin.

We took one step. Then two. To my horror I began to feel the one peeling away from me, lifting at the edges like an old stamp. I gathered all my strength, forcing another step, clinging on to the cloak of a body round me.

'John?' A puzzled voice called out. 'What are you doing here? I thought you weren't back in until tomorrow.' I heard the door to the side of the little reception office open.

We took two more steps. If I stretched out my hand I would be able to touch the cool of the metal door handle.

'John!'

I daren't turn round. Patches of my body were being exposed as the one continued to thin. He was vaporising.

I sent him a whispered prayer of thanks as we burst through the doors and out into the dark. The one vanished into a cloud of energy, scattered for a moment, but as I watched it coalesced and gathered back into the outline of his earthly shape. He disappeared into the station; he wasn't ready to move on, I thought. But I was grateful to him for hiding me long enough to get out of the building.

I ducked behind a giant waste bin as someone rattled open the doors and stuck out his head. Thurlow. He was looking directly at me, his eyes silvery in the moonlight.

Using the last of my strength, I pulled myself into the shadows, the metal of the bin cold against my back. I hid my face in the neck of my jumper, worried my face would flash white under the security light that flicked on and off as he moved.

Time stretched elastic, thin and taut between us. I was conscious of every whisper of sound. The tinny rattle of a can as it was blown across the forecourt, the muffled drone of distant traffic, and a single siren, wailing from across the horizon.

Thurlow kept staring. I held my breath until finally, finally, he shook his head and withdrew, letting the doors swing shut.

I gasped, sliding down the bin until I hit the floor. Straightaway I gazed up at the stars and gathered their light in my hands, letting the surge recharge my blood. My heart beat hard and fast. Not yet daring to stand I took my time, smelling the sweet, secret fragrance of a nearby bush covered in dusky pink buds. The road glittered, hard and bumpy, and I let its coarse texture bring life back to my hands.

Time to go home.

*

There was enough light from the library to show a few inches of a stone floor, but beyond that Penny could see nothing but a velvety darkness - a black hole that sucked the light into itself. She wavered for a moment remembering Angie's warning that someone was prowling round the house. But the scent of sandalwood continued to reassure, and curiosity pushed her forwards.

Cautious not to make a sound, Penny took another careful step, tutting silently as tiny shards of stone crunched under her feet. Flicking on the torch on her phone, she held it up high. The light wavered feebly but it was enough to see the floor fall away steeply. Careful not to skid on the slick stones, she tried to see what was ahead, but her torchlight was swallowed up by the shadows.

Another step. Penny held her breath, listening hard, but it was as if silence had wrapped itself round her head. She couldn't make out anything beyond the sound of her heart beating. If the wolf Angie described was here, Penny could find no sign of him.

She stretched her hands out in front of her face sensing a change in the quality of the air ahead. It was a good thing she did, as the roof of the passage had suddenly dropped, and if she hadn't stopped, she'd have walked straight into it.

Penny had to bend almost double to continue. She was beginning to feel claustrophobic, conscious of the great weight of the house above her - built on countless tonnes of earth. Her brain rapidly calculated the consequences of any kind of slippage or fall, any instability in the stone ceiling; it wasn't a happy calculation.

She reassured herself the passage had been here for a very long time. No need to think it would collapse on her head at that moment. Stopping to listen again for any noise, Penny checked her phone battery. To lose the beam of light, faint though it may be, would be horrifying; her mouth dried at the thought.

Satisfied nothing breathing was nearby, Penny risked another step. Her foot wobbled on a broken piece of stone that slid away so that she shot forward, falling with a sharp, sudden shock that jarred every bone in her body. She cried out in surprise and scrabbled for the walls to pull herself up but slipped again, and this time tumbled forward scraping her knees and hands as she slithered into the dark, dropping her phone on the wet flints and pebbles.

Desperately she tried to stop herself, reaching out to grab anything to slow her down, trying not to think about what she could be hurtling towards. Her body slammed into something solid and hairy and she screamed.

Gibbering with fright Penny pushed herself away, scrambling for the faint beam of her phone's light. It was caught in a crack in the flagstones and she grabbed it, swinging it round to see what monster was lying across the floor. Was it the wolf?

Penny's hands shook and she rubbed the sweat and tears from her eyes, sobbing with panic. The light gradually steadied and Penny gasped. A dog lay stretched across the passage. It was scrawny and thin with matted fur, not the great wolf Penny had feared.

The sandalwood perfume hung rich and warm on the air. Had Frieda led her here? Or was it the house? Was there something special about this creature?

Slowly, Penny stretched out her hand and touched the animal with her fingertips, expecting it to be stiff and cold. To her shock it was warm, and she felt a tiny pulse of movement under her hand.

She was desperate to get out of the choking gloom and frightened her phone would fail her any moment. The house had led her here for a reason, she thought, surprised by her fanciful thoughts. Still, she couldn't help acting on them and picked up the dog, shuffling backwards towards the safety of the library.

Penny's eyes dazzled as she eased the dog over the grate and slumped onto the rug in front of the fireplace. After the gloom of the passage the beams from the setting sun streaming in through the windows were blinding.

The dog was a mongrel with a lot of terrier mixed in. His wiry grey muzzle was stained with blood that had turned brown over time. How long had he been in there? Penny wondered. She remembered the movement she had felt under her fingers and knelt to put her ear to the dog's chest. There was definitely something there.

Penny sat back on her heels. She'd never owned a pet and wasn't sure what to do. She sensed this dog was special, she'd been led down that horrible passage to find it, she was certain. Running her hands over the body she could feel the rib cage rising through the fur, every bone visible. It can't have eaten for days.

Pushing herself to standing, Penny carried the dog into the kitchen and laid it gently on the kitchen table. Gently she washed its bloodied muzzle and looked for milk. She'd seen orphaned lambs kept alive with bottles, but she had to make do with soaking kitchen roll in a saucer of milk and letting it drip onto the dog's half open mouth.

She didn't hold out much hope. The dog was emaciated, had been beaten, and its eyes had sunk back into its sockets. But the fur on his belly was soft as velvet and there was something sweet about his pointed ears. Tentatively Penny stroked her hand down the dog's back, hoping to feel it stir, but it remained deeply unconscious. The pulse she'd felt was slowing.

It became very important to Penny that the dog lived. She wasn't sure why. All she knew was that it was linked to Frieda, was special to Frieda. And she wanted to do something to acknowledge the woman who'd sacrificed so much to save her.

She looked at her hands, remembering her mother's painting coming to life beneath her touch, the explosion of light that evening in the room with Angie and the dead. A frown shadowed her face as she also remembered crying with agony as faceless beasts peeled the power from her nerves, veins, and sinews. The way she would clutch at her heart and belly to stop the draining, desperate to keep hold of her life force.

Penny shook her head letting the horrors fly loose, something she had learned to do very well in order to survive. She wouldn't think of that now. Maybe she could do something for this animal.

The dog was lying on its side, stretched out full length with its muzzle tipped up, a little milk leaking onto the table. Penny could no longer see the tiny lift she had felt in the dog's chest. She lay her hands on the arch of the ribcage and closed her eyes. For a moment her body jolted in rebellion; she was so used to curbing, containing, concealing, the thought of release was a hard one. But she had to do it.

The static crackle started deep in her chest, and she felt her arms and belly warm. She let the heat creep down her arms and into her wrist and hands. It came in a rush, quicker than she could control. The dog jerked once, twice and she pulled away quickly, not wanting to pour too much into him.

Penny almost laughed out loud as the dog wriggled and squirmed, trying to get up, his paws sliding beneath him. The joyful explosion of movement was a gorgeous contrast to the pathetic bundle of fur and bones he'd been only moment before.

She gathered the dog up in her arms, hoping to warm him with the heat of her body – the house was still frozen. Grabbing the milk, she poured more into the saucer and held it up. The dog licked at it, weakly at first then with such ferocity Penny had to move the dish away worried he'd make himself sick.

In the pantry she found dog biscuits and took a small handful, feeding the dog a few pieces at a time. When she thought he'd had enough she moved towards the basket hoping to lay him down to sleep under the blanket; he needed to build up his strength.

A crash at the kitchen window made Penny scream for the second time that evening, she almost dropped the dog who wriggled frantically in her arms.

'Angie!' she cried in astonishment.

*

I stared at Penny through the window. Heavy rain drenched my hair and clothes and sheets of it slid down the glass blurring everything into streaks of colour. It couldn't be. It couldn't be. I stumbled for the door seeing a flash of movement as Penny went to unlock it.

It opened, and something leaped into the air and crashed into my arms. 'Trevor!' I cried, tears immediately splashing down my cheeks. 'I thought you were dead... what happened? Where did you find him?' Incoherent and shivering, I let Penny lead me into the kitchen to sit down.

'What are you doing here?' she said. 'How did you get out? Did they release you?'

I shook my head, laughing as Trevor licked my chin and yapped. He was a bag of bones and his fur was matted – what had happened to him? – but his eyes were as bright as ever. 'I escaped,' I said. 'I reckon I've got until the morning before they realise, but we'll need to be long gone by then. Pagan's Reach is the first place they'll look. But first tell me – where did you find him? Is he OK?'

As Penny explained how she found the passage in the library and discovered Trevor in a terrible state, I noticed a change in her. 'What did you do? There's a look about you ...'

Penny smiled, her cheeks pinkened. 'I ... I was worried he wasn't waking up, so I put my hands out and sort of ... released some of my energy into him. I'm not quite sure how I did it, but it seemed to work.' She grinned back at Trevor who was hanging over my elbow and panting at her.

'You used your light on him? Dr Penelope Howes, who would have thought it. Weren't you terrified?'

'I was, but I wasn't sure what else to do. I couldn't bear the thought of letting Frieda's dog die.'

I was about to protest – Trevor was my dog! – but then I remembered the way Mrs B would let her hand rest on his head when she was reading in the library, or the way Trevor would follow her round, ears pricked and claws clicking until she threw him a lump of cheese. Maybe he belonged to both of us, I thought.

'Well thank you for saving him,' I said at last. 'I've been so obsessed with finding Mrs B I didn't have room to think of what had happened to Trevor. He'll have to come with us.'

'Don't you think we should stop and think about this? I mean, this Joshua Pettigrew might be anywhere in the country. It seems impetuous - to say the least - to take off on a whim just because of what we read in a hundred year old book.'

'I don't have anything else to go on,' I said helplessly. 'It's the only lead we have. If his family comes from Hurstbridge it makes sense that someone there will know them and be able to point us in the right direction. And we can't stay here, much as I hate to leave the house. We can't come back for a while. This is the first place the police will look.'

'Angie, is this a good idea? You know you haven't done anything wrong – Frieda's still alive. Surely we can prove that to the police? Running away just makes you look guilty. They've got CCTV. They can check your number plate to trace you.' She stretched to pat Trevor's head. 'Maybe we should give the police a call. Explain that you got frightened and that you shouldn't have run. Trust them to do the right thing, maybe?'

Gently, I laid Trevor in his basket as his eyes were drooping. He shivered in the cold, so I covered him with my coat. 'What do you want me to do, Penny? Get out a crystal ball and show them Frieda is alive? Maybe I should cast a spell to prove my powers? How do you think that will go down? They'll think I'm mad. Besides, I don't trust that Thurlow, whenever he comes into the house he behaves like a robot - something is controlling him.'

'But they'll find you! They think you're the number one suspect for a murder.' Penny's face shone with worry. 'They'll throw everything they have at the hunt to find you. We'll never get to Frieda – the police will find us well before we get anywhere close to wherever she's being held.'

I stopped to think. 'I haven't got any choice,' I said slowly. 'Mrs B is failing - I can sense it. They've deliberately kept her away from anything living so she can't replenish. Without that she won't be able to go on much longer. I have to try, Penny, you must see that. I understand if you want to go home. I can sense real danger ahead and I don't want you mixed up in it – you've done enough for me already, and for Mrs B. All I ask is that if you do say anything to the police at least wait until I'm well on my way to Hurstbridge.'

'Don't be ridiculous – I'm not going to go to the police. I want to come with you, I owe it to Frieda. I may be able to help – you never know. But no draining.' She smiled.

I held up my hand. 'Brownie's honour,' I said.

'What shall we do about the car?' Penny said as we locked up the house. 'They know your licence plate number - they'll pick you up within seconds. How will we get there? The trains won't be any good. When they see you're gone they'll be watching everywhere. How will we get to Hurstbridge?'

'Ah now,' I said. 'I think I have an idea.'

Chapter 13

She looked me right in the eyes. Right in the fucking eyes and didn't see me. Too busy flapping about the dead. What a rush that was. My cloaking held longer than I thought it would – thanks to Gran and her notes from her ma.

I didn't hang about. I didn't want to risk her finding me, not yet. I wasn't happy with how quickly she got rid of the dead. I thought she'd leave, but she spent all night moving them on. What a waste of good energy.

I was tempted to rile them up, get them to turn on her. Easily done – I'd done it before. But I wasn't sure what would happen next. Would they turn on me? There were too many of them. Hundreds.

Bit of a waste of time really. I'd hoped to get her clear of the house for a few days. Good job I had my back up plan. I stood in the woods and watched as the coppers took her away. There was another old bag with white hair standing at the front door. I hadn't seen her before. Didn't know the fat one had a mate with her.

No matter. She wouldn't stay long once the other got arrested. I'd make sure of it. Then I'd have a nice long stretch to find what I needed.

I had business with the old crone. She wasn't giving up a word despite Jez's unique methods of persuasion. I was pissed off by the time I got there. It took twice as long to get to Jez's as it should have done. Some posh twat totalled his Land Rover on the M25. I smelled blood as I drove past.

She sat propped up against the wall. She was fading. I could taste it in the air. But her eyes still flashed with the old fire. I smiled to see her. She couldn't be more than four foot, especially bent over double as she was. Crooked little thing.

I squatted in front of her. Pushed the tray Jez had left a little further away so she'd have to strain to reach it. Not that she'd touched any of the food – but she'd want the water.

'Where is it? Where is it, Frieda? Tell me how to open it' I jerked her chin up so I could get a proper look. She muttered something. 'What did you say?'

Her mouth worked and I leaned closer. Then the bitch spat on me. I felt the wetness on my cheek and reared back. There was a crack as I hit her across the face with the back of my hand. She never took her eyes from mine. The green of them was startling.

I hauled her to her feet. The chains round her neck, waist and ankles looked ridiculous. Way over the top for such a skinny old crone, but Jez had warned me. She'd almost managed to escape too many times. She was growing weak, though. Her skin was sallow and sagged where she'd lost weight

'Tell me where it is. How I get to it. You know what I'm talking about.'

She shook her head.

I leaned in close. So close she'd feel my breath. 'I'm not stopping till I find it. I'll tear the fucking house down if I need to.'

I blinked. She kept doing this. Jez had mentioned it as well. One minute there was a crumbling old bat in a ragged dressing gown, the next minute there'd be a young woman, black hair streaming down her back. Just for a second. Like when the sky box freezes and you see two frames at once. She couldn't hold it for long. That reminded me. I had the pendant in my pocket and I hung it round her neck. I didn't know what the stone was but I'd been promised it would act as an inhibitor – no more magic. Keeping her in this concrete box didn't help either. The longer we kept her here the more she withered.

'Wait,' she said as I held up my hand to beat her again.

She looked up at me with a twisted grin. Held up her fist. She waited for me to look then spread out her hands like she was doing a conjuring trick. In the centre of her palm was a coin. A gold one. What the fuck? Where did she get that?

I bent over it. Reached for it.

With a sudden gesture she flung the coin in the air and it liquified. Spattering molten drops of flames over my face and hands. They wormed into my flesh. The more I brushed them off the harder they stuck.

With a roar I kicked her until she fell still. Bitch.

'I'm not putting up with this crap for much longer,' I said to Jez as we locked up. 'She's not talking. I don't think she will talk. She'd rather die. Stupid cow.'

Jez shrugged. Nothing he'd done had worked. He said she was able to tune out of the pain. Would sit there with a blank look on her face as he'd inflicted his little cruelties. 'You can't push it too far,' he said. 'You'll kill her. She's not got long left.'

'I'm going to move her. I think there's someone who can help. I'm gonna take her up to my aunt's house. Get her ready, Jez. Lock her into the van. I'll leave in the morning.'

*

'I've never seen such a ridiculous car in my life.' Penny said, staring open-mouthed into the gloom of the underground garage. 'How old is it? Will it even work?'

'Oh, I should think so. Mrs B hasn't driven since I've known her, but she gets old Peter Brooks in the village to keep it ticking over. He loves old cars and in return she lets him take it to vintage car fairs.'

'It's very … yellow,' Penny said.

'Lemon, actually. That's what Mrs B said.'

'Looks more banana. Do you know how to drive it?'

'I hope so, it's rather bigger than I was expecting.'

'It's huge!'

We took a cautious step into the garage. The Zephyr took up most of the space and its chrome grill gleamed. I liked its little round headlights that made it look like a worried child, but Penny was right. It was massive. It would be like driving a boat.

'I can't imagine Frieda driving anything like this.'

'Apparently she used to drive a Jag,' I said. 'But gave up on driving altogether when she crashed it. Couldn't bear to start up with another car and she always thought this one was vulgar. She's had it since the 60s. Would have been falling apart now if it wasn't for Peter.'

I unlocked it with the keys Peter had brought over. 'We can even have the top down – look – it's a convertible.'

'Don't be ridiculous!' Penny looked most disapproving as she opened the passenger door. 'We're going to draw enough attention as it is.'

I clicked my tongue at Trevor who was sniffing about the entrance. He shot me a look before taking his time peeing up the door post. I was glad to see him starting to act like his old self, though he was still very thin, and a lump rose in my throat when Penny had to help him into the back seat, strapping him in with his little harness. Normally he flew into any car he was allowed to occupy, carelessly knocking aside anyone who dared stand in his way. But today it looked like his hips and knees were hurting, and he couldn't jump with his usual fluid grace.

Sitting in the car, I stared at the enormous steering wheel. The lemon-yellow seats smelled of leather in the early morning sunlight. There was no gear stick, I realised in shock. Well, there was, but it stuck out of the top of the steering column. Feigning a confidence I didn't feel but desperate to get out on the road, I turned the key, pushed down the clutch, and pushed the stick up. It clunked into gear and the car lurched forwards with a throaty roar. Penny's head jerked back and Trevor gave a warning yap from the back seat.

We shot out of the garage and I steered the car to the left and out onto the road. We were off, I thought. Moving at last. One step closer to Mrs B.

As we drove past Pagan's Reach, I offered it a silent prayer of protection. Every part of me cried out in protest at my decision to leave the house alone, but I had no choice. And without Mrs B it was an empty shell anyway.

I gripped the steering wheel with both hands and stared straight ahead.

'You'll have to go into second gear at some point,' Penny said. 'You can't go the whole way at ten miles per hour.'

'All right all right,' I said. 'Just make sure you've got the directions up on your phone.'

It wouldn't take us long to get to Hurstbridge, but I was frustrated by how late it was already. With all the faff of sorting the car it was already late morning by the time we left the village. Turning onto the dual carriageway my heart quailed as three police cars, sirens wailing, shot down the other side - heading towards Pagan's Reach, I presumed.

Penny didn't say anything. I glanced over. She was staring straight ahead, a grim expression on her face. But I noticed there was a change.

'You seem softer,' I said.

'Softer? What do you mean?'

'Well, before it was like sitting next to a frozen tornado – all that life force wound up and fizzing away inside you. Maybe that weird explosion with the one, and helping Trevor, has discharged you a bit.'

'I do feel a bit … looser,' Penny admitted, stretching out her hands.

'How have you coped with it all these years? No wonder you were like a bomb about to go off when I met you. Didn't Mrs B teach you how to use your energy?'

'She tried. But I didn't want to listen. What happened at Brokkton was like the worst nightmare you could imagine. It was so terrible for years I'd get hysterical whenever the memory resurfaced. I suppose you'd call it a panic attack nowadays.'

'Penny, even without the magic part what happened to you as a kiddy was abuse. No wonder you were traumatised. When we find Mrs B you have to let her help get you through it. She'll show you how to use that incredible energy. I mean look what you did! You saved Trevor.' I looked with affection through the rear-view mirror at the little terrier whose tongue was out as he panted happily – excited to be going on a trip. There wasn't a trace in him of the suffering he must have experienced trapped in that awful tunnel. That's the nicest thing about dogs, I thought, they never bear a grudge.

'Angie … you have to accept we may not ever find Mrs B. And even if we do it may be too late. She's very old and frail, you know, despite all her powers. There's only so much they can do. I'm sure even witches don't live forever.'

Tears immediately sprang to my eyes. 'I can't think like that, Penny. I just can't. I've got to find her. I'd never forgive myself if ...'

I couldn't even say the words. Penny didn't say anything, but I saw her expression. 'I know what you're thinking – I'm just a housekeeper, why am I risking life and limb – and arrest,' I gave a shaky laugh and scrubbed the tears from my eyes, 'to find her. But you don't understand. I was a mess when we met. Like an absolute mess. I wanted to top myself.' I stopped to draw a deep breath.

'What happened?' Penny's voice was soft.

'I was fifty, Andy had just left me, and I thought my life was over. I couldn't work out how I could go on alone. 'You see ...' I paused again. My heart was racing. 'The thing is ... we lost a baby, Andy and I. He was stillborn at forty-two weeks, and I couldn't have any more babies after that. We never really recovered, though I thought we were plodding on OK. But he just couldn't get over it. He was desperate for kids and ... well, he had an affair and got her pregnant. He was 50! Same as me. Crazy, really, but I'd never seen him happier than when he told me why he was leaving.'

I felt Penny's hand on my arm and appreciated the warm pressure. Tears were really starting to fall, and I had to keep blinking to focus on the road. 'I ended up living with Mrs B, looking after her when she broke her hip. And ... the thing is ... she showed me my life hadn't ended. That I had something special in me that meant I could do amazing things. She listened, you see? Got me through what had happened and gave me the guts to say yes when Gary asked me out – I'd never have married him if it wasn't for her.' I paused. 'She helped me find my happiness, so I owe her. Let alone the few times she actually saved my life.' I smiled and saw recognition in Penny's eyes. 'She saved you too, didn't she?'

'Yes, she did.' Penny squeezed my arm again. 'I'm sorry. About the baby. I never wanted children, but I can appreciate what a loss that was.'

'Mrs B helped me come to terms with it, but I must say, I hadn't really realised how hard I'd find not having grandkids. Gary's a fantastic dad and grandad to his family. I just wish things were different. But then, if they were I wouldn't have discovered the powers my mum gave me – or had all the adventures I've been on since I moved to Pagan's Reach.'

The sat nav interrupted us and Penny muted it before it intoned any more complicated instructions.

'What do you think Joshua Pettigrew wants?'

I was glad of the change in subject. 'You know what, considering the effect he's had on the house I think he's powerful enough to have killed Mrs B straight away.' I swallowed away the lump in my throat at the thought. 'But he didn't, he took her with him. So it had to be that he needs something from her.' I indicated to turn off the dual carriageway - Hurstbridge was only twenty-four miles away.

'It's a funny old place, Pagan's Reach,' I went on. 'I'd lived there for two years before I found it had a music room. Once, Gary's grandkids were coming round and I wanted to make one of those big old-fashioned jellies. The day before I found a giant

Victorian copper mould – it was perfect for the job. And it was in a cupboard I'd never seen before, and I knew that kitchen inside and out.'

'First exit then second left,' Penny said, looking at her phone.

'Mrs B said you had to earn the house's trust. I thought it was a load of nonsense but then so many weird things happened I started to believe it. I think there's something in the house he wants. And he's not going to want whatever it is to cure cancer or bring peace to the world, you can bet your life. It must be powerful, very powerful. And dangerous in the wrong hands. The house, and the mistress of the house, will have protected it with the most powerful of magic. And only Mrs B will know how to get to it. That's what I think.'

'Makes sense. A frightening thought, Angie.'

'Yes,' I said grimly. 'Look, we're not far now.' I pointed at the sign.

'So, what's the plan?'

'I'm not really sure.'

Penny made an exasperated noise. 'I hope the plan isn't you stand in the middle of Hurstbridge and wander about in the hope you find someone who knows the Pettigrew family?'

I didn't answer.

'May I suggest something?' I nodded for her to go on. 'I think the best place to start is the parish records. Most of them are online or kept at the local county record office. I did have a quick look, but some villages are so small they haven't got to digitising them yet.'

'Don't tell me, Hurstbridge records aren't online.'

'That's right. Witchford's records weren't either, I noticed.'

'Well, that's crap. Why are you talking about parish records if we can't find them online?'

'Because the originals may still be in the church. Every village in England has a church attached to it, and the priest or vicar has a duty to record every birth, marriage and death.'

I gripped the steering wheel with excitement, sitting up straight over the enormous steering wheel. 'Fantastic! We'll start at the church.'

'Good idea,' said Penny mildly.

Chapter 14

It took an hour of endless circling before they found a space big enough to park the car without scraping off its yellow paintwork. Penny was getting more and more worried about Angie. She seemed to be running entirely on adrenalin. She was very pale, and her hands trembled. No matter how hard Penny tried to persuade her, Angie refused to eat, saying she felt sick. Every time she saw a police car Angie flinched. Penny wondered how she'd managed to get caught up in all this chaos.

Penny was about to get out when she saw Angie hadn't moved.

'There are cameras everywhere,' she explained, pointing to a pair looming over them from the top of a nearby petrol station. 'I can't risk walking about. They've probably put my face and name out there by now, do you think?'

Penny hesitated, remembering the sirens wailing towards Pagan's Reach and the look on the officers' faces as they'd arrested Angie. 'Yes. I think you're probably right.'

'We need to get to that church and find out what we can about the Pettigrew family. I'll have to transform. Can you see a garden anywhere, or a park?'

'There's a square down the end of the road where the war memorial is,' Penny said, looking at the map on her phone. 'Why?'

'I haven't got the energy to transform without replenishing. Come on,' Angie said, creaking the door open and getting out of the car. 'I'll have to keep my head down until we get there. Put Trevor on his lead, I don't want him running off.'

Late spring flowers bloomed all round them. Penny hurried for a few steps before slowing when she saw how Angie was struggling. Her breath was laboured, and she lumbered along despite being a good ten years younger than Penny. Eventually they got to the little square and the entrance to the main village street. Up ahead they could see the spire of the church. Choosing a spot hidden by tall trees, Angie sat on a bench with a sigh of exhaustion.

Between them was a silent acknowledgement that Penny had the ability to restore Angie within seconds, but Angie had made a promise and Penny believed her.

Penny perched on the bench, conscious the seat was damp, and watched as Angie began to take slow, deep breaths. Something dazzled along her skin, the hectic flush receded and her flesh plumped, turning creamy with good health. Even her lips were fuller, her hair thicker. Penny wanted to rub her eyes.

She was conscious of the scent of grass and scatter of flowers - a confection of colour; the trees bending over them, letting green shadows fall and dance across Angie's eyelids. Something, some energy made the atoms lift and Penny felt a stirring deep in the centre of her body. The scientist in her tried to work out what it was, what had shifted. Some change in energy? How was Angie able to control it, consume it, the way she did? And what about the energy she carried? Penny wondered, looking at her ordinary, liver-spotted hands that had the power to bring Trevor back to life.

'There's a cancer shop over there,' Angie said, her eyes still closed. 'Could you look for a coat, something an old woman would wear, baggy. An overcoat – that sort of thing. It will help me transform.'

The trees swayed, skimming bright pebbles of sunlight across the path as Penny walked past the monument to the parade of shops on the other side of the green. She stopped for a moment to read the names. Long dead men. It made her mourn again the loss of the legacy she'd hoped to leave behind. Publishing her paper and saving her career seemed more distant than ever.

But she couldn't think about that now. She had committed to follow this journey to wherever it was destined to end. She felt for her purse; she could see in the window of the charity shop the perfect thing. Angie would be pleased, she thought.

'You'll have to turn away,' Angie said as Penny handed over the camel wool overcoat. 'I can't do this with anyone watching.'

'What are you going to do?'

'Just turn round.'

Penny turned and stared towards the church spire. She hoped there would be someone there to talk to and the journey wouldn't be wasted.

'I haven't done this for a while,' Angie said. 'I hope it will last long enough.'

A moment of silence passed, and Angie spoke. 'You can turn round now.'

Penny almost cried out in shock. In front of her was a respectable looking woman in her 70s dressed in a smart looking camel overcoat. Penny couldn't see a single trace of Angie, even the eye colour was different.

'They never look at old women,' the apparition said with Angie's voice. 'Everyone's eyes just slide by.'

'Good God I can't believe it.' Shocked to her core, Penny stretched out her hand to touch the woman's shoulder. 'You're unrecognisable.'

'It won't last long,' Angie replied. 'We'd better get on.'

Penny took the old lady's arm and they walked towards the church, Trevor trotting behind getting his lead caught round his legs. Penny couldn't help staring, trying to find a trace of Angie until she was told, rather sharply, to stop. 'You're distracting me,' said Angie, 'and I need to concentrate, otherwise it will all fall apart.'

'It's the churchyard,' Penny whispered, seeing the crooked gravestones and tombs ranked ahead of them. Some had fresh flowers placed at their feet, others were bare except for strands of overlong grass and climbing weeds. She noticed Angie touching the tips of the reeds and flowers that nodded over the stone wall dividing the churchyard from the road.

The gate screeched as they pushed it open. The church stood square ahead but Angie surprised Penny by heading straight towards the older tombs and graves round the side.

'Look!' she hissed. 'Pettigrew. Pettigrew. Another over there. Pettigrew. They're all over the place.'

'Can you see Ada's grave?'

'No.' The old lady circled more stones, bending down to read the carved words that were filled with cushions of moss. She began to pick it away before shaking her head. Penny's brain still couldn't accept this was Angie so didn't look at the strange figure but concentrated on listening to her familiar voice instead.

'At least we know we're in the right place. Let's hope they didn't all move to Bournemouth,' Penny said.

The church was closed. A large rusting padlock swung from the door. Above it, a handwritten sign – water stained despite its plastic cover - explained anyone wanting to visit the church could call the vicar - 'Ed'.

'What kind of vicar calls himself Ed?' Angie grumbled.

'Probably trying to make the church seem more accessible,' Penny said, getting out her phone. 'Though locking the door seems to defeat the object. It's probably because they get vandals breaking in … Hello? Is that Ed? We were hoping to visit the church. Is it possible to …? Oh, yes. That's fine. We can wait.'

Angie paced from one side of the stone porch to the other. Penny didn't want to say anything, but her figure was looking plumper, the white hair in its neat bun beginning to thread with red and purple. Was the transforming spell wearing off? Seeing her look, Angie leaned out and pulled at a branch that rustled with tender green leaves. She buried her face in them and her hair turned white again. She was still plump though, Penny thought – worried.

'He'll be ten minutes,' she said.

They waited in silence. Penny was conscious of how hard Angie was working to keep her transforming charm going. She was tempted to say that once inside the church Angie could show her real self, the vicar was unlikely to know who she was, but the internet was so quick nowadays. Angie's face might be all over the news and social media. 'Ed' sounded rather too internet friendly.

Trevor was straining at his lead. 'Oh, let him off the lead,' Angie said. 'He won't go far and it'll be good for him to stretch his legs.'

Penny leaned down to unclip the terrier who jumped up on his back legs, resting his paws on her knees so she could give him a pat before he bounced off and disappeared into the long grass - tail wagging.

They heard a car draw up and Angie stiffened, buttoning her coat over her swelling body, and adjusting her hair. Footsteps tapped from round the back of the church. A man appeared at the entrance to the porch and Angie immediately hissed under her breath and turned so she faced the shadows. Her body vibrated with an energy Penny didn't understand.

He wore grey trousers and a black shirt with a dog collar. Despite the 'Ed' he must have been in his 60s, Penny thought, not much older than her. He had a weak face with a rather rabbity mouth and colourless eyes.

'I'm Dr Howes,' Penny said, stepping forward to cover Angie and holding out her hand. The vicar shook it, his palm soggy and cold; Penny had to fight against the urge to wipe away the damp residue. 'We'd love to have a chat if you've time?'

'What are you doing?' she hissed at Angie as the vicar retrieved a handful of keys and began unlocking the door. 'What's the matter?'

But Angie just shook her head. Penny couldn't read the expression on her face, but it looked very much like fear.

Ed began his spiel as soon as he crossed the threshold. 'This small but beautiful church is dedicated to St. James The Great, Apostle and Martyr. It's rooted in the fourteenth century, but you will find traces of both Saxon and Norman work in the building ...'

'I'm sorry, Ed isn't it?' We haven't come to see the church, well not only see the church. We wanted to see the parish records. We couldn't find them online.'

'Oh? Well, you didn't say on the phone ...'

'I'm sorry,' Penny cast another exasperated look at Angie who had refused to come into the church and was still hiding in the shadows of the porch. Was she worried her disguise was slipping? She didn't look different to Penny; the old lady apparition was still convincing. 'I'm tracing my family history,' Penny improvised. 'And wondered if you could help.'

Ed looked irritated. Penny remembered his damp hands.

'Have you been the vicar of Hurstbridge for long?' she asked, following him as he walked down the aisle and past the alter to a room lined with books at the back.

'A while,' he said, sitting rather self-importantly behind a large desk. He steepled his fingers and rested his chin on them. 'Some of the records are here but the older ones are kept in the church archives. It depends on how far back you want to go.'

'Oh, not too far back I don't think,' Penny said.

The vicar opened a thick, leather-bound volume that when laid flat took up most of the desk. 'What name is it you're looking for?'

'Pettigrew,' she said. The vicar's hands stilled.

'Pettigrew?' he said. Penny felt rather than saw Angie approach, still keeping well back.

'Yes, that's right.'

He kept his head down, seemingly fascinated by the entries on the pages in front of him. 'An old Hurstbridge family,' he said at last after a strange pause.

'Are any of them still living in the village?' Penny held her breath.

'Most of the family died out years ago. Descended from Lord Philip Pettigrew who was gifted the house and village in King James' time. You'll see their names on the front pew and many in the graveyard.'

'Are there any Pettigrews left?' Penny repeated, impatient. 'Do they live close by? In the village? You said there was a house - like a manor house?'

'Sarah Pettigrew is still alive,' the vicar said at last. Penny wondered at his reluctance. 'I think she's the last one.'

'Where is she?'

'I'm not sure I can disclose that information,' he said pompously. 'What is it you're looking for? I thought you were researching your family history.'

'Yes, of course. That's right. I just wanted to know if any relatives from that side of my family were still living.'

Suddenly he looked up. His eyes raked her up and down and she felt strangely intimidated by his searching gaze.

'You don't look like a Pettigrew,' he said sharply.

'Well, as I said, it was a distant connection.'

'I'm sorry not to have been more help,' he said, closing the book and standing.

'Oh no, don't worry. You've been more than helpful,' Penny said, suddenly desperate to get out into the fresh air and away from this man's colourless eyes. She started to back away, back towards the nave of the church. The vicar picked up the book, and with another penetrating look at Penny, bent to lock it in his desk.

Penny raced out, not sure why she was feeling so claustrophobic. She bundled Angie in front of her until they were in the churchyard once more. Without speaking they followed the path until they were back on the road. They watched the vicar lock the door and walk round the side of the church.

'Quick! Follow him,' Angie said, her tone urgent. She pushed Penny in front of her and she stumbled. Angie dragged her upright. 'I want to see where he's going.'

'What's going on?' Penny whispered. 'Why didn't you come in?'

'He's a wolf,' said Angie. 'Couldn't you smell it on him?'

'Do you think that's Joshua Pettigrew?' Penny said in horror as they panted up to the door and peered round the side of the church. The vicar was already at the end, holding a phone to his ear.

'No. But there's definitely a connection. Who is he calling? Get closer! I want to hear what he's saying.'

'… two of them …' the vicar's voice floated back towards them. 'Poking around – how should I know? … didn't tell them …White hair … I'm on my way.'

Penny and Angie pulled back as the vicar angled into a car, slamming the door and starting the engine almost immediately.

'Who's he talking to? He's warning someone. Did you hear that? He must be calling Joshua.' Angie's strange, muddied brown eyes were alight with fear. She grabbed Penny's arms. 'Did you hear? Penny?'

'Yes, I heard. It sounds odd, I'll admit. But we don't know for sure.'

'We have to follow him,' Angie's eyes were wild and Penny saw the green returning. The colour flashed in the blinding sunlight.

'OK but we'll have to be quick, the car's miles away.'

'I've got a better idea.' Angie grabbed Penny's arm and pulled her towards the entrance to the church. 'We've got to get up onto the roof before he leaves!'

'What are you talking about?' Penny yelled, but Angie wasn't listening.

The padlock was no match for Angie who burst it open with a stream of darts from her fingers. Her disguise had completely faded, and she shook off her overcoat, throwing it onto a nearby pew.

'Hurry!' she shouted spinning round, scanning round the church looking for steps. 'There!' she pointed, and Penny followed as Angie moved towards a doorway.

Their footsteps echoed as they clattered up the stone spiral. Penny heard a crash as Angie pushed over a door and felt a strong gust of cold air.

'There he goes,' Angie said as Penny emerged into the daylight. Sure enough, they saw the vicar's silver car pulling out onto the road behind the church. Penny gasped as the wind blew into her face and she had to take a step back. They must be twenty feet above the ground, protected only be a knee-high stone wall.

'What are we doing up here, Angie?' Penny shouted into the wind.

'I told you! If we don't follow him, we've lost our only lead.'

'But how can we follow him? Frieda's car is way back there.' She gestured back towards the village.

'Penny. I know I promised I'd never do this, and it may not even work but I have to try.'

Penny took a step back, feeling the press of the roof. The countryside swayed dizzyingly behind Angie's desperate face. 'No. I know what you're asking and no. I can't. Please don't make me, Angie.'

'I'm sorry but I must. I won't take everything, but I need some to carry both of us.'

'Carry? What do you mean?'

But it was too late, Angie had taken hold of both her hands and the draining began.

*

I hated to do it. I hated to see the look on Penny's face; I had betrayed her. Broken my promise. But that man, that vicar, knew where Mrs B was. I knew it. I could smell it in the animal stink he gave off.

I gripped her hands and felt the jolt as the energy zapped into my skin travelling on into my blood and muscle. Penny twisted and tried to push me away, but I held on. I couldn't look at her face. She'll never forgive me, I thought.

Keeping hold of her I turned to the edge of the roof. I couldn't let myself have time to think. I focused on the fizzing in my blood and looked for the eddies and pools in the air. I sang the words Mrs B had taught me over and over again until they began to resonate, a hum that filled my ears, making my head ring. I saw Penny try to put her hands over her ears but stopped her, keeping them tethered in my own. She looked at me, terrified and I tried to smile to reassure her, but the sound was too loud. We needed to go.

With a cry I stepped over the edge, feeling the humming wind buffet my face and body. Penny screamed beside me as we dropped, a sickening plummet until, with a monumental wrench of effort I swooped us up, up, up into the air. For a second I saw Trevor's face, looking up in astonishment but then he was gone, and we were following the car from high, high above the tops of the trees.

I couldn't think. Everything was driven from my brain except for the exhilaration of diving through the sky, rising and falling, feeling the glorious buoyancy of the thermals. Part of me knew this was impossible. My body was too solid, too heavy to be able to soar into the sky. I pushed the thought away, forcing myself to concentrate on the car as it wound along country lanes that looked like rivers from above.

The countryside rippled below. I couldn't believe what I was doing. Look at me now, Mrs B! I wanted to shout like a child. I'm doing it!

I daren't look at Penny. I could feel her hand tightly gripping mine and hoped I could hold her until we could get back down safely. I prayed the vicar would stop soon, my energy levels were dropping rapidly and I daren't draw anything more from Penny.

We were winding deeper and deeper into the hills that rose round the village. We must be three or four miles away from the church. I hadn't seen a house for a while. Did Ed the vicar know we were following? Was he leading us on a wild goose chase?

Penny cried out and I saw we were dropping lower and lower. I tried to push up but was exhausted. My legs bumped against the top of passing hedgerows and I shouted more words, desperate to keep us up in the air to see where the car had gone, but they came out as little smoky drifts. We continued to fall.

A huge oak tree lay dead ahead, Penny cried out again and I tried to swerve but the last smoky charms accelerated us forward and it was too late. We hurtled towards the wall of green with an unstoppable force. I closed my eyes.

Chapter 15

We landed with a crash. We had to raise our arms to protect our faces from the whipping twigs and branches. For a moment all was still and Penny and I locked eyes before, with a terrifying groan, the branch we'd landed on gave way and we plunged to the ground.

Luckily it could only have been a ten-foot drop, but it was enough to knock the breath from my body and I lay, gasping for air, flat on my back. Every last trace of exhilaration had disappeared from my blood; I'd never felt such complete and utter exhaustion. I couldn't move.

My brain screamed at me to get up. Check on Penny. Follow the vicar. But it was no good, I could do nothing but stare at the sky, willing the throb of energy from the grass and earth beneath my back to begin a restoration. It would take a while, and in the meantime, I couldn't even turn my head to check on Penny.

'Penny?' I croaked. My lungs were on fire. 'Did you see which way he went? Penny?'

'Don't talk to me.' I heard a rustle of movement, but I still couldn't turn my head.

'Penny! What's wrong?'

She loomed over me looking absolutely furious. 'What's wrong? What do you think is wrong? Do you think it's OK just to drag me over the side of that roof? I thought we were going to die! You didn't even ask! And to drain me! When you promised you'd never do it again. I only have your word for it that this vicar person is even connected to Frieda.'

'Penny … I'm sorry … I …'

'Have you any idea. ANY idea what it feels like to be drained? Especially when you haven't consented.' She loomed over me again. 'Do you? Well, let me tell you. It's like having your skeleton pulled out of your skin. Not to mention all the trauma it triggered. How do you think it feels to have a friend use me in that way? Especially a friend who knows exactly what I went through and how much I suffered. I trusted you, more fool me.'

'Penny, please let me …'

'There is nothing you can say that makes this all right, Angie. You were completely irresponsible dragging me along with you like that - using my energy to do it, like I'm some kind of … some kind of battery! And you just took it. I tried to stop you and you forced it out of me. You should be ashamed of yourself.'

I tried to lift an arm, desperate to get up to explain, reassure, apologise, but the flying had taken everything from me and I couldn't move. I felt terrible. I knew I'd used Penny, even as I took her hand I knew it was a dreadful betrayal but, to my shame, I knew I'd do it again to find Mrs B. Penny's life force would always regenerate, I couldn't say the same for Mrs B. Even as Penny ranted my mind was speeding along, remembering the car we followed, which direction had it gone in? Would we be able to find him again?

'You're not even listening to me, Angie! Are you? Just thinking about that fucking car.'

I flinched. Penny must be very angry indeed.

'Well, you don't have to listen to me any longer. I'm leaving. I can't believe I stayed with you on this ridiculous goose chase for so long.'

'No! Penny! Wait!' With a monumental effort I pulled myself up onto my elbows and called after her departing figure. I saw her stumble, her legs bruised from the fall. 'What about Mrs B?'

Eyes flashing, Penny wobbled back towards me. She had a great scratch across her face that looked sore. 'You lost the right to ask me for help when you betrayed my trust, Angie Tully. You could have killed both of us with that ridiculous …' She gestured towards the sky, 'whatever that was. When you said there was danger ahead it didn't cross my mind that it would be because of you.'

'I don't know what to say.'

'Because there is nothing for you to say.' She took a deep breath and I felt awful to see her chin tremble as she struggled to hold back tears. 'I don't trust easily, Angie. And now I know why. I wish we'd never met.'

She walked away. I rolled over and pushed myself to my knees, blinking away the wave of nausea and vertigo. I couldn't replenish quickly enough. I'd never been this drained before and I felt queasy again at what it must have felt like for Penny when I'd dragged the force from her. I was also very conscious of time ticking past, it must have been half an hour since we'd seen the vicar's car, he could be anywhere now. Anguish kicked me in the belly, and I doubled over with a groan.

Penny was right, I'd been thoughtless and irresponsible and worst of all I was no nearer to finding Mrs B. I didn't need Penny to carry on searching, but as I watched her reach the edge of the field, I realised I wanted her to be by my side. It had been so lonely searching on my own. I had to get her to come back. She had to finish the journey with me, no matter what was going to happen.

'Penny!' I called, dragging myself up by leaning on the trunk of the oak tree. I relished the sizzle of its energy under my fingers and felt a little stronger. 'I'm sorry, Penny.' My heart jumped a little as I saw her stop, but she didn't turn to face me. 'You're right. I did betray you, and in the worst way. I can't justify it. I knew what I was doing.' I began to limp forward, my legs strangely weak; I had to concentrate hard to stop them folding.

'No tricks, Penny. All I can do is ask you to forgive what I did and give me another chance. Help me find Mrs B and you never have to see me again. I know I've broken the bonds of our friendship and I can't tell you how much I hate myself for it. Especially, as you said, when you were used so badly before.' Her face softened, just a fraction, and a tendril of hope uncurled in my heart. 'I'm so sorry, Penny. I know I've dragged you into this mess and I abused your trust. You didn't deserve any of this.' I stopped, wheezing. Breath was still a struggle.

A flicker of concern crossed Penny's face. 'Are you all right, Angie?'

Carefully I sat back down in the cushion of grass. 'Not really. I think I may overreached myself jumping off that church roof. I'll need to replenish before I can go on.'

I heard the rustle of movement as Penny came to sit next to me.

'I'm not sure I can forgive you quite yet, Angie. I'm too angry.'

I nodded. 'I understand that, Penny. You've every right to be angry.' I craned my neck to look up at her. 'But will you stay?'

A dreadfully long pause hung between us, and I found myself desperate, desperate to hear her say she wouldn't go.

She sighed.

'Please, Penny,' I said, my voice soft.

'I didn't deserve to be treated like this.'

'No, you didn't,' I agreed.

'I was terrified,' she said flatly. 'The draining was bad enough but then to grab me and hurl into the air without any warning. It was …' she shook her head. 'I haven't been that scared since I was trapped in that house in Brokkton when I was thirteen.'

Shame stung my face red. I couldn't meet her eyes.

'Are you feeling better?' she said after another long pause. Birdsong and sunshine filled the space between us, but I felt hollowed out with sadness at the look on Penny's face.

'A little.'

'We'd better get on then,' she said, getting to her feet. 'Just before we crashed, I saw the car turn into a driveway. It looked like it led to a big house.'

Incoherent with gratitude I let Penny pull me to my feet. I started to gabble out more apologies, more promises, but she held up her hand - her face stern.

'Don't talk anymore, Angie. You've said enough.'

*

'Are you sure we're going the right way?' I said to Penny as we clambered over a stile at the edge of the field and dropped down onto the road. It was getting really hot, the sun sailed high overhead, shrinking our shadows to dots beneath our feet. I had to take off my hoodie and tie it round my waist. Penny looked cool and elegant in her oversized black jumper and trousers.

She cast me a glance.

'Sorry, I'm sure you know where you're going.'

'Just before we crashed into that tree, I saw the car turn off. I remembered that collection of pylons over there. The house must be close by.'

'He knows something, I'm sure of it.' I said as we followed the lane round a corner. The hedgerows were bosky and smelled of summer. 'Interesting how he ran off and made a phone call the minute you mentioned you were interested in the Pettigrew family.'

'Yes. But don't get carried away, Angie. It might not mean anything. We must be careful how we approach this. We can't just storm up to his house and demand to be let in.'

'Of course not.'

'I think you should let me do the talking. Wait. I think this is it.'

Tucked into the hedgerow to our left was a wide, five barred gate. Weeds swarmed about it and the track beyond was full of potholes and overgrown with dry looking grass.

'Are you sure? It doesn't look like anyone's gone through this in ages.'

'Look,' said Penny, leaning over and running her fingers over the latch. 'This is clean and the hinges have been oiled recently. I wonder why they've done that but not bothered to cut back all this overgrowth?'

'They don't want anyone to know they're here,' I said, excitement lighting a fire in my blood. 'Come on, Penny.'

'Wait, Angie! I told you, we can't go storming in – we need to have an excuse for being here.'

'OK, you're right. What do you think we should do?'

Privately my plan was to grab hold of the vicar and blast truthing charms and fire balls at him until he told us what he knew about Joshua Pettigrew, but perhaps Penny had a better idea.

'I think I should knock on the door and say I was still looking for my distant relatives and ask them outright if they know Joshua Pettigrew. Perhaps I could suggest there is money he is due to inherit? People usually respond to money. Ach, it's a shame I don't look smarter, I could have pretended to be a lawyer.'

I looked at her in surprise. I thought Penny always looked quite smart, except for the day we first met, and she'd consumed a boat load of vodka.

'Sounds good,' I said and pushed the gate. It swung silently open. Penny was right – someone was keeping this gate maintained despite the neglect in evidence everywhere else. Gravel crunched under our feet as we walked down the drive. Ahead was a flash of white that kept disappearing in and out of the trees as we got closer. If it was a building it was sunk into the ground.

I clutched Penny's arm in excitement when I spotted the silver car parked carelessly on the lawn. 'It's his! Look!'

We'd moved further round so we could finally see the house. Immediately a shiver rocketed down my spine. I took a step back.

'What's wrong?'

'This can't be right,' I said. 'I thought we were following him to the Pettigrew house – didn't he say the king bestowed a house and village onto their ancestors? I thought it would be a big four-hundred-year-old mansion. Not this!'

Before us, sheltered in a curve of grassy bank was a low, white, building that glittered with glass. The roof swooped in an undulating curve down to the ground. Everything was hard, and white, and cold. I felt an urge to touch the ground to feel the living energy of the rich soil to counteract the emptiness I could feel in the building.

I'd seen modern buildings before. They'd lacked the layers and layers of lives lived of old houses, but I'd never responded like this before. Dread filled my stomach, splashing up into my throat.

'I don't like this place, Penny. There's something very dark about it.'

Penny laughed, 'I would have said the complete opposite - look at the size of those windows! All that glass. It must have cost a fortune. Do you know, I think an old building was here and they've torn it down to build this. See over there? It looks like a walled garden and the barn beside it looks very old. They must have been part of the original estate.'

'I think that place is much bigger than it looks,' I said with a shiver. 'I think it goes deep underground. It must hide all sorts of secrets.'

'You're not scared are you, Angie? It's just a house.'

'No, not scared. Well, a bit. But I think there is more to this house than meets the eye. We should be careful.'

'I'm always careful,' Penny said and began walking down the path to the front of the house. I followed, but every hair on my body stood up and waved a warning. I shivered again.

The front door was a tombstone of white that stretched high above our heads. A discreet, stainless-steel button circled in a ring of copper eyed us and Penny gave it a firm push.

It felt as if we were waiting in silence for an hour, but it was probably only five minutes before we heard a step and the door opened. A warm breeze blew a woman in her late sixties towards us. She moved so gracefully she seemed to be floating in the darkness of the hall behind her. In a second, I took in her well-tailored suit, her carefully curled and pinned white hair, and a face so painted it looked like a mask.

What was it that made my heart thump so? As Penny shook the woman's hand, introducing herself, I tried to see beyond her, into the house. As I suspected, the building rolled away for miles into the earth. I could sense rooms and corridors stretching back like the roots of a tree.

Then I recognised what it was that had triggered such a strong and immediate response.

'It's her! She's here! Penny. She's here!'

Pushing Penny aside I barged past the white-haired woman. Startled, she fell to her knees and dimly I heard Penny exclaim and help her up.

'Where is she?' I demanded, spinning round, wanting to shake the woman. 'I know she's here.' I was in a long windowless corridor but two bright, sun filled halls on either side bounced in light that picked out the woman, Sarah Pettigrew I presumed, who looked furious.

'What on earth is going on, Angie?' Penny said.

'I can tell she's here. Can you smell it? Sandalwood. Only a trace but it's here. Roses and sandalwood.' I stifled a sob and spun round again. I stepped over and grabbed the woman by the arms. 'Where is she?'

Penny wrenched me away. 'Angie! Stop it!'

'I don't know what or who you are talking about,' said the woman, staring straight at me with silvery eyes.

'You're Sarah Pettigrew, aren't you?'

Surprise flared and she looked at Penny before nodding. 'What do you want? I think you should leave.'

'Where's the Vicar? Ed? We saw him drive here. What's he doing?'

'My brother is upstairs,' she said.

'We're looking for Joshua Pettigrew,' Penny said calmly. 'Do you know him?'

'There's only me and Edward here. I don't know who Joshua Pettigrew is.'

'You're lying!' I yelled, my blood pumping to a roar in my ears. 'She's somewhere here, I know it. Penny! Hold on to her!'

I panted down the corridor to a large kitchen at the end. It was completely empty of everything except a tap over a shallow indentation. Cupboards, work tops, floor, all in the same, dense, plasticky white. Not a plant or a book to be seen. It felt sterile and dead.

'She was down below when I saw her,' I shouted back to Penny who was watching me, frozen with shock. 'The room had shiny concrete walls, there must be a basement or something.'

I started opening doors. One cupboard after another. Nothing. I ran back out to the corridor and crossed a glass-roofed hallway and plunged into darkness again – another windowless corridor. I felt like a dying moth banging against the glass trying to reach the light that would kill it.

I sensed a cooling of air and moved towards it. The corridor began to slope downwards. There was a metal door at the end. I headed for it, the breath tearing at my chest. 'Mrs B?' I shouted.

Suddenly I was pushed into a sprawling heap by a thump of pressure. Sparks flew over my head. Stunned, I turned to see Sarah Pettigrew standing at the end of the corridor, her hands above her head. Penny was slumped on the floor at her feet.

The woman grinned and clapped her hands together. I only just got the words out to spin a mantle of protection before the next lot of bolts were sent my way. With a roar of defiance I rubbed my fingertips until they burned and flung arrows of blue-green fire. One hit her on the shoulder, knocking her back and I shouted with satisfaction.

Mrs B must be here, I thought in exhilaration as I waited for Sarah Pettigrew's next move. She was no match for me, her charms were thin and easily shrugged off. Thank goodness I'd fully replenished on the walk from the field to the house, I thought. It gave me an edge.

Holding my hands out in front of me I walked towards her. She growled and cast another handful of cinders that I threw aside with an easy wave of my hand.

'Where is she?' I said, wrapping a binding charm round my wrists.

Sarah just shook her head, her mercury eyes never leaving mine. I felt a thrill to see the fear in them. 'I know she's here,' I said, so close now I could see the sweat dotting her forehead and throat, her hair beginning to turn lank.

'Edward!' she shouted. But before she could call again, I pulled the binding charm into long threads and began to twine them in cobweb strands round her head and body. She clawed at them, but they stuck like ivy, sending little hooked darts into her skin. It wouldn't hold her for long; I had to hurry.

I took a second to check on Penny who was unconscious but breathing well and her heartbeat was strong. I had to get to that steel door.

It was locked, of course, but the smell of roses and sandalwood was stronger than ever. 'Mrs B!' I cried joyfully. 'It's me! It's Angie! I'm here. Stand back.'

I slammed against the door, using all my weight but it didn't waver by an inch. I slammed into it again, stupidly, thoughtlessly, as I couldn't bear to waste a second by stopping to think. The lock was too thick and heavy to melt. Eventually I came to my senses and retreated along the corridor to search Sarah for keys. There were none, but after a frantic search I found a set hanging in the kitchen.

Fumbling to push the right one into the big lock I heard a voice behind me.

The vicar. Ed. Holding a phone and stepping gingerly round the slumped form of Sarah Pettigrew.

'I know who you are. You've been on the news. I've called the police.'

I turned back to the lock, forcing in another key, then another. I dropped the set with a clang and swore, bending down to pick them up and try again. They were slick with my sweat.

'They'll be here any minute. I shall tell them how you assaulted my elderly sister in a completely unprovoked attack.'

He was a wolf, but a weak one. A follower not a leader though both him and his sister have proved loyal to Joshua. Was he their son? No matter. I had to get Mrs B out from underground.

At last a key moved with a sudden, sweet, slide into the lock and I pulled the door open. Immediately I recognised the rubber floor and concrete walls. 'Mrs B!' I screamed, rushing forward. A thick pair of chains swung loose on the back wall; a crumpled, blood-stained blanket lay humped into a ball on the floor.

Gasping for breath, a stitch punching my side, I fell to the ground. The room was empty. In the distance I could hear the wail of sirens.

'

Chapter 16

Penny came to as the vicar knocked against her, reaching to help his sister to her feet. Her eyes glared at him, but something was wrapped round her face and shoulders, rendering her mute.

The pair shuffled away from Penny, disappearing down yet another corridor. She could hear animal wails and was struck with fear. Where was Angie?

Head thumping, stars dancing in front of her eyes, Penny stumbled towards the noise. That cow must have knocked her out, she thought.

The house was a maze, a network of corridors and hallways leading to locked doors. Penny blinked as she moved from blindingly bright halls to pitch-black-dark corridors, her eyes never adjusting in time so she had to fumble her way towards the cries.

'Angie?' she called, rubbing her head. She ran her hand along the wall, edging her way closer and closer. 'Angie! Where are you?'

'She's gone! She's gone, Penny!'

Penny stood in the doorway to a stark, empty room. Angie lifted her face and Penny shuddered to see the despair marked there. She was slumped over a stained blanket, tears rolling down her newly gaunt cheeks. Penny could see bruises and cuts on her arms, a crimson swelling blossoming on the side of her jaw.

She ran forwards and gathered Angie up in her arms, trying to get her to stand. 'Angie, don't,' she said. 'Please. It's going to be fine.'

'She was here,' Angie cried. 'This is her blood. Her energy is everywhere. We were too late.'

'Shh, Angie. It's fine,' Penny soothed with nonsense words, her heart breaking to see Angie's utter devastation.

'We were so close,' she said, her chest heaved with sobs.

'The police are coming,' The sirens were a constant noise. 'I think you need to go and speak to them. Explain what you found here. They'll find evidence all over the place to prove Frieda was here and very recently.'

'Even if they believed that they'll arrest me for hurting that woman - Sarah Pettigrew.' She wiped her face, rubbing her eyes on the sleeve of her top. 'The vicar, Ed, must have told Joshua. He must have called him and warned him we were close. We could only have missed her by minutes.' The tears spilled again. 'We can't stay, Penny. I told you, I don't trust the police, I think Joshua is manipulating them in some way. We must find out where he's taken Mrs B. They can't be far away.'

With a grimace of effort, she stood up and walked towards the door. 'We need to get out,' she said. 'Both of us.'

'We can't, Angie. We'll walk straight into the police. We've got no choice, we'll have to just be honest with them.'

'We have got a choice,' Angie said. Penny saw she was desperately trying to pull air into her lungs, she was knuckling her chest, frowning in pain. 'Come here.' She stopped to see the look on Penny's face. 'No, I'm not going to drain you, I promise.' Penny didn't move. 'I promise, OK? Hurry, we haven't got much time.'

Penny stepped forward wondering if she was mad to trust Angie again. But she didn't see she had much choice. The police would be running into the house as they spoke. She watched as Angie drew her close and began to hum. To her amazement, thin ribbons of light began to scribble words on the air. They rippled and undulated, moving too quickly for her to make out. As they moved, they wove together, more and more quickly until they formed a glossy, golden mesh that hung in the air.

Penny looked over at Angie who had her eyes closed, her lips constantly moving. Then she looked up, the green of her eyes flaring and she smiled to see Penny's bewilderment. She lifted her arms and spread the golden mantle so that it folded round the pair of them.

'Now stay close,' she whispered, and together they moved down the corridor. 'Nobody can see us beneath this, but we need to be quick as it won't last forever. Don't, whatever you do, make a sound.'

They got to the kitchen where Sarah and Ed Pettigrew were talking to two police officers. Sarah was leaning heavily on her brother, looking pathetic – quite a contrast to the fiery eyed woman who'd managed to knock me unconscious, thought Penny.

She nearly cried out when she saw Angie's face leering out of a TV screen in the sitting area of the kitchen. The Pettigrews pointed at the TV, bursting into chatter as Angie and Penny edged past them. For a heart-stopping moment Penny caught Sarah's eye and the woman frowned, squinting as if trying to see past a bright light. 'She can see us!' Penny breathed in Angie's ear. Angie shook her head, but Penny noticed she began to move more quickly.

At last they were out into the fresh air and they only needed to navigate past an officer leaning on a squad car, before they were out of the main grounds and heading for the road. The golden mantle dissolved and fell into shimmering shreds that sunk into the grass, not leaving a trace.

'Where to now?' Penny asked as they closed the gate behind them. Clouds had gathered overhead, dark and ominous, saturated with rain that looked as if it was going to fall any moment.

'I don't know,' said Angie. Penny had never seen her looking so dejected. 'He could have moved her anywhere.'

'Well, let's get back to the car and think about our next move. We need to rest and get something to eat.'

They trudged on. Angie didn't speak. Penny tried to talk to her but fell into silence when Angie refused to respond, sunk into the depths of misery. It took them two hours to walk back to the church, by now drenched to the skin by a sudden downpour.

Even Trevor, his face a picture of indignation, jumping out of the long grass of the church yard into Angie's arms didn't raise a smile. Penny shepherded Angie back towards the car, walking past the memorial square. It seemed like a hundred years ago she had sat on the bench beside Angie, watching her replenish.

Now, Angie stared dully ahead, not responding to Trevor as he licked her face. Penny recognised she was in no fit state to drive so opened the passenger door for Angie and folded her onto the seat, Trevor tucked onto her lap.

Inside the car the windows immediately steamed up as the heater drew the rain from clothes and fur. With difficulty, Penny worked out how to turn the wipers on and the windscreen cleared. She hoped the heavy rain and fog that had rolled in out of nowhere would keep Angie hidden from the CCTV camera. Not that Angie seemed to care that her face was all over the media. Her misery at only just missing finding Frieda was all encompassing. It filled the car with its darkness.

'Where shall we go?' Penny asked, looking across at her friend. Angie shrugged. 'Come on, Angie. We can't give up now.'

'Well, what do you suggest Professor? If we'd got to Hurstbridge earlier we might have found Mrs B and been able to save her.'

'Are you saying this is my fault?'

Angie turned to glare out of the side window.

'You can't blame me, Angie!'

'Is it my fault then?'

'No, of course not. I'm not saying that at all. But we must make the best of it. Look, let's think about what we need to do. We'll get on much better with some decent food and some rest. There's a service station on the dual carriageway. Shall we go there for a bit? I don't know about you, but I could do with a sit down and a cup of tea.'

Angie shrugged.

With a sigh Penny started up the engine and tried to work out how to put the car into reverse.

*

I couldn't believe it. To be so close, to smell her fragrance, see her blood on the blanket, and for her to be gone. My head was throbbing as it tried to take in what had happened.

I wasn't sure how much I had left. My body was pummelled and sore. I wondered dully if I'd broken a rib falling from the tree as a sharp pain sliced through my side whenever I took a deep breath. Sarah Pettigrew's darts had left their mark too; lesions, raw and red, were scored into the side of my face and along my arm. I hadn't noticed them at the time, too fixated on finding Mrs B.

What was going on with that family? I asked myself. Sarah Pettigrew had powers, though I didn't think she was a full witch – it was as if she'd learned some spells second hand, her powers didn't lie in her bones and blood the way they did in those who carried the sigil in their palm. It was why I was able to defeat her so quickly. And that vicar – useless animal he was, holding onto his phone like it was a weapon, calling the police to do his dirty work.

I groaned at the mess I'd created. Now every move we made I'd have to think about how close the police were on our heels. I'd been shocked at how quickly they'd responded to the vicar's call, and to see my face and name on the television had been more than sobering.

My clothes stank of sweat and fear and my hair itched with grease. The unceasing worry about Mrs B, as well as the guilt I felt for the way I'd treated Penny, had gnawed a hole into my stomach lining so I felt continually nauseous: I was forever swallowing down bile. Penny kept trying to make me eat but it felt like a betrayal – the only thing I should be doing was finding Mrs B.

I thought of Brokkton, that strange torn-in-half village with the sea roaring ever closer; the face of Lilith as she'd tried to help me on my way. Pagan's Reach, the way it had protected and shielded us from evil and was now dying, its heart freezing over. I'd failed everyone and everything important in my life.

It was getting late on Friday evening by the time Penny pulled into the service station. Nearly two weeks had passed since the day I found the ruined bed and Mrs B gone. All trace of the sunny afternoon had vanished and though the rainstorm had stopped, the night had turned cold, and freezing puddles spread across the forecourt as Penny led me towards the bright lights of the restaurant.

It stank of fried food and damp coats. My stomach heaved to see two men gulping down enormous plates of bacon and egg. Trevor's ears pricked up with great interest though, and Penny had to give his lead a sharp tug to call him to heel. 'He's a service dog,' she called to a sceptical looking passing server.

'I'll go and get something to eat,' she said to me. 'Look after Trevor.'

He jumped up and I felt the warmth of his wiry little body. He tucked his nose between his paws and curled into a ball on my lap. I gave him a stroke, remembering how I'd raced off after Mrs B leaving him alone in that churchyard adding another iron-heavy weight to the burden of guilt that was threatening to press me into the ground.

Penny pushed a bowl of soup across the table along with a bread roll and a little pack of butter.

'I don't want it,' I said as she sat and began cutting up her food. Trevor stirred and poked his nose over the edge of the table, studying her plate with hopeful eyes.

'There's coffee as well,' she said. 'I've added lots of sugar. I think you need it.'

I craved the obliteration of sleep. My eyes were gritty and raw, the whites criss-crossed with red scribbles of blood and my skin was so bruised it protested at the slightest of contact.

'One spoonful, Angie, or I walk out right now. You're going to pass out or have a heart attack if you don't stop. You look awful, all grey and your hands keep shaking. You can't keep pushing yourself like this, especially with all the magic you've been doing. Do you often turn into other people, cast invisibility spells, and go flying?'

Despite my exhaustion and despair, I couldn't help a smile. 'No. Not really. Maybe spread out over a couple of years. Usually, I use my powers for easing pain or making salves and things. I've never flown before, though Mrs B spent a whole summer trying to teach me.'

'Well then. You can't be doing yourself any good using all your energy on spells and then recharging and using it all up again. Your body can't take it. Look at your hands!'

We both glanced at the cup in my hand – it was shaking so hard coffee splashed onto the table. I quickly set it down and padded up the spill with a napkin.

'Since you came to find me I can't think of a single night when you've got a decent amount of sleep. You've just kept going until you've passed out. It's not healthy, Angie.'

'OK, I'll have some soup. I need the toilet first though, where is it?'

I followed Penny's pointing finger and squeezed out from behind the table. As I washed my hands, I was shocked to see the state of my reflection. My hair stood on end in greasy, matted spikes. Great black circles under my eyes held the only colour in my face which was so pale I was a revolting yellow- grey. My eyes looked like they were bleeding. Instinctively I rubbed my fingers for some refreshing sparks but came up empty; I'd nothing left.

With a sigh I returned to the table and took a spoonful of soup. It was good – rich and thick. Saliva flooded my mouth, and I was suddenly ravenous. I tore the roll in half and slathered it in butter, soaking in the soup and devouring it until liquid ran down my chin.

To my surprise within a few mouthfuls I was so full I thought I would burst.

'It's because you've not been eating,' Penny said. 'Your stomach has shrunk.'

I gave the rest of the bread to Trevor who was watching every move I made. We must get him some dog food, I thought.

'Better?' Penny said, she looked very worried.

'Yes. I do feel better. Thanks. I needed to be told – you're right, no point in not looking after myself, that won't help me find Mrs B.'

I sat back, feeling hot. My body was plumping every cell with the nutrients from the soup and the rush of the fresh coffee. I closed my eyes; sleep was pulling at the lids; they were as heavy as lead.

'I don't know what to do, Penny,' I said in a murmur. 'Actually, I do. I just want to sleep and never wake up.'

'I won't have you talking like that, Angie. Don't be such a coward.'

My eyes sprang open, and I looked at her, outraged. 'I'm not a coward.'

She gazed back, head tilted to one side. Her glorious sweep of hair swung loose in soft, pearl waves. I realised with a start she had stopped pinning it tight to her head.

'No, that was unfair. In many ways you are very courageous, Angie. But you also don't think ahead, and you try to batter your way to a solution. I'm not sure it's very effective.'

I swallowed the last mouthful of coffee. 'No. You're probably right. But you tell me what I should do. Where do I look next? We can't go back and shake it out of those weirdos in Hurstbridge because the police will be waiting for us. What do you suggest?'

Silence fell between us broken only by the sound of lapping as Trevor drank from the water bowl Penny had organised.

'I don't know, Angie,' Penny said. 'Can't you try and connect with Frieda? Like you did with the crystal?'

'I've tried, countless time, of course I have,' I said, heartbreak washing over me again at the thought. Every night I'd sent myself out, a thousand pieces on the four winds, desperate to make a connection but she'd been carefully hidden – somewhere that easily blocked my probing thoughts.

'Maybe we should go back there, to Hurstbridge?' Penny said.

The sudden, shrill ring of my phone made us both jump. I didn't recognise the number and very few people had my mobile details. I was tempted to ignore it, but curiosity won out.

'Angie? It's Laurie.'

'Laurie? Is everything OK?' I said, bewildered. Why would Laurie be calling me so late? My heart lurched, maybe something had happened to the house?

'Everything's fine, don't worry. It's just you said to call if I saw anything …'

I flashed back to standing in Laurie's shop, writing my number of a pad of paper.

'Oh, yes. What's up?'

'It's probably nothing but I saw the van, you know, the one that kept parking up over the road.'

I sat bolt upright, sharing a look with Penny.

'Where was it?'

'I was out walking Ruby, sorry to call so late but I thought you'd want to know straightaway.'

'Thank you, Laurie, that's fine, don't worry. We're still looking for Mrs B so anything you can tell us would be great.'

'Well, as I say, I was out walking Ruby and we took a different path that we usually do. That playground is getting overrun with teenagers at night and nobody's doing anything about it. I keep complaining to the council but …'

I wanted to bite my hand off with frustration but kept my tone light. 'Sorry, Laurie, I'm in a bit of a hurry. Where did you see the van?'

'It was up on Humphrey's farm. You know he's converted those little cottages by the barn? The ones at the edge of his new orchard? It was there. They must have rented one of them, he lets them out as Airbnbs. Joanie Edwards said he's been making money hand over fist.'

'Thank you, Laurie, that's really helpful. We aren't far away so we'll go and have a look. Let me know if you see anything else.' I cut her off and shoved my phone back in my pocket. 'I know where she is!' I said to Penny, getting to my feet and grabbing the keys from the table. 'Let's go!'

*

Penny watched as Angie zoomed out of the restaurant. She sighed and leaned down to unwind Trevor from his lead that he'd wrapped around the chair and went to pay the bill. There was a queue and the server behind the till was unable to change the till roll so called over a colleague. Penny felt irritation rise and craned her neck to see whether Angie was waiting for her.

She frowned to see Angie had stopped, her arm out for support as she leaned against a pillar at the entrance to the forecourt. What was she doing? Penny looked back at the queue and took a step forward as a customer paid and moved away.

She was just opening her bag to look for her purse when she heard an exclamation. She looked up. Two people were standing at the window craning their necks to see what was happening by the entrance. A strange ripple in the air turned Penny's vision dark and she looked up, alarmed. Her hair rustled and stirred.

She couldn't see Angie. Leaving the queue and ignoring the shouts from the server she walked to the exit. She began to run as she saw Angie on the floor, her body crumpled into a broken heap. A puppet whose strings had been cut right through.

Chapter 17

I could have smashed the bloke in the face when he told me the fat cow had disappeared. How did she get out? I asked. I thought you had her locked up? We did, he said. She was in a cell. Nobody knows how she escaped.

He tried to calm me down. We'll find her, he said. Her description will be on every police channel he said. She won't get far.

But she had got far. Two days later and still no sign of her. I was desperate to get into the house again, have a proper look about but now it was crawling with police. Even with the control I had over them I couldn't get away with finding what I needed. Besides, even if I did I couldn't unlock the fucking thing.

After Jez admitted there was no more he could do I had to think again. I had to move the old woman and work out what to do next. There was no way I could take her back to my apartment. I needed somewhere well out of the way but close enough I could have another prowl round Pagan's Reach.

It was ma who gave me the idea. Asking for money as per fucking usual, moaning about why she was so skint and what she was owed. And that's when she said it. About my great aunt and uncle up in Hurstbridge. How they'd got the house and all the money leaving my Gran in the cold. God she's a bitter old cow. I'd heard the rant so many times I tuned it out but this time she caught my attention.

Where are they, ma? I said and that same afternoon I drove the van through the gates and up the drive to see a house that looked like something out of fucking Grand Designs.

Staying with Sarah and Ed did my fucking head in but they had their uses. I didn't talk to them much, kept myself to myself in their weirdo house. What the fuck were they thinking, pulling down the old place and building that pile of shit. I lost count of the number of times I got lost wandering up and down those bloody corridors.

I could see why ma and Gran wouldn't have anything to do with them. They got all the money and my Gran got nothing. She never forgave them. I was expecting to have to bring out the charm when I arrived – the old bag banging away in the back of my van – but they knew who I was straight away. He knew a true Pettigrew when he saw one, he'd said – the vicar with his 'call me Ed'. Twat.

They treated me like a king – golden bollocks I was to them. They knew what I was and thought they'd take advantage. I saw the way they looked at me, her especially – Sarah. She gave me the creeps with her skinny fingers and voracious eyes.

They'd lit up like fireworks when I carried the old hag into the house. They knew how powerful she was and looked at me with fucking stars in their eyes that I'd tamed her. Gleefully Sarah had shown me their cellar, pointing out the lack of windows, the rubber floor and concrete walls that would encase the old witch in a stagnant pool of air that she'd find suffocating.

I took my time. The longer I left her down there the weaker she got. I kept an eye on the news, pleased to see the fat cow was being hunted for the old woman's murder. It wouldn't be long before she'd be caught and locked away again.

When Ed called to say someone was poking about the church asking about the Pettigrews I knew it was time to go. Far too soon. The old witch still had enough energy to bite me as I unchained her from the wall.

After carrying out the old bitch and chaining her in the back of the van I went back and told Sarah that if anyone came to the house, she should do whatever she could to bring them down.

Out on the road excitement ripped through me. Though it was earlier than I would like, I was on my way back towards Pagan's Reach. The hag didn't have much left in her, I could smell it, smell her weakness. It wouldn't take much to tip her over the edge and I knew just the thing to do it.

If Sarah didn't kill the fat cow I knew she'd come looking for me. I wondered how long the old woman would last if she saw me holding her friend up in front of her with my knife to her throat.

*

'I've called an ambulance, they're on their way.' A mother and daughter knelt next to Penny, the younger one holding up her phone as if in proof.

'Thank you, that's very kind,' said Penny distractedly. Angie was lying on her side, someone had rolled her into the recovery position after she'd collapsed. She was breathing but it didn't sound right, like a staccato snore. 'Angie, Angie, can you hear me?'

She daren't touch her, though she longed to, perhaps she could restore Angie the way she had Trevor – but she had no idea what she was doing. Her touch could send her heart into an arrhythmia or stop it altogether. She wanted to cry with frustration. 'Angie!' she said again.

There was a thundering noise as the server pounded over carrying a huge box. 'We've got a defibrillator on site!' he said proudly and dropped to his knees beside Penny and began to unpack it.

'Wait!' Penny said. 'You don't know why she's collapsed, it might not be her heart.'

The server looked down at Angie, 'I'd say it was – look at the size of her, and she's well into her 50's. Looks like heart attack to me.'

Penny was surprised to find a great waterfall of anger nearly knock her sideways. If she'd had a bat in her hand she would have smashed him over the head without a second's hesitation.

'Don't worry, Mrs, it checks the heart first anyway before it does anything. I just need to attach these thingies.' He held up two wired pads in one hand and tried to unfold the instructions with the other. Penny resisted the urge to grab everything from him but presumably he'd had training, though he certainly didn't inspire any confidence. She wrung her hands.

Angie's face, her dear face, was wiped clean of any expression. Robbed of the passion and ferocity Penny was used to seeing, she seemed strangely empty - and old. Penny had to lean in to check again she was still breathing.

Why didn't I force Angie to stop? Penny thought in anguish. She knew Angie was driving herself to this – not eating, not sleeping. She remembered Angie pushing herself with all that magic. It had robbed her of every drop of strength she had every time she used it.

'I'm sorry, Angie,' Penny whispered. 'I'm so sorry.'

Just as the server was about to push Angie onto her back so he could stick on his pads, Penny sobbed with relief as the ambulance, sirens blaring, screamed into the car park. Two paramedics dressed in green ran towards them and Penny saw a crowd had silently gathered. They parted to let the paramedics through and with a jolt Penny realised they thought Angie was already dead.

'I'm sure she's still breathing!' she shouted as they grew nearer. 'I don't know what's happened. She's been pushing herself a lot recently …'

'All right, all right, don't worry.' The first paramedic, a woman with a mop of red hair, spoke with complete reassurance. 'What's her name love?'

Penny opened her mouth and then stopped herself. Angie's name would be everywhere, she thought. 'Penny,' she said at last. 'Penny Howes. She's my best friend.' Her voice ended on a croak. The paramedic nodded.

'Penny? Can you hear me love? Can you open your eyes?' She checked Ange's pulse. 'It's very fast,' she muttered to her companion. 'It's 160 bpm and climbing.'

Penny gasped in horror, stumbling backwards, hitting against the wall. 'Is she going to be all right?' she asked.

'Let's get her into the ambulance so we can do a proper assessment,' the companion said. He was tall and bald with a broad, plain, weather-beaten face Penny found comforting. 'You can hop in the back if you want to come with us.'

'Yes of course.' Penny watched as they lifted Angie onto a stretcher and carried to the waiting ambulance.

'You can sit there.'

Penny climbed into the back, an unusually docile Trevor hidden under her arm, and tried to make herself as small as possible. They slid Angie in and began wiring her up to an array of machines. She couldn't look as they bent over her prone body, whispering to each other.

She jumped as the siren blared and they set off with a jerk. Should I call someone? she thought. Perhaps Gary, his number was bound to be on Angie's phone. Penny's mind dithered with shock.

She wished Angie would come round, say something. She couldn't bear seeing the dense weight of her, unmoving and slack.

'Is she going to be OK?' she asked again but as she spoke a machine began to beep urgently and the paramedics stirred into action.

'She's gone into AFib'

Penny buried her face in her hands. For the first time in her life, she prayed. Prayed to whoever and whatever was listening to save Angie. The thought of losing someone so passionate, so loving and impetuous, was obscene. Penny gripped her hands together and closed her eyes, hiding from the noise and shouted instructions and then the horribly familiar 'clear!' as they shocked Angie, once, twice.

In a dream, Penny walked with the stretcher when they reached the hospital. The red blanket covering Angie's body was the only colour she could see as people in scrubs swarmed out of the main entrance, swirling round the stretcher and running with it down long corridors. She could hear only the squeak of rubber soled shoes and the buzz of the electric lights, as the double doors swung shut with a hush and Angie was taken away.

Penny collapsed onto a chair, her legs giving way at the horror of what had just happened. How could they go from arguing over soup to this nightmare of sterility and death in half an hour? Her brain spun with shock. She remembered Angie's grey skin, her laboured breath. Why didn't she make her stop? Penny asked herself for the hundredth time. Trevor whimpered and she bent to give him a reassuring rub on the head. He looked small and unsettled.

A slideshow of memories flashed remorsefully across Penny's vision. Angie's face, a mix of exhilaration and guilt after they'd crashed into that damned tree; the love that shone from her when she talked of Gary and her beloved Mrs B; the way Trevor curled round her with absolute trust. It doesn't seem possible, thought Penny, that I only met the woman less than two weeks ago.

But in that time she'd captured Penny's heart with her kindness and strength, never giving up despite the odds against her in the hunt for her mentor.

She hasn't died yet, Penny told herself, cross for being so dramatic. She's in the best place. It was a good hospital with a strong reputation for cardiac care, she looked again at the report she'd found on her phone. But should she be pushing for Angie to be looked after privately? Penny wondered. She would pay whatever it took – she had plenty of money, earning a good salary and spending little.

Not able to help herself she returned to her phone. Atrial fibrillation was a serious condition that could lead to strokes and heart failure, she read. Angie could die if they couldn't get her rhythm back to normal.

Penny stared at the walls until her eyes lost focus. Time limped past; she kept checking her watch but the hands didn't seem to move. She was terribly thirsty but couldn't bring herself to get up and look for water. She chided herself for being foolishly superstitious; sitting in the corridor in an uncomfortable chair staring at the doors through which she'd disappeared wouldn't stop Angie dying. But still, Penny didn't move from her silent vigil – she owed it to Angie.

It was the early hours of Saturday morning when an exhausted looking doctor approached Penny. She was small and thin with shadows under her eyes and a brave slash of vermillion lipstick.

'You came in with Ms Howes?' she said. Penny stood, her knees and hips creaking with the movement after so long sitting.

'Yes, that's right. Is she ... is she OK?'

'I'm sorry not to have come to see you earlier, it's been a busy night.' She smiled at Trevor. 'Hey, you shouldn't be here, should you, gorgeous?' He opened one eye before going back to sleep.

Penny waited, her pulse jumping in her throat.

'Ms Howes is fine,' the doctor said at last, patting Penny's shoulder as she slumped with relief. 'But her blood pressure was sky high and she was severely dehydrated and malnourished. Her bloods weren't good so we have her on a drip now, which will help. Has she been under a lot of stress?'

'Yes, she has,' Penny said. 'She's not good at looking after herself and her friend has gone missing.'

'Well, we need to keep her under observation for a couple of days. She needs to rest and I'd like to put her on a 24 heart monitor to check the rhythms are stable. Is she on any medication at the moment?'

'I ... I don't think so,' Penny replied, wondering if they'd searched up Dr Penny Howe's medical records. Not that they'd find much.

'OK, so we'll set her up with blood thinners and blood pressure tablets. She'll be back on her feet in no time – but she'll have to take better care of herself. Tell her this is a warning – she'd be mad not to take heed of it.'

'Thank you, doctor. Can I see her?'

The doctor explained Angie - though she called her Ms Howes – had been moved from the high dependency unit to a small ward and directed Penny through the doors.

'You can't take him in with you, I'm afraid,' she added, nodding at Trevor. 'You might be able to persuade the nurses' station out front to keep an eye on him.'

It was dawn by the time Penny found herself next to Angie's bed. She was relieved to see colour in her cheeks, but worried she still hadn't come round. Her pulse beeped steadily. Not daring to touch her skin, Penny rested her hand on Angie's arm, willing her to come round and look at her.

'Angie,' she said quietly, conscious of the silent bodies in the other three beds in the ward. 'Angie, it's me. Penny. You're in hospital – you had a bit of an … well, an episode. But you're doing OK. They're looking after you.'

There was no response, but Penny was comforted by the regular rise and fall of Angie's chest, and the steady beep from the machines. The rhythms lulled her until her head nodded with exhaustion and she pulled over a chair covered in a scratchy plastic cover.

Penny watched the sun creep across the room from one side to the other before falling asleep. She dreamed of flying, and the silvery eyes of wolves.

Chapter 18

I woke up feeling like I'd been hit by a car after a night drinking bottles of gin. Every muscle in my body was painfully tender. Terror galloped through me. I didn't know where I was. I didn't recognise the way the light fell in the room. My face itched. I lifted my hand and cried out at the wrench of pain. I couldn't even sit up as my stomach muscles were as weak as tissue paper.

'Penny?' I called out, my voice high with pain and fear. 'Penny!'

'Shh,' I'm here. Relief soaked away the panic as I felt Penny's presence, her hair fell across my face as she leaned in close. 'You're in hospital. You're fine. I've told them your name is Penny Howes. Got it?'

I tried to nod but the movement made my head explode with pain. 'What happened?'

'You collapsed. You're fine, but your blood pressure was very high, and it affected your heart. They've got you on a drip with a cannula, so don't move your hand. You were really dehydrated.'

'I need to get out of here, Penny! They'll be looking for me.' I wriggled from side to side but the sheets were tucked in tight, holding me down.

'Stop it, Angie! You're safe for the moment, they think you're me – understand? I told them your name was Penny Howes.'

'Oh, yes, you said that.' I frowned. I couldn't make sense of anything. My thoughts circled round and crashed together; the pain in my head was so severe I could barely see. 'What time is it?'

'It's Saturday, just gone midday.'

'Oh my God! How long have I been here?'

'Since last night,' Penny said.

'It's too long already.' With an effort I peeled the sheets open and tried to swing my legs round. Penny danced along the side of the bed, reaching for a buzzer. 'And don't you dare call anyone,' I said. 'We need to get going.'

'You're not well enough, Angie!'

'I'm fine. I feel much better. I can rest when I've found Mrs B. We need to get back to Witchford. Where's Trevor? Where's the car?' Gritting my teeth, I pulled out the cannula and looked for my clothes – I was wearing a thin cotton gown. Penny moaned to see the blood dripping from the back of my hand, and I gathered a handful of the bed sheet to blot it until it stopped.

It took me three goes to find the way out of the hospital. Despite what I'd said to Penny I felt odd – light-headed and sick. I just needed to get into the car and have a bit of a rest and I'd be fine, I told myself. I kept trying to follow signs but they made no sense, no matter how hard I blinked and rubbed my eyes.

At last I pushed open a fire door and found myself outside in the deliciously damp mist. I let it settle on my hands and cheeks, the chill draining the hectic flush from my skin. My head began to clear and I sank into a small nearby patch of grass and pushed my fingers into the black soil until the blade skewering my brain began to retreat.

Penny caught up with me as I stood staring at the taxi phone just outside the main entrance. She was holding a huge paper bag of medication and looked furious. 'I suppose you want to get a taxi back to the car,' she said.

'Yes, we're not far, are we?'

Penny didn't reply.

We rode in silence back to the service station. Mrs B's yellow car welcomed us with a wide chrome grin. I hadn't dared talk to Penny. I knew she thought I was an idiot, and she was probably right.

'Let's get back to Pagan's Reach,' I said. 'Humphrey's farm is walking distance from there …'

'Angie, if you want to kill yourself by having another heart attack because you can't rest, then that's your decision …'

'It wasn't a heart attack …' I tried to protest but she cut me off.

'As near as damn it. But it's not fair to leave me to pick up the pieces. What happened yesterday was horrendous. I was terrified you were going to die and I had no idea what to do …'

'I'm sorry, really I am – I can't believe I put you through that and you've no idea how grateful I am that you stayed with me. I certainly didn't deserve it. But … we're so close, Penny! I can feel it. As soon as I've got Mrs B back in Pagan's Reach then it'll all be over.'

Penny glared at me, thinking hard. She was at a crossroads; I could see it in her expression. I'd taken advantage of her, frightened her out of her wits and betrayed our friendship in the worst way – she didn't owe me anything. Even now I was tempted to sound an inducing charm; it would be so easy to daze her into doing everything I asked. I hated myself for it, but in this fight to find Mrs B I'd discovered I was not as nice as I thought I was. Part of me knew I could manipulate Penny without a second thought if it got me closer to finding the old woman.

I let my hands fall by my sides. Turned out I couldn't do it. I had to let her make the decision to stay. Besides, my powers only stretched for so far for so long. If she was held to me by magic it could fade, and I'd be left alone anyway.

'You were going to cast a spell to make me stay, weren't you?' Penny said, her hair lifted by the wind into a cloud of pearl round her head.

I paused and then nodded. 'But I didn't.' I held up my hands.

'I'm only staying because you've promised to help me with my paper,' she said after an agonising pause. Her face broke into a grin, and I was so relieved I could have hugged her. When she smiled like that I saw the mischievous child she must have been. 'Come on, I'd better drive.'

We climbed into the car, making sure the back window was open a crack so Trevor could stick his head out of it and yap at passing traffic. Just before we pulled out onto the road heading back to Witchford I touched Penny's shoulder.

'Thank you,' I said. 'For staying. I don't deserve it.'

'No, you don't,' she said and wrenched up the gear stick with a flourish.

*

I must have fallen asleep instantly. We were turning onto the ring road when I came to, my head thumping. My heart fluttered in my chest and I laid a calming hand on my sternum. I promised myself I would take the meds, eat properly, get some rest. My body was letting me down when I needed it most. Just a little longer, I thought.

Penny argued, but eventually I persuaded her to drive to Pagan's Reach first.

'There's a side entrance to the grounds we can use,' I said. 'I just want to check the house is OK, then we can walk to Humphrey's farm.'

'It's a stupid idea,' Penny changed gears with an angry tug. 'The police will be all over the place looking for you.'

'That's why I want to go round the side, it's a hidden entrance and we can look to see if anyone is there first.'

We'd reached the final stretch and were winding towards the valley. I stretched in my seat to look for the first glimpse of Pagan's Reach. It reminded me of trips to the seaside when I was a child and we'd all cheer the first person to see the wash of blue, shouting out, 'The sea! The sea!' The cry that meant the holidays had begun.

My heart lifted to see the familiar curve of the woods that sheltered the house. The sky was clear at last, and the sun caught the topmost window as if signalling a welcome.

But something was wrong. As we started the final climb to the side gate, the familiar landscape looked different: distorted, and the wrong colour; there was light where there should have been a wall of green.

I couldn't work out what had changed until I saw with a gasp that a horse chestnut, one of a mighty pair, had lurched to one side. Had there been a storm? Surely Laurie would have mentioned it if there was a storm big enough in Witchford to bring down the trees.

Then I saw the crane.

It looked monstrous, a mechanical triffid glaring orange and white against the green of the trees. Three men in hard hats stood by the gate looking up at two others on the crane. There was a dreadful roar and a colossal branch dropped to the ground with a massive crash.

'Pull over, Penny,' I said, my heart fluttering again. We stopped and I struggled out of the car. I stood for a moment, frozen with shock, before running to the gates.

'What are you doing?' I shouted, horrified. I loved these beautiful trees that were just starting to light their candles to welcome summer. Their great rustling skirts sung in the wind above us. The buzz of the chainsaw rattled out again and another massive bough fell. The noise was deafening.

'Stop! Stop!' I cried, and without thinking about how I should be conserving my power and resting, I smashed my hands together until a pulse of light sprang to life. I flung it at the belly of the crane and the metal shimmered like a heat wave before turning molten. The two men above shouted in alarm as the crane began to fall.

It landed in the road with a satisfying metallic crump. The men who had tumbled into the hedgerow groaned as they got to their feet, rubbing their backs.

'What the hell happened?' one of them said. I recognised him, he was the son of an old mate of mine from school. I couldn't remember his name – Scott? Sam? Something like that.

'Buggered if I know,' the older man was looking at the damaged crane and scratching the back of his head. 'Looks like … I dunno … lightning maybe? Did you hit a pylon, you twat?'

I ignored them and looked up at the tree, my heart breaking. It was nothing but an upright chewed log, all its gracious finery torn away. Its mate on the other side seemed to stretch its arms towards it in despair.

'Why did you do this?' I turned on the men who had gathered around the crane. 'What right did you have to cut it down?'

They looked at me as if I were mad. I was conscious of the tears running down my cheeks and my red face.

'Just doing our job, love. We've got all the paperwork.' He handed me a folder filled with papers.

'There's been a mistake,' I said, shoving it back in his hands. 'The house and grounds belong to Frieda Beaudry. She'd never allow this to happen.' As I spoke, a chill ran down my back; there was movement up at the house, a flash of blue light. Penny was right. The police were waiting for me. I backed away. 'I'm going to call the council!' I said. 'You'll regret this – you bloody monsters!'

'He's cutting down the trees!' I sobbed to Penny as I got back into the car. 'He knows how important they are to us and the house. He's chipping away at everything.'

'Who? Joshua? How could he do that? Angie, you look awful.'

'I'm fine,' I insisted, clipping in my seat belt.

'What do you mean they're important?'

'It's for replenishing. Those big mature trees are something we can connect with, the house needs all the growing things around it and he knows that.' I tried to catch my breath which seemed trapped at the top of my chest. 'He's going to destroy everything in the grounds, which will cut off us and the house from restoring.'

'You can't be sure,' Penny said mildly, trying to calm me down. 'It could just be a mistake by the council – they look like council workers.'

'No. It's more than that,' I said. 'I can feel it. I don't know how he's doing it, but he's behind all this. Joshua Pettigrew. I'm as sure as anything.'

I couldn't bear to look at the desecration of the once glorious tree that had guarded Pagan's Reach so faithfully for so many years. Mrs B would be heartbroken, I thought.

'We'll have to drive up to Humphrey's farm,' I said. 'I could see police up at the house.'

'Police? Good God, Angie, why didn't you say? We'd better go.'

'Just drive up that track – we won't go far, nobody ever comes here.'

'I'm not sure the car can take it Angie.'

'Just a little way.'

The earth was muddy and stuck in clumps to the wheels as Penny inched forward. Eventually she braked. 'If I go any further I'll get stuck.'

'OK. Wait here. I'm just going to have a quick look.'

Leaving Penny to hold onto Trevor - who was going mad at being kept in the car when he could smell home so close by - I made my way up the track. My breath was laboured within minutes; I pushed down a spasm of fear that my heart couldn't cope with this constant movement. But I'd find Mrs B and then I would concentrate on getting better. Besides it wasn't really a heart attack, I reassured myself. It was a warning. Too much stress, high blood pressure and dehydration – that's all it was.

The gate for Humphrey's farm was just ahead and I turned right to walk along the fence to the workmen's cottages he'd been having renovated. The cottages Laurie was walking past when she saw the van.

I stopped. There were police strolling through the wood that ran along the edge of Humphrey's land. Over the fence I saw two more uniforms walking up the drive to the main farmhouse. Christ. They were everywhere.

Rubbing my chest, I made my way back to the car. Dizziness was blurring my vision; the woods swooped and buckled, not offering their usual comfort. I felt very ill. I had to find somewhere to retreat and lick my wounds. I couldn't do anything useful in this state.

'They're at the farm as well.'

'Who?' Penny said, turning on the engine.

'The police! They're bloody everywhere.'

Penny turned off the car and dropped her hands in her lap. 'So what are we going to do?'

'We'll go to the Doc's house. He's been a friend of Mrs B for years and him and Maeve have been very kind to me. They're away at the moment, and I know where they keep the key. We'll be safe there.'

'All right, Angie. Whatever you like. But promise me you'll rest. You look awful.'

I directed Penny back to the village. I didn't think it wise to park a huge yellow car outside the Doc's house on the high street, so we drove the long way round and parked by the village hall.

Penny took my arm as we approached the Doc's house. I showed her the side alley to the back of the house and dug out the key from the clematis pot by the conservatory door.

'What a lovely garden,' Penny breathed.

'You should see it when summer really gets going,' I said twisting the key and pushing the metal door open with a shove of my elbow. The movement sent my head reeling.

I hurried through the conservatory to the kitchen. It was cold, and I flicked on the thermostat. 'We need to stay in the back rooms,' I explained to Penny. 'The village is a nosy lot and if they see the curtains shut or any lights on, they'll be calling the Doc quick as a flash.'

'Sit down, Angie – you're white as a sheet.'

I pulled out a chair and sat before my legs completely gave way. The Doc's house smelled so familiar I almost wept. I'd lived with them for a while before moving in with Mrs B and he and Maeve had treated me like family. I wished they were here.

Penny was opening and shutting cupboards with a bang. 'There's nothing here,' she said, exasperated. 'Not even a tea bag.'

'They're away for two months,' I said, resting my head on the table. 'A second honeymoon. There's a freezer through that door - in the little utility room – you might find something in there.

Penny disappeared and I closed my eyes. I was desperate to get up to the farm and search the cottages. I was also very worried about the trees being torn down. It was such an aggressive move. I knew Joshua Pettigrew was behind it – he knew how to weaken us, and the house. I groaned aloud in despair at the thought of more trees being torn down: the oaks leading to the orchard, the willows by the stream, the silver birches that whispered and chattered in the breeze by the paddock – they were the guardians of Pagan's Reach, dear and familiar.

Penny returned holding a couple of packets. 'This is all I could find,' she said. 'Some frozen vegetables and two pies. I'll put them in now.'

'You can't use the oven,' I said pointing at the Aga. 'They've turned it off and I've no idea how to get it back on – the one at Pagan's Reach is different.'

'Microwave?'

'Yes. Up on the side.'

While it was whirring away Penny poured a glass of water and placed it by my elbow along with a pile of pills she'd methodically popped out of packets.

'I don't need these,' I said. 'I just need to properly replenish – spend some time in the woods.'

'I told you, Angie. You don't take these then I'm walking straight out of that door.' She glared at me.

'Fine.' I swallowed them down one by one and stuck my tongue out at Penny so she knew they were gone. She made an exasperated noise and turned to the microwave.

'I'll go to the village shop first thing tomorrow,' she said over our paltry dinner. 'There is a shop isn't there?' I nodded. Satisfied, she went on. 'Nobody knows me here so no reason for them to connect me with you - it should be fine. We can then work out what to do next.'

It was strange to be lying in the little box room I'd last stayed in years ago when the Doc and Maeve took me in. I hadn't closed the curtains and propped myself up so I could watch the woods that ran along the back of the village and curved an arm round Pagan's Reach further along the hill.

No matter how hard I tried I couldn't shake off the dragging sense of exhaustion. My heart still kept fluttering and, worse of all, I couldn't summon up a single spark. That one burst of energy I'd used to stop the crane had drained me completely and nothing had returned. Without my powers I was useless. Fear curled round my chest. I was so close to finding Mrs B but was I strong enough to fight the monster who'd taken her?

I had to hope the medicines would work, that rest would replenish my body that ached so. But time was running out. Pagan's Reach was suffering, and I had to restore its mistress before it was too late.

Chapter 19

'Oh, you look better,' Penny exclaimed as I came down the stairs. I couldn't believe how late I'd slept. I'd fallen into a dreamless oblivion the second I'd closed my eyes, even the sun blazing in through the open window and the flood of bird song hadn't the power to force me awake.

'I turned on the immersion so I could have a shower.' The feel of hot water sluicing away the sweat, fear, and dirt of the past weeks had been heaven. I'd scrubbed my hair with Maeve's shampoo until it squeaked and taken the time to comb through conditioner and moisturised away the dry patches on my face.

'Well, you look a hundred times better for it,' said Penny as she pulled on her coat. 'I'm going to pop up to the shop before it shuts. I forgot it was Sunday.'

'OK,' I said. 'I thought it might be a good idea to try some scrying – I haven't got a crystal but could always use a bowl of water – that sometimes works well. It would be much safer to scry into the farm from here.'

'As long as it doesn't drain you,' Penny said, frowning with concern. 'You have to be careful, Angie. I won't be long, all right? The kettle's just boiled – I've made you a cup of fruit tea – there was a packet in the utility room. Don't drink any coffee.'

I watched from the kitchen as she crossed the garden to the back gate. I hadn't said anything to her but I was hoping that after a good night's sleep, dutifully swallowing the pills Penny had left by my bed in the morning, and a good wash, my powers would begin to restore. I rubbed my fingers together but no sparks appeared. It would seem my body wouldn't co-operate until I'd rested. Again, I pushed away the image of Mrs B beaten and bruised. I had to rest. I couldn't help her until I'd replenished properly.

The wind rattled the window frames, but the sun continued to shine. I took the cup of fruit tea and went out into the garden. Magnolia blossom nodded to the right and the sun turned the lush grass into shining silver ribbons that swayed and rippled in a joyful movement that lifted my heart. Trevor leaned against my legs and panted happily.

Sipping the tea that was disgusting but good and hot, I sat on the Doc's favourite bench and lifted my face to the sun. The wind was fresh and buffeted my face and hands, reminding me of leaping from the church roof and flying into the air. My blood surged with the remembered thrill. Whenever I thought of it, I couldn't help a smile.

Maeve's flowers were dancing in their serried ranks and I inhaled restorative breaths, pulling the spring-soaked, healing air deep into my lungs, willing the energy of it to move into my blood and heart. I half closed my eyes and let the colours of the garden and the woods beyond blur into a swirl of a thousand different greens.

I had to replenish. A proper, deep replenishing, not the panicked gulping down of energy I'd been relying on these past weeks. I needed to slowly pull the force from the woods and garden deep into the marrow of my bones and soak myself in the richness the world offered.

After days of constant movement fuelled by nothing but fear and rage, to be forced to sit and be still for a moment was glorious. I couldn't worry about Mrs B because without replenishing I couldn't help her. It had taken collapsing at the service station for that message to be finally received; the message my body, and Penny, had been trying to tell me since Mrs B was taken. I didn't even have enough in me to scry the farm.

So, I sat and enjoyed the sun. The birds swooped and dived in the ocean of sky above, it was the most tender of blues, as if newly unwrapped; the dismal dense blanket of winter cloud finally dissipating. I itched to leap into one of them and soar over the village to see if I could find the van, but I hadn't replenished for long enough.

Instead, I shut myself down so I was just a seeing, hearing, smelling thing that could do nothing but absorb. I imagined myself as a lake holding within itself the light and movement of the trees.

It took an hour or two, but by the time the sun had begun to sink behind the ridge of the woods I felt much stronger. Strong enough to scry out that bastard Joshua Pettigrew, I thought.

Back at Pagan's Reach I'd an old copper bowl I used to use. Maeve didn't have anything like that in her kitchen, but I found a wooden salad bowl that would have to do. It took a while to settle my thoughts. I pictured Humphrey's farm in my mind's eye. I'd been there often and was familiar with its layout. I'd turned out all the lights and pulled down the blind so the water moved darkly. I lit one of Maeve's Christmas candles and moved it so the reflection of the flame rippled across the water. The scent of orange and cinnamon filled the room.

I let my eyes relax and skimmed my vision across the surface, watching the light fracture and reconnect. There. A field, trees, buildings on the horizon. A flash of white and adrenaline dried my mouth. Was that the van? I leaned forward but something was wrong. A vacuum, a black hole of emptiness smeared the vision into incomprehensibility. I pulled back with a jerk. My heart jumped but I wasn't sure if it was in fear or excitement, one thing I knew for sure was that Pettigrew was there and was shielding the place from prying eyes – my prying eyes.

I pushed back my chair and called for Penny, suddenly realising how much time had passed. I checked my watch – it was gone four o'clock, she should have been back ages ago. My heart thudded an alarm. I couldn't think of any reason why Penny wouldn't be back by now. Even if Laurie had uncharacteristically engaged her in chatter, it wouldn't have taken this long.

My phone was charging upstairs. My hands were shaking as I retrieved it from where it had fallen down the side of the bed. I brought up Penny's details and clicked the number. Immediately I heard a phone ringing in the kitchen. She'd left her phone behind.

From the Doc's bedroom I could see all the way down the high street. The wind had blown clouds that scudded across the sun so light and shadow chased each other down the road; I had to blink hard to focus. There was no sign of Penny. The street was empty, a typical Sunday afternoon when the village slumbered through the showers of April waiting for the clear skies and sunshine of May.

I couldn't see any police but daren't risk walking out of the house. I didn't want to waste energy on transforming so rummaged in Doc's cupboard until I found an oversized woollen coat with a hood – that would have to do.

Pulling the hood up and keeping my head low, I left the Doc's house and headed for the shop. Trevor had tried to shoot through my legs to join me outside, but I shut the door firmly on his furry face. 'I'll be back soon,' I told him.

Desperately I hoped Penny had been waylaid, decided to pop in to look at the old church, or got chatting to some university bloke who'd invited her for a drink in the pub. I tried to imagine every possible scenario I could think of that didn't involve her being hurt or getting attacked.

A couple walking their dogs passed and looked at me curiously as I stumbled along, barely able to see out from under my hood. The sun was already setting. How had I let the day pass without wondering what had happened to Penny? Yet again I berated myself for being so wrapped up in my own world I lost sight of others. I'd been selfish and thoughtless.

But Joshua Pettigrew would have no way of knowing there was any connection between me and Penny – nobody did except Mrs B. Penny had never visited the village nor Pagan's Reach. My breath eased a little. There must be some explanation – she'd be fine. She might have got lost trying to cut back to the house through the woods.

She was also over sixty, I thought. She could have fallen and hurt herself. I kept my eyes sharp, searching every front garden and side alley, every hollow at the side of the road, looking for a glimpse of Penny's white hair.

Laurie's was shut when I got there but I could see a dim light at the back. My anxiety clicked up a notch as I knocked on the door, hoping Laurie hadn't gone home. Using my hands to frame my eyes I leaned against the glass shop front and peered in. There was definitely a flicker of movement. Was it Penny?

I banged on the glass, feeling it cool and hard under my hand. Darkness was creeping down the street and I was starting to get really worried. Where was she?

'Laurie?' I called. 'Oh. It's you, Damian.'

He lumbered from the back office looking guilty and I wondered what he was up to. We stared at each other through the glass. He didn't seem to recognise me – was he high? I banged the glass again.

'Damian! It's me, Angie. Can you let me in?' I looked around to make sure nobody could hear me, the last thing I needed to be doing was drawing attention to myself.

Damian frowned and I wanted to thump him. I thumped the glass instead. 'It's me, Damian!' I pulled my hood back and finally his face cleared. He gave a little wave and mimed he needed the keys.

I pulled my hood up again and tried to press into the shadows underneath the awning. I stepped from foot to foot in impatience as Damian took an age to move to the back of the shop to find the keys.

I was waiting at the door as he unlocked it and I pushed my way in, keeping to the dark corners of the fruit and veg section.

'Angie? What's up? Hey ... the police are looking for you. They came round. I didn't say nothing ...'

'Thanks, Damian. I know. But that's not why I'm here. Have you been in the shop all day?'

'Yeah. Mum's away. I'm looking after the place. We're closed though – shut at four. I was just ...' he looked back at the little back office with its single light bulb. 'I was just er checking stock.'

'Right. OK. Look, this is important. Did you see my friend today? Her name's Penny. She's tall, with lots of really white hair – curly. Hangs all over the place. Oh, and she's skinny. Dressed in black.'

Damian scratched the back of his head. 'Yeah, yeah, I did see her. She came in this morning.'

'When did she leave?'

'She was only here ten minutes or so. Bought milk and ham, bread, you know – that kind of thing.'

'Did you see where she went?'

He shrugged.

'OK. Look, can I ask you a favour? If you see her again, can you give me a call? Pass me your phone.' He handed it over and I typed in my number. 'If you see or hear anything at all. Her name's Penny. Penny Howes.'

'Sure.'

I wasn't sure I believed him, but I doubt he'd be able to help me anyway – he was the most unobservant person I knew, and the heavy weed habit didn't help either.

I pushed out of the shop, letting the door slam behind me. The obvious course for Penny would be to go straight back down the high street to the Doc's house but I'd not seen a single trace of her on the way to the shop.

It was getting cold. With my hood up and my head down, conscious of the CCTV cameras above the shop I considered my options. It wouldn't take much to send out a seeking charm.

Keeping in the shadows I spoke one or two words, nothing that would draw attention or cause me to weaken, but hopefully enough to give me some idea what had happened to Penny.

The words fell green and gold. It was such a relief to see them after coming up dry for so long. I had to be cautious though, conscious of the vulnerability that ran through me like a crack in glass. If I pressed too hard I'd shatter into a million pieces.

I watched as the glimmers of the charms fluttered and floated ahead of me like glow worms. I spoke again, mentioning Penny's name, and they brightened and flew together. Picking up speed, they cast their light on the ground and began to move, curving around the shop and heading for the path that led to the woods.

Where were they going? Why would Penny have gone that way? Could I trust my charms?

I had no choice but to follow. Again, I was faced with one choice and it seemed as if my path had narrowed and narrowed as the days passed. I just prayed I would find Mrs B safe and alive at the end of it.

The sun had sunk behind the ridge and the moon hadn't yet risen. I pulled out my phone to turn on the torch as the charms danced and glittered along the path ahead.

I had to quicken my step as they bounced over a thick tree root that crossed the path and disappeared. I climbed over it and stopped. My lights had gone. I was standing at the edge of a hollow in the soil framed by twisted tree roots as thick as a man's arm. Something was humped on the ground, fumbling for my phone I almost dropped it before pressing the button to get the torch going.

In the flickering beam were two bags lying on their sides. Thin, plastic ones striped in red and blue. I'd seen Laurie snap them out from under the counter a hundred times. Two loaves and a bottle of milk had spilled out onto the earth. The scent of Penny's fear stung the air.

*

Penny wasn't impressed with what was on offer in the shop. She was hoping to stock up on fresh fruit and vegetables but all she could find was two wizened carrots and a lonely tomato.

She hoped Angie was resting back at the house. Penny couldn't shake off the feeling that something horrifying was approaching. She'd felt it for days now – something was following in their footsteps as they chased after Frieda's trail.

She shivered to remember the desperate message scrawled across the walls of Pagan's Reach – over and over again. And the face on that woman in Hurstbridge, the venom in her eyes, the ease with which she had knocked Penny unconscious … Penny shook her head. As a child she'd believed in evil, but years of study had taught her it was a human construct – the devil nothing but an invented entity designed to frighten the population into obedience. But now she wasn't so sure. Spending time with Angie had brought her childhood memories into sharp focus and that same look of venom had lain in the eyes of those who had abused her.

The house at Hurstbridge was the setting of nightmares with its maze of corridors and locked rooms. Penny couldn't bear the thought of Frieda being chained to the wall in that awful, dead-aired cellar. She blinked away the vision of Angie's utter devastation at being so close to saving Frieda. The horror they'd both felt seeing the evidence she'd been imprisoned was overwhelming. That phone call had convinced Angie that Frieda had been taken close to Pagan's Reach. Penny wondered why Joshua Pettigrew would risk bringing Frieda so close when he must realise there were police everywhere looking for Angie.

He wants her to open the house to him, she thought. Angie had said the mistress of the house owned all of its secrets. He needed Frieda to get whatever he was after. Resolve filled Penny at the thought – they had to stop him. That house had been in the hands of women for centuries, they couldn't allow this monster to pry his way in.

One thing was odd: those records of the house from the turn of the last century had detailed a whole community of witches living there. How had it ended up with just Frieda - and lately Angie and Gary - living there? Penny thought. Where had they all gone?

She opened the fridge to get orange juice and tutted with irritation as a man in heavy jeans and a fisherman's jumper bumped into her.

'Sorry,' he muttered. Penny took a step back and turned towards the array of tinned soups. She added a couple to her basket and moved to get bread. Her shoulders prickled and she turned to see the grey-haired man behind the till staring at her. His eyes were vacant as if he was trying to work something out.

Wanting to get back to Angie, Penny took her basket over to pay. The man, who was the only other person in the shop, came over holding a jar of coffee and a carton of milk. He stood close behind Penny, too close; she turned to throw him a sharp look.

Her stomach fell away as she saw his silver eyes.

Chapter 20

'You don't look like a Pettigrew,' Penny remembered the vicar's words. He and his sister had shared the same eyes: the colour of mercury. And here they were again. Thank God whoever this was would have no idea she was connected to Angie or Frieda.

Swallowing hard, Penny turned back to the till and passed over her basket keeping her eyes fixed dead ahead. Her skin prickled with the awareness of the man standing so close behind her she could feel his breath on her neck.

He was big. Hands like dinner plates as her mother would have said. His shoulders pressed against the seams of his jumper – he was well over six foot, Penny calculated. And broad with it. She took him in in quick glances, observing the hair crawling out from under his cuffs, his thick neck bracketed by protruding trapezius muscles.

Her response was irrational Penny told herself. She had no evidence beyond an unusual eye colour to connect this man with Frieda's disappearance, but her body told her differently. She noted her heart rate accelerating as adrenalin pumped into her system.

She had to warn Angie, she thought, even if she was wrong it was better to be safe than sorry – another of her mother's sayings. Penny's mother had felt very close over the past few days, she felt if she turned quickly enough, she'd see her out of the corner of her eye. Foolish thoughts.

The man behind the till took an age to add everything up – he was using the calculator on his phone rather than the till and Penny wondered if he was pocketing the money for himself. As she waited, she slid her hand into her pocket feeling for the familiar oblong of her phone. At the same time she remembered leaving it in the kitchen to charge and wanted to cry out with frustration.

Finally, two bags were filled and paid for and passed over the counter. Penny tried to keep her head down as she turned to leave but couldn't help glancing up at the man who seemed to fill the little shop with his presence.

Their eyes met, just for a second, and Penny had to stifle a quail of fear – worried he would smell it on her. He looked blank but then frowned, as if cogs were whirring in his brain. He opened his mouth to speak, and Penny scuttled past him, feeling an urgent need to get out of the shop and away from this big animal of a man.

Outside she dithered for a moment, not daring to look back. Should she head straight back to the house and Angie? What if that man did mean harm and she led him straight to her?

Instead of turning left she turned right, thinking she'd wait to see where the man went. The shop was at the end of the high street and a couple of houses were strung along the road, eventually petering out. A track led away from the road towards the woods and the hill beyond. Penny decided to walk along it for a while; she'd be set back from the main road, and she'd remain hidden unless anyone followed her up the track.

She waited for what felt like an age, loitering under an enormous oak that spread its canopy in shelter overhead. The handles of the bags bit into her flesh. Slowly, she felt her heart rate calm and her breathing return to normal. There was nothing to worry about, she told herself crossly.

Penny waited for a few more minutes but all she could hear was birdsong and the rustle and hush of the trees. She took a step, then another, and stopped. What was that noise?

It was a thundering, like hundreds of conkers falling to the ground, or apples, she thought distractedly. The woods distorted the sound so she couldn't work out where it was coming from.

Penny spun round but could see nothing. She squinted into the green gloom of the wood, but the path was empty. She turned back to the main track and a scream ripped from her.

The dark-haired man with silvery eyes was slithering towards her, horrifyingly on all fours - his face almost upside down as he craned his neck to look up at her. Before she could move, he sprang into the air.

*

I stared at the ground where the mud had been churned into mounds and hollows. Leaves were smeared into a slick mush right by the abandoned bags. An animal had been here – a large one.

I felt very cold. It couldn't be more than two miles to Humphrey's farm from here, I thought. The end was close. I could feel it. I wasn't sure I was ready, but Penny's disappearance had forced my hand. In looking for Penny I'd find Mrs B. And Joshua Pettigrew, I reminded myself with a tremor.

Twigs snapped underfoot as I took a step forward. I froze as I heard a crackle of static and two uniformed men appeared from amongst the trees complaining about the cold. They stamped down the track and I stepped back into the shadows of a broad-beamed oak.

I held my breath as they passed. It was dangerous for me to be out. The police were actively looking for me, and still about, even late on a Sunday evening. I wished I could go back to the house, replenish a little more, maybe search the kitchen for knives I could slide up my sleeves.

But it was too late, time had finally run out.

Cautiously I wound around the trees keeping away from the path. My feet were sure and certain as I stole through the darkness to Penny, Mrs B, and Joshua Pettigrew.

*

No matter how hard Penny thrashed, the iron-hard grip holding her in place didn't falter. She was upside down and the darkening sky above spun dizzyingly, bile swung into her throat.

To restore some sense of where she was Penny moved her head so she could see the animal's boots as they strode easily along the path, her extra weight seeming to have no impact on him.

The ground looked to be hundreds of feet away, as if she was being carried on the shoulder of a giant. Fear was a constant hum in her blood, but her brain clicked coolly away like a machine, trying to work out a solution.

Physically she had nothing. There was no way she could even begin to overpower him, and she had no weapon. She tried to talk to him, reason with him, bargain – but he was deaf to her pleas and just … kept on walking.

Penny stopped struggling and let her body fall limp. It was easier - fighting him had no effect, and the jolts didn't hurt her bones as much when she relaxed. She thought of Martin's words in his office, talking of retirement, how she'd failed the university – it felt like a century ago. The past week had contained more excitement and adventure than the last twenty years, she realised. Had she now come to the end? She couldn't see a way out and knew Angie simply wasn't strong enough to fight this beast that carried her like she was a bag of rubbish – hopefully she'd be sensible and call the police when she discovered Penny missing, but she didn't hold out much hope; Angie was many things, but she had never struck Penny as being sensible.

They were approaching a group of buildings – four small cottages, all dark except for one. Just behind them squatted a square barn, some kind of cow shed Penny thought, with a corrugated roof. That's where they were headed.

With a grunt, the man shifted Penny onto his other shoulder so he could reach into his pocket for a key. Penny could see a large padlock swinging from a pair of rusty metal doors. They screeched as he pulled them open. She could hear a strange thrumming sound – it seemed to hang above them as if the sky was electrified.

There was a stink of cow dung though the barn was empty. Rubbish was piled in the corners and bits of broken furniture littered the floor. The man moved forward and lifted Penny into the air, dangling her from his hand. She tried to twist round, to see where he was taking her, fear was turning her into a panicking animal – was he going to kill her?

With a sudden movement he threw her to the floor. The flagstones ripped at her hands and knees, and she cried out it pain. Something was hammering in her head, and she rubbed her temples. She tried to get to her feet but he pushed his foot into her back and sent her sprawling onto her front again.

He leaned forward and, grabbing her by the hair, jerked her head up so she was staring straight ahead. She gasped in horror.

Frieda. It was Frieda. Lying on her side in a torn and ragged scrap of cloth. So thin she was a jumble of bones - her face a death's head. Her wrists were manacled behind her back with cruel cable ties wrapped tightly about her ankles. She was dirty and looked frozen. Round her neck hung a black pendant, it seemed to draw the light into itself.

Penny opened her mouth to cry out in despair when to her astonishment Frieda's eyes opened. A bright, brilliant flare of green. 'You don't know me. Say nothing.'

The words sounded inside her head as loud as if Frieda has shouted in her ear, but her lips hadn't moved. As Penny watched, Frieda closed her eyes as if exhausted.

'Who is this woman?' Penny croaked. 'What have you done to her?'

The man laughed. 'You know exactly who this is and she knows you.' Despite his tremendous size his voice was light and high - a hissing tenor. Without warning he booted Penny in the side and she screamed in pain, curling her body away from him.

'I haven't a damned clue who this is, Joshua, so you can stop torturing her.' Frieda's words were sharp and clear, they belied the crumpled, crooked, and bony heap of her tiny body.

He snatched a thick hank of Penny's hair again and pulled her up to her knees. 'You sure you don't recognise her, hag? Have a good look.' He batted Penny's hands away as she reached for her hair, desperately trying to ease the pressure. She felt it begin to tear away from her scalp and moaned in agony.

Frieda shook her head, glaring at him with defiance. He laughed and waved his hand, the air rippled, knocking Frieda back but she rallied quickly.

'Still not very good are you, Joshua? Surely, she taught you better than that? You're just a thug – you can't even summon a decent buffeting charm. Shame there's no dead here you can draw from. You're pretty useless without them.'

'I can still do this, though can't I?' With two great strides he marched towards Frieda and hit across the face with a hammer-like fist. Penny yelled at him to stop but he just smirked, leaving Frieda with blood running from the side of her mouth.

'I'll kill her,' he said matter of factly. 'You know I'll do it. Just tell me the charm and I'll let you both go.'

Frieda managed a shrug. 'Let her go. I don't even know who this woman is.'

'Oh no?' he said, his tone brutally mocking. 'What's this then?' He took something from his pocket and threw it onto the floor between them. A wooden photo frame spun once, twice before skidding to a stop. Penny and Frieda, smiling into the camera. Penny remembered the day with a shocking sharpness. The day she graduated. Daphne had taken the picture. It was an afternoon of cake and tea and the sun shining – it felt a million miles away from this filthy barn that smelled of blood and manure.

'Angie's called the police,' she blurted. 'They'll be here any minute.'

'I very much doubt that,' Joshua said. With a glance at Frieda he bent over Penny, so close she could smell his rancid breath. 'I've waited long enough. I'm sick of it. Tell me the charm!' his voice rose to a roar and Penny flinched. Before she could move, he slammed his fist into her temple and agony burned black behind her eyes. She swayed and felt darkness begin to gather her up. Frieda's yell pulled her back and she saw with horror how the old woman was trying to summon her powers to help but something was stopping them.

'Leave her alone,' she said.

'Tell me the charm.'

'You know I can't do that,' she was so weak her voice had sunk to a whisper. 'I'm mistress of the house. I'm here to stop animals like you from coming anywhere near its secrets.'

'You'll die then.'

'So be it.'

'You may not give a shit about yourself – and why would you? You look a thousand years old – you've lived enough. But what about Curly here?' Penny screamed as he threw her across the floor so she was inches from Frieda's face. 'And the other one – the fat cow – whatshername, Angie? Has she lived enough?' He snarled, 'I'll burn the whole fucking village to the ground.'

Frieda's eyes widened and Penny craned her neck to see what had frightened her. Joshua had swelled to monstrous proportions, and it took a second before she saw the glitter of the blade.

*

I ran my hand along the bark of every tree I passed, feeling for the life bubbling inside, drawing it into my flesh so my blood thrummed. The moon sailed in and out of the drift of stars and I reached for its light; I needed every drop of power I could absorb.

I heard the electric buzz of Joshua's shield before I saw it – a blank grey sheet pulled low over the buildings ahead. A simple charm but one that would be enough for searching eyes to slide past.

There were four cottages ahead. I didn't know how well he would be able to sense my approach so I wove a mantle of golden words and drew them round me. I felt strong, for the first time in days. The replenishing and rest had done me good – I would just have to keep a tight hold of the fear that threatened to spiral out of control.

Joshua Pettigrew was a wolf. Wolves fed on fear: they grew gross and swollen and even more powerful if they snuffed up the merest trace. What worried me was he seemed to be more than a wolf. It was unusual for a wolf to create a shielding charm the way Joshua had. Had Ada Pettigrew taught him the ways of the witch? It would make him a formidable opponent.

That's not anything new, I told myself. He would have needed powerful magic to subdue and abduct Mrs B. She knew enough to keep her fear hidden so he must have other ways to charge himself up.

These thoughts ran through my head as I grabbed the crumbling stone of the nearest cottage and pulled myself up to look through the window. The room was empty with a neat arrangement of new furniture, I didn't sense anything.

The next one had light gleaming from the front porch. Not daring to go round the front I slipped into the darkness behind. The back door led straight into the kitchen. There was enough light to see a large rucksack slung onto the table and my pulse ticked up a notch. I had to keep calm. I took a breath and settled my hand on the centre of my chest.

I rested my palm on the wall and leaned in. There was nobody there, but there had been. My breath shortened as I traced the memory of the rooms and saw a huge man with the thick, tightly curled hair of a ram's fleece. Joshua Pettigrew, I was sure of it.

Desperately I increased the sharpness of my focus to search for Mrs B and Penny, but there was no sign. Where were they? Had he taken them somewhere else?

I had to know. Was she nearby? The shield above stifled everything so I couldn't tune into anyone's presence. I breathed words silently onto the cold night air and like someone slipping a hand into mine I felt her. Mrs B. She was close. She was reaching out to me.

I had to force myself not to run. He didn't know I was here, I was sure of it, I had covered my tracks well, but I didn't want to risk him hearing me approach.

Rubbing my fingers together so they sparked fire, bright and hot, I crept round the side of the cottages and saw Humphrey's long abandoned cow shed. A surge powered through me – I could sense Penny, feel that astonishing life force she'd kept locked up inside herself for so long. She was there, I knew it, though the signal was terribly faint, it was there.

I summoned a shielding charm and used all the words I knew to make my movements swift, my eyes sharp, and my flesh strong. There was no need to hide my presence now. I wanted him to come out and face me.

Keeping my head high I moved forward, not allowing a flicker of doubt or fear to hold me back.

With a roar I kicked open the metal doors so they crashed and rattled against their frames. For a second the scene in front of me was a frozen tableau spot lit by a single bulb that swung crazily overhead.

The man whose dark energy told me immediately was Joshua Pettigrew stood dead centre. A huge, animal of a man whose muscles bulged grotesquely. Behind him my heart burst with joy to see Mrs B, thin and weak but alive. Thank God, thank God, I thought. I'd found her – at last.

But then I saw why Mrs B's face was filled with rage and a smothered fear. She was looking at Penny who was on the floor, trying to get to her feet. Her white hair writhed around her head, her eyes filled with terror as Joshua lifted his arm.

'No!' I screamed.

He paused and turned to me with a terrible smile and I saw the knife in his hand. It was long and thin, ground so often the edge was almost invisible. It seemed to cut the air in two as he moved.

'Stop,' I screamed again but it was too late. The blade plunged into Penny's side, and she fell.

Chapter 21

Fury screamed down my arms and legs, flames licked along my skin, and I roared until the rafters shook. I hissed the most brutal of words, feeling them catch on my lips as they fell sharp as iron shards. I gathered them in my hands and hurled them at the wolf's back. They hammered into him and he stumbled. I threw another handful, hoping he'd fall.

Instead, he turned towards me, pushing Penny's body carelessly aside with his foot. I daren't look at her, instead I concentrated on bringing him down. I planted each foot securely on the stone floor and braced myself as he grew close. I remembered everything I'd learned from Mrs B and the books passed down from witch to witch in Pagan's Reach.

Palms out, I drew upon the rage that pounded so hard in my blood it made my skin throb and cast the strongest summoning charm I knew. A cloud of debris flew into the air and swarmed between me and Joshua. I watched fragments of wood and stone fly towards him, saw the cuts and nicks appear and blood run in a thin crimson rivulet down his neck. Disappearing into the blinding storm I saw him tear at his face. It gave me enough time to run to Penny and Mrs B.

Blood was seeping from Penny's side. Keeping my hand up to hold the summoned storm in the air I tried to turn her over, refusing to let grief sap the power of my fury.

'Angie. Angie!' The whisper was quiet but clear in the maelstrom that billowed around our heads. It was Mrs B. She was scrabbling at her neck. 'Take it! Take this off ... I can't ... '

Reluctantly I left Penny and crawled over to the old woman, barely able to see through the thick cloud that continued to buffet Joshua into immobility. It would fall very soon, I calculated – I only had seconds.

I wrenched at the black pendant round Mrs B's neck, howling as I touched it; an agonizing shockwave shot up my arm as if I'd been electrocuted. I threw it as far away as I could and heard it smash against the stone wall.

'My hands,' she whispered again.

I reached behind her. The summoned debris was running out of energy. Joshua was beginning to move; I couldn't hold him for much longer. I wrenched at Mrs B's chains, but they were too heavy and strong. Screaming with frustration I shot a thin stream of fire into the lock until it grew molten and I pulled the links apart, burning my hands.

Before I moved I took a second, just a moment, to lay my hands on her belly and chest. Quickly I pulsed a jet of energy into her - enough to replenish for a few crucial moments.

'Go to Penny,' I gasped as I heard the spatter of stones on the floor and knew the storm had fallen.

I waited long enough to see Mrs B inch toward Penny then I turned to face Joshua, my chest heaving.

His eyes were liquid metal, his face twisted in fury. A ball of flame jumped to life in his hand and before I could blink it struck me on the shoulder, scorching the cloth. I grunted in shock as I was knocked backwards.

Another hit me in the stomach and rolled down my body leaving a trail of flames; I had to roll onto my front to smother them. I cried out in pain as they caught at my skin.

Spitting out dust and bits of straw I tried to summon a djinn, but the shield Pettigrew had cast above prevented me from drawing on the power I needed from the sky.

Out of the corner of my eye I saw Mrs B pressing her hand to Penny's side.

To give myself time to think I blasted two stunning charms, one after the other. They smacked him square in the chest. It was enough to send anyone flying but Joshua was so huge he barely moved. I saw they'd knocked the wind from his chest, though, and it gave me a moment to look at him properly, this animal who thought he could just beat and brutalise women to get what he wanted.

His charms were basic, it was his size that gave him the advantage - I needed to keep well away from him.

I couldn't help a flicker of fear as he held up his knife and I saw the shimmer of crimson. Penny's blood. He grinned as he sensed me quailing, and I saw his chest and shoulders swell.

Invigorated, he opened his mouth and exhaled a sooty cloud, thick and black, that floated towards me. It moved so fast I couldn't get out of the way in time, and my breath carried it into my body.

Immediately I coughed; my lungs were filling. I pounded my chest and coughed again, wisps of black smoke curled from my lips and nostrils.

Panic clamped an iron brace round my head, and I couldn't see. I tried to clear the mass, but it was no good. Joshua was moving closer as I frantically tried to draw breath. I couldn't summon words, my hands uselessly clawing at my mouth to pull out the blockage. All I could hear was the terrible choking noises as my body convulsed, desperate for air.

The world darkened. Red and purple flowers blossomed in front of my eyes, and I fell to my knees. My heart pounded as if it would explode. Then I heard a terrible cracking.

Almost instantly the pressure on my chest eased and Mrs B was there, smiling her crooked smile, her fingers glowing as she pulled the sooty thickness from my throat. Behind her Joshua was looking up at the roof as another great crack sounded, loud as a gunshot.

'Help her,' said Mrs B. Penny lay between us. I bent to lift her into my arms and as I did, Mrs B stood as straight as she could and pointed to the roof. Sparks shot from her fingers hitting the joist she'd already weakened.

With the sound of a bomb going off, half the roof fell. Joshua disappeared beneath it and Mrs B pulled at my arm.

'Angie. Help me. We need to get Penny out of here, she's dying.'

'But what about …?'

'He'll be after us soon enough, I've bought us about ten minutes. Hurry!'

*

I dragged Penny out through the metal doors. Already I could hear the crunch of stone and creak of wood as Joshua began to stir. As one, Mrs B and I turned and, holding hands, chanted an entrapment charm that spun from us dizzyingly fast, layering a mesh of criss-crossed light that would hold him for a little longer.

Oh, it was good to have Mrs B by my side. I looked down at her shrunken figure, smaller than ever.

'You look awful,' I said.

'You took your time.'

Penny stirred in my arms. Mrs B had done something to stop the bleeding, but she was deathly pale. 'She looks like she's lost a lot of blood,' I said, and coughed until my eyeballs felt near to bursting, my chest still heaving from the oily gunk Joshua had blown into my lungs.

'We need to get her back to the house. He'll be coming for us, and outside of this shield he's put up he'll be able to reach the dead.'

I shivered. 'What do you mean?'

'I haven't time to explain!' she snapped. 'Just pick her up – we need to get moving.'

Penny was tiny so I was surprised by her heft as I lifted her onto my shoulder. It felt like she weighed a ton but it didn't help I was completely drained. I couldn't make out her force, there was a slight hum but barely discernible. That bastard Joshua. I prayed her body was channelling all its energy into healing.

We stumbled past the cottages and into the woods. Mrs B was limping, and I saw the bruises on her cheekbones and the swelling round her mouth. The blood had dried into a painful crust, and I could see the gleam of her scalp through dirty tufts of hair. I reached for her hand and squeezed it. She acknowledged it for a second before moving away.

'Wait,' I said, seeing Mrs B shivering so hard her teeth knocked together. Gently I laid Penny down and pulled off my hoodie, handing it to the old woman.

'Don't be ridiculous.'

'Put it on or I'll not move another step – you're frozen.'

With a look that could melt metal, the old woman pulled the hoodie over her head. It was so big on her it fell below her knees, but I felt happier seeing her more covered, her dressing gown and nightie were no more than threads.

I gathered Penny up in my arms and pointed to the gate hidden in the overgrown hedgerow – it was rarely used so was barely distinguishable. It was a useful shortcut and hopefully Joshua wouldn't know it existed.

'He's coming,' Mrs B warned. My stomach dropped. 'Cover that fear,' she said crossly. 'You know he can smell it – makes him stronger. We need to get inside the house.'

We moved as fast as we could, my heart hammering, breath panting as I struggled to keep Penny on my shoulder. The house seemed to move further and further away; I could see the bulk of it dark against the night sky. Eventually we were through the paddock and heading towards the back door.

'The big trees are gone,' Mrs B said, her voice sharp with concern. 'What happened? Two of the oaks and the birches …'

'He's been getting them torn down. I don't know how. The horse chestnuts at the side gates are gone too.'

Mrs B didn't speak. She knew as well as I did what bad news this was for us and the house.

At last we burst into the kitchen and the old woman snapped on the light. 'Lay her on the table. Quickly!' She locked the door as I put Penny down.

'I'll look after her, go and get the house ready. He's coming.'

'What do you mean? What do you want me to do?'

'What do you think? Lock the doors and windows! Check the protection spells!'

'Mrs B … they went ages ago. Since you went … well, the house has changed. Turned against me – it's got really cold and I couldn't light any fires. The mantle we had over the place has gone. He's been inside.'

Mrs B's face dropped in horror. She had unrolled Penny's jumper up above her waistband and I winced to see the grotesque, blood-rimmed slit that bastard had cut into her side. 'What do you mean he's been in the house?'

'When I was away looking for you he must have sneaked in – I think he was controlling the police …'

'The police? The police were here? Good God, Angie.'

'I'm sorry. I … I didn't know what to do. They don't seem to be here now. They're looking for me – they think I murdered you.'

Mrs B threw up her hands in exasperation. 'Oh, what a damned mess. I wouldn't have brought poor Penny back to the house if I knew it wasn't safe.'

We looked at each other as we heard a distant crash.

'He's here,' Mrs B said quietly.

Leaving her to look after Penny I moved up the stairs to the old woman's bedroom – it had the best view of the front of the house and to the valley beyond.

The house would tell me nothing. Wouldn't respond to me as I tried to communicate with it. When I tried to lean in there was nothing but a void.

At first, I couldn't see anything out of the window. The sky was just beginning to lighten, and I could see the terrible gaps where some of the biggest trees had been torn down. The sight broke my heart and filled me with trepidation at the same time. Was this why the house had curled away from me? Had it been cut from the roots of the trees it needed to live?

Something was moving across the end of the lawn. I saw one, two flashes of light. I cried out in horror. The huge oaks that framed the main gates were on fire, the bowl of their branches now an awful beacon of flames that lit up the sky.

I skidded back down the stairs, my breath coming in gasps. 'Mrs B! Mrs B! He's here. He's … he's burning the trees.'

*

I almost crashed into her as she came out of the kitchen to meet me, she was drying her hands. Penny lay still on the table behind her, but I gave a sigh of relief to see her cheeks were pink and she was breathing gently.

'Is she going to be OK?' I said.

Mrs B nodded but looked distracted. 'I think so. I've done all I can. She's stronger than she looks and that powerful life force she has will help. I don't want to leave her there with that monster coming. We need to get her hidden. Come. Help me.'

Penny was still unconscious, so it was a struggle to get her off the table and onto my shoulder. I was losing strength so had to let her legs drag along the floor. My brain was screaming at me to move. I could sense Joshua drawing closer and closer. My mouth dried as I smelled smoke and thought I heard the crackle of flames.

'In here,' Mrs B said, shoving open the door of the big sitting room. She moved to the back wall, the one that disappeared into the eaves and was covered in books. To my surprise she reached into the shadowy corner and pulled something. I jumped as there was a crack and the wall to my left opened to reveal a wood panelled room.

'I never knew that was there!' I said in shock.

'The lever only appears at times of grave danger,' she said.

'The house must be a little on our side then,' I said.

'Of course it is! That won't ever change. But that beast has tried to drain its heart. I just hope we can help it recover.'

The room contained nothing but a small bed covered in cushions and a little side table holding a decanter of whisky and tumbler. Mrs B poured herself a large shot and swallowed it back in one gulp as I propped Penny among the cushions and made sure she was comfortable.

'You'd better have some,' she said.

The liquor burned down my throat and flamed in my belly. Power crackled along my veins, and I saw the same spark dance brightly in the centre of Mrs B's pupils. 'God,' I said, eyes watering, 'what is this stuff?'

'Bruichladdich. I get it from the Hebrides.' She poured out another shot for me and then took another for herself.

'Is it magic?' I said, coughing.

'Not technically – but it works wonders when you're afraid.'

'I'm not afraid,' I said stoutly.

'You should be,' she said, her eyes sad, just for a moment.

'We've seen off worse before.'

Memories danced between us. 'I'm so glad I found you,' I said.

'Ach we haven't time for histrionics. Don't be a goose. Penny will be safe here. We need to go.'

Back in the sitting room Mrs B pulled the hidden lever and the door to the little room closed with a hush and a clunk.

'If she wakes up can she still get out?'

'Oh yes. Don't worry. Not that she will wake up, not for a while. She needs to sleep and replenish the blood she lost. But there's a handle she can use from the inside.'

With Penny safe we needed to go and see what was happening outside. But before we left, Mrs B paused and moved to the giant cabinet that was filled with so many fascinating and magical things.

'You used the bell?' Mrs B said, taking it down from the top shelf.

'Yes, he sent hundreds of ones into the house. It took me forever to get rid of them all.'

'He's learned to draw upon their power,' she said. 'That's why he's so much more dangerous than a wolf.'

'He can use them? We found his great-grandmother lived here in Pagan's Reach and she got thrown out for using the dead to control and terrify everyone rather than helping them to move on.'

Mrs B nodded. 'That explains a few things.'

We surveyed the shelves.

'No combs left?' I said. Just after the war the old woman had been given three magical combs by a Russian witch. One had caused Brokkton to fall into the sea, the last two we'd used a few years before. They were tremendously powerful and would have been a great help.

'No. A few walnuts.'

I pushed two into my pocket. The walnuts, when cracked, supplied whatever you needed at the time. For Mrs B it had been a stream of rats when she was attacked in Venice, for me it had given the dress I'd worn at my wedding.

'Anything else? He's not far.'

'He's burning the trees to weaken us. And the house,' Mrs B said.

'It's an awful thing to do.'

'But gives us some time,' she said.

She reached into the cabinet again and gave me a heavy gold necklace studded with square black stones.

'Tourmaline,' she said. 'Put it on. It's a source of protection. My grandmother, Lilith gave it to me.'

I opened my mouth to tell her how Lilith had appeared by her gravestone, but there wasn't time. Afterwards, I promised myself, hoping there would be an afterwards. The necklace was cold against my skin. Mrs B was wearing the gold necklace she wore when I first met her. Pools of gold that shimmered and bumped over her skinny collar bones.

'It will help hide any fear of course, as well as stopping darkness like that cloud he breathed into you.'

It made me shudder to remember it.

'Mrs B ... What is it he wants so badly?'

Chapter 22

The old woman sighed and twisted her necklace through her fingers for comfort. 'I've never told you this. I was going to. Would have done soon, when you were ready.' She paused. 'Deep in the heart of the house, you know, at the end of the tunnel from the library fireplace, is a hidden space.'

'Where Marroch was killed,' I breathed.

'Yes. Where the forest grew. This house has been home to women of power for centuries – you see their writings in the books on those shelves. Well, over time they've collected hundreds of magical things. Many of them very dangerous. He wants what's in that room. Nobody can get in there unless they know the charms and the house knows her as its mistress.'

'What is it he wants from there?'

'It's a staff. A kind of wand. Retrieved from the battlefield at the start of the Great War. Some mage created it.'

'What could it do?'

There was a pause.

'It can reanimate the dead,' she said. 'Or gather their ghosts to do as the holder pleases. Very useful on the fields of battle, strewn as they are with bodies. The mage used it on graveyards too, created an army of the dead. They destroyed village after village before he was stopped. The women of Pagan's Reach brought it back here and it's been hidden safely ever since. Nobody alive should know it exists except me.'

'Oh my God,' I said. 'That's sickening.'

'You can understand why I would die rather than let a monster like Joshua Pettigrew get his hands on it. Though he considers it his birth right, along with this house. He's been told that since he was a child by his mad grandmother.'

'He wants the house too,' I said.

'Of course. And we must make sure he doesn't get it.'

She smiled and, for a moment, touched my hand with such swiftness I could believe it had never happened. We left the sitting room and shut the door.

'The library,' the old woman said.

We could see the flicker of light reflecting on the ceiling before we passed through the door. I gasped to see the whole length of trees that protected the front of the house blazing with flames that crackled and leaped from one branch to the other. The sky burned orange and red.

'Look,' said Mrs B.

And there he was. Standing in the middle of the lawn staring up at the house, his face twisted with rage and hunger. He lifted his arms, and I cried out.

'There! Hundreds of them.'

Tumbling, bounding, snarling they came. Filthy creatures with red eyes and matted fur. They looked rabid. Behind them trailed smoke, as if they were on fire. They raced across the lawn and within seconds were swarming towards the terrace.

'Outside!' Mrs B yelled. 'We must stop them reaching the house!'

Out on the terrace the air was hot with fire, the stink of the burning trees rasping at my lung and breaking my heart. Before I could think, the first of the creatures were upon us.

One climbed straight up me, and I grabbed at its fur and threw it as hard as I could until it smashed open on the stones. Another jumped for my shoulder and sank its fangs into my skin making me scream in pain. I grabbed that one too and ripped it away.

Mrs B was struggling under three or four of them and I pulled them from her, using sparks from my fingers to blow them to pieces. They started to slow, wary of us now we had turned to face them. Joshua yelled a command. He looked enormous, the flames behind him casting a shadow that stretched all the way across the lawn.

More and more creatures appeared as if born of fire and night. Mrs B and I sung words and silvery-blue lances shot from our hands. The creatures jumped and spat and were torn apart by the laser sharp darts.

'There's more coming,' Mrs B cried.

'Should we go back to the house?' I shouted above the terrible roar of the blazing fires.

'No. We can't let them in. They're vargs. If they get inside they'll tear the place to pieces.'

I kept firing, moving closer to Mrs B as I could see her charms were losing their power. She was getting exhausted. Her face was crumpling. There was no sign of the young priestess with long black hair I was used to seeing whenever Mrs B cast charms in earnest. It was a little, crooked-back old lady who fought these armies of creatures that came in endless waves.

She was failing; I had to do something. I gathered every ounce of strength and power I had left and spoke the most powerful, the most dangerous words I could find. I felt my feet lifting from the floor as the air pulled me up towards the sky. If the creatures were night and fire, I must use light, I thought.

I felt the loss of the trees Joshua had torn down, but behind me I had the whole wood and the house whose roots curled deep, deep within the earth. I called on the flowers, their colour and scent, the new buds plump and luscious, the leaves stretching their joyful fingers as winter retreated.

I closed my eyes and breathed all of it in and gathered it into a shining, sunlit mass deep in my chest and with a shout let it burst from me where it exploded, lighting up the terrace, the garden, the blazing trees beyond with a blast of golden light that tore the gibbering ranks of vargs into nothing but charred wisps of soot that hung for a moment and then fell into nothing.

I heard Joshua roar as I fell to the ground, the air knocked from my lungs. Before I could move, he began to run across the grass towards the terrace, his eyes fixed on Mrs B. He lifted his massive hands and lightning forked between them.

I tried a few stunning blasts but he shrugged them off and kept moving. He was heading directly for the old woman who was holding onto her necklace with one hand and weaving a fragile mantle of protection with the other. She stepped back until she bumped against the wall of the house.

He was less than twenty feet away, eyes fixed on Mrs B. His arm raised ready to strike and I began to run as fast as I could. The space between us narrowed, but out of the corner of my eye I saw a flash of light as he flung a dazzling zig zag of light straight at the old woman.

I pushed myself to run faster, faster, my muscles screaming with the effort, my chest and heart cramping in pain. I was so close. In slow motion I saw her raise her hands in a futile effort to protect herself and in that moment I jumped.

The lightning hit me with an explosion that seemed to knock my brain from its skull.

'Angie!' screamed Mrs B.

*

Those BITCHES! How fucking dare they. That fat cow lumbering about the place, almost blinding me with her fucking cloud of crap. It was good to watch her choke, though. That look in her eyes, that terror as she felt herself drowning – I could have watched it all day.

They got away but I knew where they were heading, stupid hags, as if the house will offer them any protection after what I've done to it. I shifted the timber but tore my shoulder doing it. Half the shed was gone, covered in rubble and I'd lost my fucking book. The one my Gran gave me.

No matter. I remembered enough until I could come back and search for it properly. In the meantime, I needed to get going.

I moved past the cottages, nearly falling over Thurlow's body. I'd no use for him anymore and he was becoming tiresome and increasingly difficult to control. He'd come over to tell me CCTV had seen the fat one in Hurstbridge and they were moving in to arrest her.

Not that I gave a fuck. I'd pick her up before the police got to her.

Walking through the woods I rubbed my hands at the thought of what I was going to find in the house. The hag was going to lead me straight to it, I'd make sure of that. Much easier with her friends around to threaten. I'd seen the look on her face when I'd slid my knife into that woman's guts, though she tried hard to hide it.

She was frightened of me. I'd finally seen a chink in her armour, and it was killing her friend that did it – it was all I needed.

The trees were dry and went up with a boom. I let the heat scorch my face to get my blood raging. Sparks jumped from one to another until the whole row was blazing. I wanted to howl at the burning sky but I had things to do.

What a rush it was to send my creatures running towards the hags who stood shaking as I walked towards them. I thought the vargs would overwhelm at least one of them but the fat one proved stronger than she looked and got rid of them all in one fucking explosion that nearly sent me flying.

Weakened her though. I could see her exhaustion. The hag was almost on her knees. She was the key.

I knew she'd do it. Get in the way. She couldn't help herself. I don't understand these women. They hold their lives lightly.

I sent that lightning bolt straight for the old witch's face. Sure enough the fat cow launched into the air like a hot air balloon and I hit her right in the side of the head. She dropped like a stone and the old bat screamed.

She was stunned but not dead. Not yet. I kicked her until she rolled to the old witch's feet. I heard her sob - but she looked at me with defiance. I pulled out my knife and held it to the unconscious cow's throat.

'You know I'll do it. Hag. Now tell me.'

'I won't. I can't.' The old bitch's eyes filled with tears but still she was not afraid.

She hissed as I pressed the blade harder and blood ran down the cow's fat neck. 'Tell me.'

She shook her head.

I stood. With the blade in my right hand, I sprung a ball of fire in my left and hurled it at the nearest window. It smashed the glass and immediately the curtains hanging there burst into flames. All those books turned to kindling.

'I'll burn the place down,' I hissed in her ear. 'I know the treasure's underground. Nice and safe, you bitches hid it well Can't be too careful, eh?'

I saw her glance at the flames licking up the window frames. Just for a second. 'You can't get in there without me,' she said.

'I don't need her though, do I? You want to lose another one?'

With one hand I pulled the fat one to her feet, she was still out of it – the lightning had probably frazzled her brain, but she was still breathing. I angled my blade so the tip pressed against her chest, right above her heart.

'The house will be gone,' I said. 'You'll have lost everyone when I kill this fat bitch. I've watched you for a long time, hag. They're all you have. Tell me and I'll let her live.'

The old woman looked up at me steadily, her back crooked and bent. Not a scrap of power was left in her body – there was nothing she could do to stop me. Tears fell down her cheeks, but she never took her gaze from mine. Defiant. 'No,' she said.

I lifted my knife. She closed her eyes.

*

Penny was underwater. A deep, dark lake. It was cold. An oar floated past and banged into her side and she woke up, a scream echoing in her ears. Bewildered, she looked round to find herself in a small room with a lamp shedding a soft, warm light. She pushed back the covers and stood, crying out as a skewering pain flung blinding fireworks of agony in front of her eyes.

She sat on the bed and lifted her jumper to see a large dressing running across the dip of her waist. She probed it gently. The wound had been treated well, she smelled antiseptic and a whiff of calendula. With a crash of adrenaline, she remembered the monster's knife sliding into her and she jumped to her feet, crying out again as the movement tugged at her torn flesh.

Holding her hand to her waist she reached for the door. Her hackles rose as she smelled smoke. Where were Frieda and Angie? Was she trapped in a burning building? Where was she?

The reassurance of opening the door and finding herself in the familiar surroundings of the sitting room in Pagan's Reach was immediately offset by the sight of burning trees outside and the stink of smoke. Panic made her dizzy and she scrambled for the door and crossed into the hall. Just as she did so, a flower of light bloomed from the library.

She cried out in horror as she reached the doorway to see flames eating up the long curtains that framed the first big window. Already sparks were flying left and right, clinging to the spines of books and turning into yellow and blue tongues that greedily ran along the edge of the pages.

Wringing her hands, feeling useless, Penny cast round for a blanket, anything to smother the nascent flames but before she could move the second curtain disappeared into a sheet of fire. She patted her pockets for her phone, but it was gone, she couldn't remember the last time she'd used it.

She closed the library door and ran to get outside. But as she reached the front door, she froze to hear voices. She recognised the chilling tones of that animal who'd beaten Frieda with so little mercy. Where were Frieda and Angie? It would be stupid to go outside without knowing what was happening. Penny hated herself for behaving like a dithering old woman. She had to do something.

The sitting room windows flanked the front door and looked out over the terrace, she remembered. On the other side stretched the library, but she couldn't think about what was happening in that lovely room.

Closing the sitting room door behind her to try and stop the smoke that was creeping across the hall, Penny ran to the windows, making sure she kept back so nobody on the terrace could see her. What she saw was so horrifying she had to push her fist into her mouth to stop from screaming out.

The burning trees lit the terrace bright as day. Joshua Pettigrew's grotesquely huge figure towered above Frieda. Penny gasped to see Angie's body slumped over his arm. Frantically, she pulled at the doors of the cabinet looking for something, anything that could help.

Strange objects bounced to the floor as she pulled them out with desperate urgency. She sobbed to see nothing but glass birds and carved statues, nothing that looked like a weapon. There was no time. She had to go out there, do something.

Careful not to jolt her side, Penny tucked herself behind the floor-length curtain and pushed up the window. She lifted her leg and swung it over the sill letting herself drop silently to the ground. Another sharp jab of pain made her breath catch in her throat and she had to stop for a second until it receded.

She could hear Joshua speaking, and took a cautious step forward, keeping as low to the ground as she could. He was roaring at Frieda. She stared back at him, the fire reflecting in her green eyes. For a second she looked beyond his bulk and caught Penny's gaze and her pupils flared.

Penny didn't stop to think. The fire, the clouds of smoke, the glare of flames from the library windows were driving her mad. Despair and rage gathered her up and flung her to her feet.

'Get away from her!'

Chapter 23

Joshua turned. For a second she saw surprise flickered across his face. He thought I was dead, she thought. But then he smiled. He dropped Angie to the ground and as he did Frieda drove her sharp knee into his groin with such force he immediately doubled over.

Penny ran.

She crossed the big stones of the terrace and skirting Joshua's prone body grabbed hold of Frieda's hands. A question appeared in the old woman's eyes and without hesitation Penny nodded.

Frieda's body rocked with the power Penny discharged into her. Like a flower unfurling in the heat of the sun the old woman straightened and grew tall. Her hair darkened and fell down her back in a sheet. In astonishment, Penny watched as the years were stripped away and a fierce priestess of a woman stood in front of her, already speaking a stream of words that danced green and bright in the air between them.

Joshua was up on one knee and Penny's stomach dropped, but Frieda's hand was strong and warm in hers.

Frieda bent and took Angie's hand. The green words fell onto her forehead and throat, they sparked bright before sinking into her skin and Angie awoke with a gasp. With tremendous strength Frieda pulled Angie to her feet. She didn't seem to be fully conscious, but Penny realised Frieda needed the three of them.

For some reason she was wearing an oversized hoodie that hung past her wrists. The word 'Adidas' emblazoned across it, but nothing could take from the majesty of her presence. Her green eyes filled with power and starlight, her figure tall and slim. She seemed to grow even taller as she held Penny and Angie's hands.

Between the three of them something powerful was building. They stood in a semi-circle, the power of three. Slowly Frieda lifted her arms until they towered over Joshua.

To Penny's amazement she felt the ground fall away beneath her feet. A crackling energy danced between the three of them as they rose higher and higher into the air. Joshua was standing now looking up at them, reaching for them, snarling. Penny knew he wanted to tear them all to pieces but now she felt no fear. She felt triumphant, connected to these two incredible women.

Any thoughts of how this worked, how it was possible were blasted away. The scientist in her marvelled but no longer calculated. Frieda had drained her but in joining the three of them together all her lost energy was replenished.

Fear crawled over Joshua's face, and he began to shrink. Frieda had immobilised him in the triangle of light the three of them had created.

'You will never reach the objects that have lain hidden for so many years,' she said, her voice low and resonant. 'They could never be allowed to fall into careless and power-hungry hands. Your head has been filled with lies. This house doesn't belong to you. We owe you nothing.'

Penny waited for the killer blow. Joshua had been dragged to his knees by the force of energy. He pushed against its walls, but nothing moved. Then Penny realised Frieda was drawing what power he had out of his body. Streams of light flooded from him, and the brighter they were the more he was diminished.

Frieda began to chant, and Penny watched as the charms fell and Joshua was on all fours. Thick fur ran along his back and his face lengthened into a muzzle. Penny blinked and Joshua Pettigrew was gone. In his place a dog growled and pawed at the ground until Frieda let go of her women and clapped her hands. The light disappeared, and the dog bounded away towards the trees and was gone.

'You didn't kill him?' she said to Frieda who was flickering between the tall dark-haired warrior of a woman and the crooked backed old lady she had known most of her life.

'No,' she said with great weariness. 'He was misled more than he was evil.'

'He was going to kill us all,' Penny said.

With a sudden rush, Frieda fell next to Angie who had slumped against the front wall of the house. Flames still blazed from the library window.

'I need to do something. Her heart has stopped,' she said.

'What? What do you mean?' Penny stumbled towards Frieda, horrified. 'She was fine, she was standing.'

Frieda's hand was on Angie's chest, her head tilted to one side as she concentrated. 'It's badly damaged,' she said, her voice filled with tears.

'Help her!' Penny said. She sunk to the ground next to Angie and held her hand. It was heavy, and cold.

Dimly she could hear the whine of sirens in the far distance. Her head was filled with the roar of the fire, and she mourned the loss of her friend and the house that meant so much to both women.

'I can help, but you must swear you will never tell Angie what happened.'

'What do you mean?'

'She can never know. Do you understand?'

Mystified, Penny nodded.

Frieda bowed her head and placed both her hands on her chest, frowning as if in pain. She seemed to be pulling something from her body. Penny watched in amazement as a glow began to form. It started as a bead of light but gathered in strength until it was the size of a large pearl and then grew until it filled Frieda's cupped hands.

Penny found she couldn't look away though it seemed as bright as the sun, making her eyes burn.

'What is it?' she whispered.

But Frieda didn't answer. Holding the bowl of light as if it might spill, like molten gold, she held her hands above Angie's silent figure and with the gentlest of gestures, laid the light above her heart.

For a moment it hovered and then at a word from Frieda it sank into Angie and a flush of gold radiated along her skin and Penny saw her chest heave.

Frieda sat back on her heels. She looked suddenly gaunt. She watched Angie for a moment and, reassured, nodded her head. She sighed and looked at Penny. 'Years ago, when Angie and I first met, we fought a man who had hunted me most of my life. He was after something I'd stolen from him. An elixir.'

Penny waited, feeling warmth flooding into Angie's hand.

'I'd kept it protected and hidden for years. People would have paid a king's ransom for it, killed for it. And one day my curiosity got the better of me. I drank it.' She said simply.

'And it made you immortal?' Penny said, understanding dawning.

'It did.'

'So, what did you just do?'

'I gave it to Angie.'

'So you've made her immortal?'

'I'm not sure how it works. I don't think so. But it will cure the damage done to her heart and she will live.'

'But what happens to you?'

Frieda shrugged. 'Who knows? Maybe it's time for me to think about other people. I've led a long and rather selfish life.'

Penny and Frieda held hands and waited as fire engines shrieked up the drive and skidded to a halt in front of the house.

*

My eyes snapped open when sunshine rolled across my face and to my astonishment, I saw the oak ribcage of the roof arching above my head. I sat up with a gasp. What had happened? How could I be back in my flat? The last thing I remembered was Joshua's lightning smashing into the side of my head.

Had I been dreaming? I rubbed my forehead and the skin flamed with pain. I climbed out of bed and leaned over the dressing table to examine my face. A livid scar forked from my temple down my cheek to the edge of my jaw. A small puncture wound on my throat was surprisingly sore.

Not a dream then.

A stirring from the bed made me jump and I grinned in delight to see Trevor poking his head out from the bed clothes, his ears rumpled. I hugged him until he squirmed free.

I was still in my long-sleeved shirt and jeans, and they stank of smoke. I shuddered to remember the trees burning. I tore off my clothes that were grubby and stained and pulled on clean tracksuit bottoms and a big jumper. I had to find Mrs B and Penny.

They were sat at the kitchen table eating breakfast. Mrs B looked tired, and Penny had huge bags under her eyes.

'What happened?' I said. 'What happened to Joshua?'

'Frieda stripped him of any powers that he had and turned him into a dog.' Penny said putting down her piece of honeyed toast.

'You make it sound ridiculous. And simple,' Mrs B said, looking cross. 'And I didn't turn him into a dog, I just took away anything he had left that was human. What was left manifested as a dog.'

'And what did you do to the dog?' I felt odd, as if I was trapped in a Surrealist movie.

'It ran off into the wood.'

'So that's that? Thank God. It's been the worst two weeks of my life.'

'It felt like a year,' Penny said dryly.

I smiled, though the movement pulled the deep graze on my cheek, making me wince. Happiness bubbled in my belly to see

Mrs B at the table behind a pot of tea with Penny at her side. It felt good to have another woman in the house.

'The house doesn't feel cold anymore!' I said.

'No, it's healing well. Penny has been helping me clear the last traces that animal left.'

I pinched away the tendril of jealousy her words provoked and forced a grin.

'How are you feeling, Angie?' Penny said pouring me a cup of tea and buttering some toast. My mouth watered.

I paused. 'Do you know what? I feel … amazing. No pressure on my chest, no headache, I can breathe really well. It must be those pills you got me, Penny. They've done me the world of good.'

Mrs B and Penny exchanged a glance.

'What?' I said,

'Nothing, Angie. I take it you haven't seen the library?'

'No. Why would I? What happened?'

They didn't reply.

Suddenly I saw the sadness in their eyes and my heart swooped.

I took a step back.

'Angie, wait. Hang on, we'll come with you.'

But it was too late. I was out of the kitchen and down the corridor. The smell of smoke and charred, damp paper filled the air. My pulse thumped. I didn't dare think what could have happened.

I saw the puddles first. They stretched across the floor of the main hall and were edged in black. I hadn't noticed when I ran down the stairs, eager to find Mrs B and Penny. The door to the library was firmly shut.

If I hadn't seen the water sliding out from under the door I wouldn't have thought anything was wrong. But that choking stink of fire was everywhere.

Steeling myself I opened the door.

'Oh …' I said.

'It's just stuff, Angie.' Mrs B was at my shoulder, back in her woollen Chanel suit, the red one she wore on grey days. It suited her better than my Adidas hoodie, I thought distractedly.

'But …' I wiped my eyes.

'Someone in the village called 999 when they saw the light from the burning trees. That damned monster. So many torn down. So many torched. The fire engines were here within half an hour. It could have been much worse.'

I took a step into my beloved library. The one I'd spent months clearing and cleaning when I first arrived. Where Mrs B and I would read side by side, arguing over books she'd recommended.

'Careful!' Mrs B touched my arm. 'The floor isn't stable, particularly by that window.'

My heart broke to see the whole wall to the left of the window was a charred mess. Every book there had gone and whatever had survived had been forever damaged by the water used to smother the fire. The whole of the corner wall was black. The joyful oil paintings Mrs B had collected and stacked in a pile under the window seat were nothing but twisted lumps of sooty matter.

The fire had eaten away the floorboards right into the middle of the room and a black hole gaped beneath. The edges poked like broken fingers over the space.

'It's terrible, Angie, I know. And I know how special this room was to you – but look to the right. Look above. See? So much of it is untouched.'

She was right. Averting my eyes from the great burned wound round the window, I could see the rest of the room was unharmed, free of smoke damage, though it would take a long time before the stink of the fire would vanish completely.

'We'll get it all fixed,' I said with a cheeriness I didn't feel. 'It'll be as good as new.'

Mrs B nodded.

'And we'll replant the trees, though I won't be alive to see them mature. You'll still be around, you're indestructible.'

Mrs B raised an eyebrow and chuckled. 'Perhaps,' she said.

A thin line of light ran across the hall from the front doors. I pushed them all the way open to let the sun in to dry the last of the puddles on the floor. We paused to breathe in the summer air. Overnight, it would seem, the trees had filled their branches with leaves, and honeybees droned and bumped their way around the peonies and roses.

I shivered to remember the sterile morgue of a cellar where Mrs B had been held. 'You know I saw Lilith? In Brokkton? She appeared at her grave and told me where to look to find a crystal. It led me to you.'

Mrs B's face twisted with emotion. 'I saw,' she said. 'A strange light appeared, and I heard Lilith's voice. I thought it was her then saw your face. I miss her every day. I'm going very soft in my old age.' She reached for a stalk of lavender, breaking it off and crumbling the flowers between her fingers. The scent was heavenly.

'How did you know his name was Joshua Pettigrew?' I said. 'I still feel terrible I didn't see your message until Penny came to the house.'

'You had to have Penny with you to see it. I didn't have time to consider my options, it was the only thing I could think of. I hadn't realised how much he'd already affected the house. The message should have been stronger.' She gazed across the valley, always at its most beautiful in May. 'I knew who he was as he's been writing strange, incoherent letters to me for years. Telling me he was the rightful heir to Pagan's Reach. I thought if you knew his name, you'd find the letters in my desk.'

I gazed at her, open mouthed. What an idiot I was.

'I didn't think to look there,' I said. 'I was in such a state. You know he nearly killed Trevor as well?'

Mrs B tutted.

'Thank God for Penny,' I went on. 'She helped me in so many ways, though I treated her very badly.'

'She saved my life last night,' Mrs B said. 'As did you. We've been talking about how she can use that energy of hers, though it looks like you've helped her a great deal already.'

'I promised Penny we'd help her with her paper. There's something she said she needs to see. Something about gravity and space. She needs to publish, or they'll sack her.' A thought struck me. 'What happened about the police? They've been chasing me for the last week. I've been all over the papers and the telly. Have you seen them?'

'They were here last night, with the fire engines,' Mrs B said. 'I had to stop them dragging you off in an ambulance. Penny said you had some kind of heart attack?'

'Rubbish. I was just dehydrated and a bit stressed. I feel loads better now.'

'Hmm,' said the old woman. I was pleased to see her bruises were starting to fade, being back in Pagan's Reach would be the best thing for her.

'So I'm off the hook?'

'Yes. I reassured them I hadn't been murdered. Though it looks like Pettigrew killed a detective.'

'Thurlow?' I said, turning to look at her. 'He's dead? He was awful, I think Pettigrew had him in the palm of his hand from the start.'

'They found him in the woods, near one of Humphrey's cottages. There was a bag of weapons and Pettigrew's wallet. He's been in jail a number of times already, apparently. There's a warrant out for his arrest, but I doubt they'll find him.'

I slipped my arm through hers. 'I'm glad we found you,' I said. 'The house has been a stranger without you here.'

'Don't be so mawkish. You'd have been fine without me.'

'Oh! I didn't tell you – I flew! Right off a church roof.'

'Good woman!' Mrs B gave my arm a squeeze.

'Yes,' I said happily. 'It was brilliant.'

'It looks like it's time, then.'

'Time for what?'

'To show you how to reach the treasures,' she said.

Chapter 24

Two weeks later I was in the kitchen pulling out the most glorious pair of sponges I'd ever created. They'd risen so massively they were in danger of overflowing the cake tins. My mouth watered as I pictured sandwiching them together with great spoonfuls of my home-made strawberry jam and lashings of the cream that was waiting in the fridge to be whipped into thick peaks. I set them on the side to cool and sat down to my eggs and soldiers.

One of the best things about having Frieda safe and sound at home was that my appetite had returned. I'd cooked a roast chicken the night before that had been ambrosial, even Penny asked for more roasties, and the old woman wolfed down two helpings before I'd finished my first.

I was full of energy. I'd washed every piece of dirty laundry I could find and the line outside was full of clean clothes that danced in the wind and sun. We were well into May and the sky had been clear for days. I'd opened all the windows and doors to let the fresh air blow away the last of the cold that lingered in the house.

Pagan's Reach was no longer a stranger. Wi-Fi was working again, though the house still blocked it along the back of the house, and lighting fires on cold mornings was easy. There was still some resentment, though. I could sense how unhappy it was about the damage in the library and I still couldn't find the music room. I hoped when the library was fully restored the house would relent and the door would open again. I couldn't play any of the instruments in there but liked to sit at the harpsichord and pick out notes while looking across at the beauty of the valley. I wondered if Penny played anything.

In contrast to my frenzy of busyness, Penny and the old woman had rested. I didn't mind. For some reason I felt amazing. My blood pumped clean and rich, my cheeks were pink and my hair thick and shiny. It must be the pills, I thought.

I still had nightmares about losing Frieda, and Joshua's silver eyes still burned across my dreams, but I felt strong. I'd handled myself, I'd more than handled myself and I had the deep-seated confidence that only flying off a church roof can give you.

My cooking brought us together three times a day and I found great solace in baking great loaves of bread and chopping up colourful salads sprinkled with pomegranate seeds. The simple pleasure of watching the people I loved enjoying the food I'd made was one I relished. I enjoyed spending time searching for exotic ingredients and discovering new recipes. When I learned Penny loved vegetarian food a whole world opened up to me and I made a Tartiflette au Reblochon that deserved a standing ovation. My

Masala Dosas were Mrs B's particular favourite, while Penny kept making me cook Melanzane alla Parmigiana.

We were existing in a bubble, reluctant to let the outside world in just yet. Reporters had swarmed over the garden for a few days, drawn by tales of a kidnapped old woman, a murdered policeman and a missing suspect.

Mrs B's extraordinary and aggressive rudeness saw off even the most persistent of journalists and eventually we were left alone. When she wasn't shouting at intruders, she spent her days endlessly reading in her bedroom demanding cups of tea and coming down for meals.

As the weather improved Penny spent hours and hours outside walking through the woods and returning with pink spots on her cheekbones, her hair in a tangle down her back and a cloak of delicious smelling fresh air. I noticed she kept her phone on the side in the kitchen, always turned off. She never checked it.

I suspected she was putting off what she needed to face but I didn't push her as I liked having her in the house and watching her arguing with Mrs B over dinner. The old woman had developed a fierce interest in theoretical physics and spent hours grilling Penny on things like dark matter and monopoles. It made my head spin a bit and if I was honest, I couldn't help a pang of jealousy at their closeness.

I knew something was up when Mrs B appeared in her violet suit. She always wore it when she meant business. The bruises and scratches had faded from her face, but she still looked thinner than I would like.

'Come on, then. It's time to show you – I want to get down there before lunch, Penny said there was an excellent documentary on dark energy at three.'

'Can I least finish my eggs?' I complained, a buttered toast soldier in my hand.

'Oh, if you insist. I'll have a tea while I'm waiting.'

Still chewing, I poured her out a cup. 'I've only just taken the sponges out of the oven so you can't have any cake until they've cooled.'

'Any shortbread?'

I sighed, scooping the last bit of yolk out of the egg with the end of my toast. I prised the lid off the shortbread tin and passed it over to her. She took her time choosing, eventually pulling out a petticoat tail and a round.

'There's been a bearded one roaming round the garden – I'm surprised you haven't noticed him. Can you go and see to him?' She reached for another biscuit and crunched it down with a surprising relish considering how few teeth she had.

I looked out of the window to see who she was talking about. After that dreadful night when I'd had to deal with hundreds and hundreds of the dead I hadn't seen any since. But it looked like they were drifting towards the house again, as they had for centuries, knowing they would find aid. Young, old, dead through disease, accident, or through their own hand – Pagan's Reach drew them to its heart in droves.

He was in the back garden, before the path to the wood: a shadowy figure in the bright sunlight. I went to him, smiling to see the look of astonishment when he realised I could see him.

He had strong, dark eyebrows and a thick beard. He was so tall he towered over me. When I took his hand, the tension left his body. I closed my eyes to hear his story and let his words fall into me.

I was getting better at not letting myself be affected by these tales, but this one made me cry, and I held his hand tight as I placed my palm against his chest until the light could break free and he disappeared.

Back in the kitchen Mrs B was waiting for me.

'Where's Penny?' I said.

'She's in her room getting her laptop to show me the paper she's been working on.'

'Do you think you'll be able to help her? She says she might lose her job.'

'Perhaps,' she said. 'Now let's get on. We won't be long.'

Mrs B opened the door to the tunnel under the big library mantelpiece. I hadn't been down there for years; it didn't hold good memories.

'Careful!' I said as she nearly bumped her wizened old head on the edge of the hole. 'Do we really have to do this now?'

'Yes, of course. Besides, there's something down there I think might help Penny.'

Mrs B clambered into the passage and I followed. My back was screaming after ten minutes of walking as I had to bend over double. The old woman had no problem scuttling ahead of me. She seemed full of vim and vigour after her ordeal, but she was never one to brood on the past.

I couldn't quite believe she was here, back at Pagan's Reach. Gary had finally been able to call me the week before and had been puzzled by my delight to hear from him. It felt like a year had passed since he told me he was off on another operation somewhere far away.

I didn't tell him everything. I couldn't really find the words and I didn't want to cause any worry. He wouldn't be back for another month, and I hoped we will have been able to repair most of the damage by then. He would notice the trees though; I tried not to look at them. Their absence had ripped a terrible scar across the landscape – wherever you were in the house you could see the gaps where once beautiful trees had stood. Joshua Pettigrew's legacy.

'Are we nearly there?' I said, my back and hips beginning to cramp. 'I don't remember it being this long.'

Mrs B had stopped. A small opening at her feet appeared under the sparks she had thrown in the air. 'That's how he got in,' she said, and I shivered.

'Block it up,' I said.

She waved her hand and the soil slumped across the hole, closing it forever, I hoped. 'There must be thousands of tunnels under the house,' I said. 'Anyone could come crawling through them.'

Mrs B nodded. 'We'll seal them all up. Gary can help when he returns.'

We kept walking. Finally, the passage opened so I could stand. I breathed in the scent of pines and earth.

'Nearly there,' Mrs B said.

I wondered what the place looked like now – I'd not returned since those awful events of that summer when the old woman and I had stood side by side and fought Marroch. He would have killed us both if it wasn't for the last comb.

The forest had grown at tremendous speed, a magical collection of trees that writhed and thrust themselves into the vaulted chamber. But would they still be there? How could they continue to grow without sunlight?

I gasped as we walked through the huge stone arch that led to the place hidden deep, deep beneath the house, centuries underground. I was expecting darkness but somehow sunlight drifted in high above. It slanted in dusty beams across the bristling tops of the trees. There must be some cuts, some cracks in the land above that let in the light.

The huge flagstones beneath our feet were now covered in a carpet of earth and leaf mould so our steps were silent as we wound our way between hundreds of slender tree trunks. We could have been in any wood in the world except there wasn't a trace of bird song. In the distance I could hear the rush and bubble of a stream of water.

It felt like a holy place. A cathedral with an arching ceiling of green that rustled and murmured, sounding like nuns in prayer.

'Stop gawping, Angie. We haven't got time to lollygag about.'

When Mrs B judged we were right at the heart of the wood she stopped. 'Here,' she said. A small round wooden door sat in the ground. I shivered to remember what had happened here.

'Open it,' she said.

'I thought I needed special charms and everything?'

'Not for this bit,' she said impatiently. 'This is just the entrance.'

'You could do all of this with a bit more ceremony,' I said crossly. 'Isn't this supposed to be an important moment – handing over from the mistress to the apprentice sort of thing?'

Mrs B tutted. 'Yes, yes, all very important. Just open it. It's freezing down here.'

I lifted the trapdoor to find a deep round hole. I couldn't see the bottom.

'It used to be an ancient well,' Mrs B said. 'But there's no water there now. Put your hand just inside the rim. You should feel a sort of recess.'

I ran my hand along the side until I felt a shallow dent. The sigil in my hand warmed, and I moved my palm until it heated further. 'It's doing something to my hand,' I said.

She nodded. 'Only those with the mark can get this far. When you feel it has connected, give it a push.'

I did as she said and heard a tremendous groan. From the far end of the chamber there was a sudden movement.

'Come on then,' Mrs B said, holding out her hand.

We walked through the trees to the edge of the magical forest. Ahead the wall had swung inwards revealing another, smaller room. It was dry and clear with stone walls and floor as if carved out of rock. Every inch of the walls was pitted with holes of different sizes. Inside each one was an object.

Mrs B stood at the entrance and spoke words I'd never heard her say before. She said them too quickly for me to take in any of them. A vibration in the air made the tufts on her head wave and once it stilled, she took a step forward.

'What would happen if you tried to get past without the charm?' I asked.

'You'd be obliterated,' she said. 'Now, let me show you.'

One by one Mrs B showed me the treasures collected by the generations of women who'd lived in Pagan's Reach. A golden dial that could change time that had a lengthy, handwritten label of warning attached to it. A pair of dragon's eggs. Everlasting candles. A pot that would produce a never-ending supply of whatever you cooked in it. Bottles and bottles of different ointments and potions that were too dangerous to be kept in the pantry with our remedies. They ranged from preparations that could bring loved ones back to life to answer one question, to liquids that could make crops bear harvests over and over again, and creams that would keep you young forever but your insides would rot. There were crystals that could see into the future and the past, a talisman carved from obsidian that, when worn, would draw and control a cult of loyal followers, willing to do whatever they were asked.

Hundreds of things. They made me dizzy to look at them. 'You'll have to learn what they all are when you take over as mistress of Pagan's Reach,' Mrs B said, weighing a gold sovereign of invisibility in her hand.

Well, that won't be for ages, I reassured myself. 'What's this?' I picked up a large oval stone that held light within itself, its depths glowed a pure emerald. It felt cool and heavy in my hand.

'If you throw it on the ground an ocean will appear,' she said, frowning as she looked for something.

'Oh.' I set it carefully back in its nook.

'Ah! There it is.' The old woman pulled out a chain that was so long she had to loop it over and over her hands. It glittered brightly.

'That looks like it's made out of a thousand tiny stars,' I said 'Or fairy lights.'

Mrs B snorted. 'It will help us to help Penny find what she's looking for.'

'Oh, really?' I said with interest and reached to touch one of the sparkling lights. She pulled away.

'Don't touch it!' she said. 'We have to wait for the right time.'

I sighed. The old woman was often given to gnomic utterances, enjoying creating an aura of mystery, so I didn't press her on what she meant by 'the right time'.

Finally, we stood before the staff. The secret of its existence had been kept until Ada Pettigrew had broken the trust of Pagan's Reach and told her daughter who in turn told her grandson – Joshua Pettigrew. I thought of all the pain and suffering his obsession had caused.

'It doesn't look much, does it?' I said, staring at the twisted length of wood that had runes carved down it sides.

'Hmph,' said Mrs B. 'It's the most powerful and dangerous thing to be found in this space. It must never, never be spoken of outside Pagan's Reach – not even to Gary, or Penny. You must always protect it.'

I felt strangely solemn; I could see in her eyes how important it was that I listened.

'I swear, Mrs B. I'll make sure nobody comes here. I'll protect the staff.'

'Right. Let's close everything up and get back upstairs. I'm frozen and I think it's time for lunch and some of that cake, don't you think?'

*

Penny had been putting off turning her phone back on for too long. Standing in the kitchen with Frieda and Angie off on some secret mission she pressed the button until the screen sprang to life. Immediately it vibrated and pinged signalling the arrival of hundreds of emails.

She sighed. She'd spent the early hours of the morning cleaning the damaged books in the library. She'd looked online and found a chemical sponge that would help clear the smoke that had rolled along the shelves next to the window.

It was absorbing, mindless work and wiping away the sooty stains to reveal the glowing jewels of the leather covers had been tremendously satisfying. Within a few hours she had worked through four shelves; they looked so much better when she was done. The house seemed to warm round her and, unnoticed, on the other side of the room a door opened with a click.

The emails were all from the university. The early ones from Martin saying he needed her to make a decision and more recent demands from the head of HR.

Penny had tried to work. The events of the past weeks had been exhausting physically and mentally. She had needed the time to recover in this lovely house. Reconnecting with Frieda and getting to know Angie had been an unfamiliar pleasure. It was as if she'd been hungry for years and years not realising how starved she was until someone had offered her a delicious feast.

Speaking to Frieda about her research had allowed a tiny spark to develop after so long repressing any thoughts of work. She'd even noted down a few ideas after a particularly fruitful discussion with the old woman about dark energy.

But this flood of emails threatened to drown out the spark before it had a chance to grow. The thought of dreary meetings with HR and the board was wearisome but she knew she wasn't ready to give up.

She decided to leave her phone. She'd sit down the next morning and work through everything. She knew she wasn't ready to retire, but the plain fact of the matter was that she had to have something to show them. Something that would convince them her idea was sound.

Back in the library she waited for Frieda and Angie. Thinking hard about how she would word an email to Martin, she took another book down from the shelf and wiped it clean. A breeze blew from the hole behind the fireplace where Frieda had left the entrance to the passageway open.

Penny shivered as she remembered creeping into the oppressive darkness of that tunnel, discovering Trevor's body deep within. She'd taken him for a long and muddy walk that morning and she'd left him, belly up and paws in the air, in the kitchen.

As she thought of him she heard a clicking sound and he trotted in, ears pricked.

'Speak of the devil,' Penny said fondly. 'You've already been fed.'

A noise made Trevor start and he cocked his head to one side, looking towards the end of the library where a spiral staircase was hidden behind a door of fake books. Trevor padded across the rug towards it and looked up.

Curious, Penny followed him. The hidden door held only the staircase that led up to the mezzanine that ran across the top floor of the library. She'd never been up there before. Trevor wagged his tail, as if in encouragement.

'There's nothing up there except books,' she told him. She pulled the book as Angie had shown her and the book panelled door swung open. 'See?' she said to Trevor. He looked back at her his eyes bright.

Perhaps she should have a look up on the mezzanine, she thought but when she turned to climb the spiral staircase she'd seen there before, she found it had disappeared. Instead, an empty wall greeted her with a large gold button, right in the centre.

Without hesitation she pressed the button feeling it move with a satisfying click under her fingers.

A whirring sound reminded Penny of the grandfather clock in Daphne's sitting room. She'd had it for years; it would sound like an old man as it groaned its gears together ready to strike the hour.

As she watched, her eyes wide, a piece in the wall fell away into a cavity. Penny leaned forward to see what was hidden there when, to her amazement, a complicated machine rose in front of her eyes. It pushed forward like the model of a huge city held high in the air. Penny had never seen anything like it. As she raised her hand to touch, it sprung to life, whirling in a crazy movement Penny couldn't understand.

Parts began to uncurl: long, thin golden arms that held spheres of all different sizes. There must be hundreds of them, if not thousands, she calculated. A golden net, made up of threads as thin and fragile as a cobweb, undulated beneath the spinning cogs and tiny orbs of gold. It was dizzying to watch. The arms unfolded and unfolded in an infinite loop of movement. The web's pattern constantly changed. In some places it gathered in knots round the base of an arm, at others it stretched until great gaps appeared like holes ready to be darned.

Something about the undulating movement chimed a note in Penny's mind but she couldn't grasp it. She jumped in shock when she touched a blooming flower of gold to slow its motion and a great crackle of static and sparks leaped from her fingers and the pace of the machine seemed to double. The machine had drained her a little. After the events of the past few weeks Penny found she coped better with her energy being pulled from her. It wasn't such a dizzying, uncomfortable experience.

The movement of the machine was mesmerising, but Penny couldn't work out what it was. The complexity of the design was extraordinary, she thought, her mind humming. She looked at her hands and again, her fingertips tingled. Sharp pins and needles that pricked at her skin. She held them to her lips and felt a soft pulse of energy. The beds of her nails glowed. It was an uncomfortable feeling, and she shook her hands as if they were wet.

The machine seemed to be trying to tell her something, demonstrate something to her that she found impossible to grasp. There was something about the very edges … a slowing … Penny shook her head in frustration. The machine took up more space around it than was possible. An hallucination? She looked down at Trevor's upturned furry face and was reassured.

And then, with an abrupt ripple and snap the machine closed in on itself, reducing to an impossibly small block of metal before something tugged it back into the cavity and the door shut. A vacuum formed in the air so profound Penny felt its pull – strong as gravity; she almost fell.

Her fingers felt for her notebook in her back pocket, but she'd left it in her bedroom. She had to sketch the machine while the memory was still fresh. What she'd seen felt important in a fundamental way, but she couldn't explain why.

It took Penny an hour to sketch everything she remembered of the machine and how it moved. If anyone had asked her she would have been at a loss to explain why what she'd seen was so important. No matter how hard she thought, she couldn't work out what the machine was for - nothing made sense. What was it doing here in this strange old house? And why did the thought of it stir something deep inside Penny, an excitement that proved impossible to ignore.

Chapter 25

Penny was in the kitchen sketching when Mrs B and I returned. My mind was still spinning with what I had seen in the room underground. I got on quickly with lunch, Mrs B was looking pale and cold – some hot pumpkin soup sprinkled with sage and thyme and some fresh bread would cheer her up.

While the soup was heating, I spread jam thickly across the now cooled sponges and whipped up cream into plump clouds that I spooned on top of the jam, sandwiched the two cakes together and dusting with icing sugar. Mrs B never took her eyes off what I was doing. It was good to see her how much she was looking forward to her food.

'What are you drawing?' I said, looking over Penny's shoulder as I spooned out the soup that smelled delicious – rich and spicy.

She put down her pen. 'I saw something very peculiar in the library. A strange machine that just appeared out of the wall. It was huge and complicated. Somehow it opened out from a wall behind the secret door in the library and moved endlessly in a really unusual way. I couldn't work out its purpose – I assume it must have been a piece of art perhaps, something decorative. It was quite marvellous.'

Mrs B smiled. 'The house is rewarding you,' she said. 'I think it's still upset with Angie as she still can't find the music room.'

'You've seen it?'

'Of course! We both have. Though I haven't seen it for twenty years. Was it in the library when you saw it, Angie?'

'Oh, I know the one you mean – made of gold with, like, spokes and spheres on it?'

'Yes! That's it. What on earth is it for?'

I shrugged. 'I've no idea. Mrs B must know?'

We turned to look at the old woman, but she tapped her nose and gave a smug grin. 'If everything goes as planned, you'll see later.'

I tutted and carried on ladling out the last of the soup into three bowls. Sitting down I tore off a chunk of bread and dipped it into the steaming liquid. Lovely. 'I saw it in one of the bedrooms,' I said, my mouth full. 'How odd you found it in the library. The house likes to play strange tricks sometimes.' I touched the nearest wall of the house with my fingers, feeling the reassuring warmth and pulse of life I had missed so dearly.

'It's just it's making me think of something, but I don't know what it is.' She scribbled through her drawing whilst taking a spoonful of soup. 'This is very nice, Angie,' she said, and went back to frowning over her notebook.

'I'm going to see the Doc,' I said. 'The Victoria sponge is all ready for you on the side, you just need to cut it up. Your documentary's on soon so I'll love you and leave you.'

'Why are you seeing Lockwood?' Mrs B looked at me, her eyes bright.

'The hospital wanted me to go back for a check-up but I told them we had a GP in the village and could I see him. They said it was OK.'

Mrs B and Penny exchanged a glance again. They seemed to be doing that an awful lot – it was really irritating.

*

Doc was sitting at his desk with a thick folder in front of him and a slim laptop to the side. He was tanned from his second honeymoon and had put weight on.

'Dear oh dear you have had a time of it, Angie,' he said. 'Have you been taking your blood pressure and blood thinning pills?'

'Of course I have, Doc.' I said. 'Did you have a lovely holiday?'

'Marvellous, thank you. Can't believe it's all over. Roll up your sleeve.'

He muttered as he pumped up the blood pressure monitor. It squeezed until I thought my arm was going to fall off, at which point he let the air release with a hiss and checked the reading against the notes on his laptop. '110 over 65. That's excellent.'

'What was it before?' I asked, craning my neck to try and read the notes sent from the hospital.

'A rather alarming 185 over 112,' he said, wrapping up the tubes and plopping it back into its case. 'Now let's have a listen to your heart.'

He seemed to stand over me with his stethoscope for a very long time. I could feel my heart beat faster. Had he found something wrong? The Doc made me unbutton my shirt and listened again at my back before returning to my chest. The stethoscope felt cold against my skin.

'What is it?' I said at last.

He sat down at his desk and rubbed at his jaw as he reread my notes. Again. I watched his face, my mind racing. I was desperate to lean into him to feel what he was thinking but knew he wouldn't take kindly to it; he'd tell me soon enough.

'Angie when you collapsed the doctors at the hospital found evidence of a significant heart murmur. You were also suffering from arrythmia and subsequently arterial fibrillation.'

'That doesn't sound good,' I said, trying to keep my tone light.

'It wasn't. Not at all. But …'

'But what?'

'I can't find anything. Your cholesterol is low, your blood sugars are no longer pre-diabetic.'

'Must be all my healthy eating and tablets,' I said, suppressing the memory of the two large choux caramel cream pastries I'd eaten the night before.

'There's no sign of a murmur, your heart sounds as strong as an ox.'

I looked back at him, not sure what he was getting at. 'I am taking the tablets. Penny checks I do every morning and every night.'

'Yes,' he said slowly looking at me with speculation in his eyes. He seemed about to say something but then stopped. 'Frieda doing well?' he said. 'I heard there was some nasty business.'

'Yes, some madman kidnapped her from the house but we managed to track her down in the end.'

'I read about it in the news. They're still looking for the man they think killed the detective?'

'They give us updates every now and then. I think they feel bad for suspecting me for so long. They know he killed Thurlow – that's the detective – they found the knife he used on him …' I paused for a moment remembering Penny's blood on that vicious smile of a blade. 'Anyway. I'm sure they'll catch him soon enough.'

Doc frowned. 'Pettigrew, I remember that name. I think I may have treated his mother, or perhaps his grandmother. A strange family. Quite …' he paused to find the right word. '… feral,' he said at last.

Dolly, Doc's white labradoodle pushed the door open with her nose and sniffed her way over to me, smelling Trevor on the hems of my trousers. I scratched her cheeks, and she closed her eyes in bliss. I smiled.

'So I've got the all clear, Doc?'

'Yes. As far as I can see you're doing very well indeed. Especially at your age.'

'Doc! I keep telling you, you're not that much older than I am.'

He laughed and polished his glasses. 'Send my love to Frieda. Oh, and Maeve's been asking about holding that baby play group up at the house – will you ask her about it again?'

'Of course! I keep telling her, we've got so much space. It would be lovely to fill it with babies once a week.' My tone was wistful, and Doc leaned forward to pat my hand.

'The village would be so grateful,' he said. 'The hall is getting rather run down.'

I left the Doc's full of exciting ideas. I loved the thought of inviting a parent and baby group up to the house. The library would be a perfect place to hold sing-a-longs and Dumpling would jump at the chance to be pulled out of retirement to haul a few toddlers round the paddock.

Pagan's Reach was a place to be shared, I realised as I walked past the playground and up the hill. Those records stretching back hundreds of years contained the memories of a community. It wasn't right that there was just the three of us living there – four if you counted Gary. We should open the house up more, I thought as I reached the wood. I'd just have to persuade Mrs B.

Something had shifted since that dreadful day when I found the old woman gone. Perhaps in rescuing her I'd proved myself as worthy of Pagan's Reach. Her manner when she'd shown me the hidden treasures had been diffident, but we both recognised the importance of the moment. She was preparing me. And for the first time in my life, I felt as if I was ready.

'I got the all clear!' I said bursting into the kitchen but it was empty. I checked my watch, the documentary they'd been banging on about would be long finished by now. Trevor's lead wasn't hanging by the back door – Penny must have taken him out for another walk. She'd been walking his legs off recently – he must be worn out, I thought, but the time she spent in the woods and valley seemed to be helping her process all that had happened.

I'd make a cup of tea for the old woman I thought. While the kettle boiled, I cut a slice of the Victoria sponge which tasted as good as it looked. Two great chunks had already been carved out I saw, so I covered it up to save for later - she'd had enough for today.

Crossing the hall, heading for the stairs with the teacup in my hand, I saw a gossamer thin thread of light hanging as if caught on the air, like a cobweb. I stopped. Something was different. I circled slowly.

The bureau that sat under the mirror. I remembered it having four drawers, but now it seemed taller, with a brass handled cabinet set into the top frame. I'd never seen it before. My heart rate accelerated. It had been a while since the house had shown me something new.

Biting my lip to contain my excitement, I opened the doors. They were stiff but opened with a tug. I breathed in the smell of old wood, reached inside, and pulled out an antique golden rattle. It was ridiculously ornate with carved cherubs adorning the sides, and tiny gold bells that tinkled brightly. The handle felt cool and smooth under my hand and as I ran my fingers over it, I saw it was made of polished coral.

Carefully putting it aside, I pushed the doors back further to let in some light and found a beautifully illustrated copy of Hans Christian Anderson fairy tales, the cover tooled in gold with an etching of the little mermaid. Last, a jolly mug, painted with rabbits and ducks. I sighed with happiness. I wondered if Mrs B knew these were here. I doubted they belonged to her, perhaps one of the women who had come before her, another guardian of Pagan's Reach.

I had to show them to the old woman – this was just the sort of thing the old house needed. She wasn't in the library or sitting room so I guessed she'd gone back to bed to read. I shoved everything into the pocket of my hoodie and carried the tea up the stairs.

I bumped the door open with my hips. 'Mrs B!' I said, making her jump.

'Haven't you heard of knocking?' she said, closing her book.

'The house!' I said. 'I knew it!' I moved forward to lay the book and rattle on her bed.

'What are you on about, Angie?'

'I've been to see the Doc he said everything was OK,' I said in a rush. 'And he said Maeve was asking again if the village could use the house and gardens sometimes, you know for the kiddies.' I plumped down into the armchair next to her bed. 'But what about this? The bureau in the hall – I noticed a new cupboard thing and I found these inside. Can't you see? The house is telling us it wants us to hold the baby playtime here.' I held up the painted mug in triumph.

'Don't be ridiculous, Angie.' She poked at the rattle with the end of her glasses. 'You can't give this to a child. It would choke!'

'It's symbolic!' I said. 'I mean it's solid gold and hundreds of years old – of course I wouldn't give it to a baby.' I snatched the book and rattle back. It's the house talking to us -'

'Well I am still mistress of the house,' Mrs B said imperiously. 'And you know how I feel about strangers swarming all over the place.'

'They wouldn't be strangers,' I said. 'Oh, never mind. I still think it's a brilliant idea. We'll talk about it again. It's crazy us having all this space and not sharing with the children in the village. It would mean so much to Maeve. And, from all the research we've done this house has always held a community. We should open it up a little.'

I could see I was getting through to her and could barely suppress an excited grin. She had a heap of jewellery in her lap, and she held up a ruby in the shape of a teardrop, contemplating its scarlet depths. At last she looked up at me to find me staring at her. She rolled her eyes. 'I'll think about it,' she said.

'That would be brilliant, thanks. How was the documentary?'

'It was fascinating,' the old woman said, sitting up to take the tea I'd made. 'Though Penny said cosmologists are often wrong, but never in doubt.' She chuckled. 'But it did give me an idea how to help her with that paper that's so important to her.'

'With that rope thing from the vault?' I said. Mrs B had it coiled, twinkling and pulsing, on the bed post.

'You'll see,' she said.

Chapter 26

Penny's dreams were dominated by the movement of golden flowers blooming in and out with the earth rippling beneath. She woke up three or four times to frown over her notebook. What was that machine trying to tell her?

Feeling tired and grumpy she put the kettle on. Frieda and Angie were out with Trevor and the house felt empty and cold. She lit the fire in the grate, irritated it took a good ten minutes to find the matches. The clouds were low and oppressive. Even the woods looked bedraggled after a night of rain.

She realised her bad mood was due not just to a lack of sleep but an awareness she had to phone the university that morning. She couldn't put it off any longer. If she didn't call them, she risked being fired for not making contact.

With a cup of tea steaming at her elbow Penny sat at the table glaring at her phone. She took a sip and burned her mouth.

Before she could change her mind she pulled up Martin's details and pressed call.

'Penny? Where have you been? I must have phoned a hundred times.' His voice was tight and impatient.

'I'm sorry, Martin. I've been having rather a difficult time of it and you did suggest I took some leave.'

'I know I did, Penny, but that was quite a while ago now and I've heard nothing from you.'

Penny fell silent.

'So will you take the retirement?'

She gnawed at her thumbnail. Spending time with Angie and Frieda had shown there was a vibrant and joyful life available to her. Pagan's Reach could be home for the rest of her life – she could sell her flat and move in permanently whenever she liked; she knew she'd be welcome.

But then she remembered the joy of exploring the patterns of the universe. The puzzles and mysteries she could turn into numbers and shapes that revealed secrets. To her it was a kind of magic, she admitted. She couldn't give that up. Her work and research were such an important part of who she was.

'How long do I have?' she said.

'What day is it today, Friday? You'll need to come in on Monday. I can't hold them off any longer. I've known you a long time, Penny but you're taking advantage of our friendship …'

'I wouldn't call it a friendsh …'

'You have, Penny. I've defended you so often I'm sick of it. Make sure you have something to show us on Monday or be prepared to submit your resignation.'

He rang off, leaving Penny staring at her phone open mouthed with rage. Leaving her tea to grow cold she stalked up the stairs into her bedroom where her laptop lay open next to the window. There was no choice remaining. She'd have to give the university something. The weekend stretched ahead – not long enough – but it would have to do.

Powering up her laptop, Penny gazed out of the window to see it had started to rain again. The heavy clouds and damp chill seeping in through the frame reflected her low spirits. With quick strokes she brought up the notes and simulations she had stored on the hard drive. It was a good job she'd transferred her work onto her laptop rather than relying on the university's intranet. She couldn't access it from Pagan's Reach. Whether this was because the university didn't like the house's Wi-Fi connection, or her access had been taken away Penny wasn't sure.

Hours passed and the room was silent except for the soft clicking of Penny's fingers on the keyboard and the sudden billow and spatter of rain against the window. Eventually she took off her glasses and stretched out her arms to release the tension in her back. She was getting closer but it still wasn't enough.

It was just gone seven when, with a scrabble of claws and a pair of wet umbrellas, Angie and Frieda returned with a drenched Trevor. They carried with them a barely contained air of extreme excitement. Penny was too tired and disheartened to be good company so told them she was going to bed for an early night.

'You can't,' said Angie with a grin.

'I'm sorry Angie but I've had a bad day and just need to get some sleep.'

'You can't go to bed. Not yet.' She nodded at Frieda who walked up the stairs with Trevor. 'She's been on Facebook.'

'What? Why?' said Penny, bewildered.

'I never, in a million years, ever thought I'd say anything like this …' she said. Her eyes were positively dancing with delight.

'What?' Penny demanded.

'She's been in touch with some groups to help us.'

'What groups? Help us how?' Penny was fed up. She was tired and her mouth was sore. The day had been long and miserable and despite hours of staring at the screen had got nowhere. She just wanted to go to bed and pull up the covers to shut out the world.

'Come look,' Angie said, taking Penny's hand, noting sparks still leaped from her skin, but Penny had learned from Frieda how to contain her life force so touch no longer triggered an instant and dreadful draining.

'Where are we going?'

'Just to the front door,' she said.

Outside on the lawn three women stood. Penny could barely make them out in through the drizzle. Despite the cold and rain they were laughing uproariously. One was well into her eighties and hooked over a cane that was sinking into the turf. The other two were younger and wore long crimson skirts that stretched and billowed in the wind.

'Who are they?'

'They're from a coven in Edinburgh,' Angie said in triumph. 'We went out to collect them from the station this afternoon.'

'But … But …' Penny shook her head. 'A coven? You mean they're witches? Why are they here?'

'For you!' Angie said simply. 'Here she is.'

Mrs B was making her way down the stairs holding what looked like a twinkling length of tiny stars. She held it in the air as Trevor kept leaping up trying to snap at the rope.

'What's going on?' Penny asked Frieda as she led them out to the garden.

'We need to be outside,' she said. 'The moon will be up soon and we have to get to the top of the ridge.'

'This is Margot, Jenny, and Susan,' Frieda said, waving her hand at the three women. They turned to Penny with curious eyes and smiled.

'Hello,' Penny said. Her face felt stiff. Angie gave her arm a reassuring squeeze.

'Trust us,' she said. 'I think this may end up being something amazing.'

The walk to the top of the ridge took an hour. Progress was slow in the dark and the dampness in the air soon soaked Penny's hair and clothes so she shivered. As they moved, the clouds began to slide apart until the whole of the night sky, studded with glittering clumps of stars, shone brightly above them.

'Perfect,' said Frieda nodding approvingly. She was walking well but Penny noticed she favoured her right leg and as time went on her breath was short in her chest.

'Where are we going?' Penny said but the woman just grinned.

At last they reached the top of the ridge and the beauty of the sleeping valley spread before them with Pagan's Reach, windows glowing warm and amber, nestled in the arms of the wood.

Frieda led them to a clearing where the grass had been scoured away by the wind, leaving a polished stretch of chalk that gleamed in the moonlight.

The women fell silent. Penny, still bewildered, recognised a strange sense of ceremony. The three women huddled round Frieda's little crooked silhouette. Penny hung back for a moment to talk to Angie.

'Tell me again why those women are here?'

Angie dropped her voice to a respectful hush. 'Frieda contacted them. She tried loads of covens, but she's fallen out with all the local ones. She had to go further afield to find a group who didn't know who she was.'

'But why does she need them? She's so powerful.'

'She wants to do something special for you. I told her I promised you we'd help with your research, and this is the only way she could think of that might work.'

'I don't understand!' Penny exclaimed.

'Keep your voice down!' Angie hissed.

Penny dropped to a whisper. 'What on earth has this got to do with the Theory of Everything? Or Physics?'

'You'll see,' Angie said with a grin.

'Come here, Penny,' Frieda called, stretching out her hand.

The women moved into a circle and Frieda passed out the rope of stars so it twined round the six of them three times. They held hands.

'Close your eyes,' Angie said. Penny, caught up in the strangeness of it all, did as she was told.

Around her the women began to hum. The resonant note sounded in Penny's bones. Then they began to sing, and Penny opened her eyes in shock to see they had lifted into the air, tightly bound by the chain of light. The stars above moved towards them in dizzying spirals and darkness gathered beneath their feet in soft clouds.

How was this happening? Penny thought. It's a dream. It must be. The women climbed higher and higher. Stars and planets circled round them and still the rushing upwards, carried by the women's song.

She gasped to see the Milky Way ripple past and still they flew. Halos of stars grew more and more diffuse as they accelerated towards the infinite night that seemed to be seeping towards them like a dark puddle.

Penny, her head reeling, looked at the other women. Their faces were blank, only their mouths moved as they chanted the same words over and over again. A light fell on them as if they stood in sunlight while Penny shivered in the cold emptiness of space. She longed to rub her eyes but her hands were held tightly by the women on either side.

She remembered Frieda's questions about dark matter, gravity, galaxies and gas. Her eyes opened wide. They were taking her to the edge of the galaxy. Stars had thinned and disappeared. There was nothing but darkness. They were still. Frozen.

Lights appeared and stars and planets performed a ballet. Penny saw the movement of gases and the forces of gravity, picked out for her in pulses of energy. She frowned to see something else. Not as a colour or a light but a kind of faint pressure she could feel with her skin.

Penny's face cleared and understanding radiated bright and clear and she smiled. 'Eureka,' she said.

*

We stumbled through the dark laughing with exhilaration as if drunk. Arm in arm with Mrs B I couldn't remember a time I'd felt so happy. Penny walked ahead of us like an automaton. She positively vibrated with purpose.

The minute we got back to the house she disappeared to her room. Mrs B, Jenny, Margot, Susan, and I gathered in the kitchen and Frieda retrieved four bottles of her favourite Pétrus from the pantry. Margot smacked her lips over glass after glass of Bruichladdich showing no signs it had any effect on her eighty-year-old body.

At two in the morning, we realised we were all starving so I made goats' cheese and caramelised onion tarts which were gone within minutes, so I made another batch.

The kitchen was warm and happy and full of laughter. 'See?' I kept signalling to Mrs B with my eyes. As I searched in the chest freezer for the enormous chocolate cake to defrost, I thought of making mince pies and inviting the village up to celebrate Christmas. I could make jelly for the children.

I wanted to do more reading of the books left by the women of Pagan's Reach. Learn more about how to use my powers to heal and offer comfort. Fighting Joshua Pettigrew had also reawakened my dream of getting rid of evil wherever it could be found.

'What are you daydreaming about?' Mrs B said, appearing at the door to the utility room.

I turned to her, a beam spreading across my face. 'Oh, you know. What we can do, what we can achieve. How we can help the village, and anyone who asks.'

'Dreams of saving the world.'

'Well, why not? We have the powers to do it. I'm sure that's what the community who lived here would have done all those years ago.'

The old woman frowned. 'I don't like having lots of people about,' she said.

'You've enjoyed tonight. You can't tell me you haven't. Look what we managed to do together, the six of us. It was incredible … I mean …'

'Angie I'm old and tired, I'm not sure I …'

'You won't have to do anything! I'll make sure you won't be disturbed. And you never know – you might find you want to join in.' I reached to hug her, but the stiffness of her posture put me off. 'Look how much you've enjoyed spending time with those women tonight.'

She shrugged. 'Margot's Scottish accent is so strong I haven't understood a word she's said all evening.'

I laughed. 'I think it's more because she's drunk. What do you think? About the house? It needs a community don't you feel like it's really come to life with Penny here, and tonight has been so lovely. We should organise witch conferences!' My heart thumped at the idea.

'I don't think so,' Mrs B said with a snort. 'We're like cats, we don't like company …'

'But we like to know where witches are in case we need them,' I said. 'Yes, I know, you've told me that a hundred times. And you've put the backs up of all the covens we know. But maybe it's time to reach out and make some connections. But we don't have to be too ambitious. What about that parent and baby group to start with? It would only be once a week. The house would love it.'

'I suppose so,' she said slowly. Glee filled me as I saw she was relenting.

'I'll make some plans,' I said walking past her with the chocolate cake that was so heavy I could barely hold it. 'Do you want some of this? I'll put it in the microwave.'

'Of course,' Mrs B said.

The women left Saturday with promises to keep in touch. We had achieved something amazing together and none of us would forget it for the rest of our lives.

Penny didn't emerge until late on Sunday. Mrs B was in her room blasting Miles Davis' 'Kind of Blues' from her room as she did every summer.

'Is it too loud?' I asked her. 'Sorry if it disturbed your work. I can go tell her to turn it down.'

'No, it's fine, I like jazz.'

'So do I,' I said. 'But only for the first five minutes.'

She looked exhausted but radiant.

'How are you getting on?'

'Oh, Angie, I don't know how to put it into words. And you know what's strange? That machine – it was showing me the same movement we saw that night. It knew all along.'

I'd tried asking her what she'd seen that magical night but didn't understand her answer.

'I haven't got anything finished,' she went on, 'but it's enough to present my theory and it's going to blow everyone's minds.' She grinned with satisfaction. 'I am proof positive, Angie, that it's never too late.'

'What will happen next?'

'Who knows? But one thing I know for sure – they can't ignore this.'

She left early the next morning with a cheery wave from the window of my little car. I didn't know it then, but within the year we'd be seeing Dr Penny Howe's face all over the news. Her findings were revolutionary. There would even be a film.

Pagan's Reach became her second home and she'd visit regularly. Once, she searched high and low for that strange machine, but the house never let her find it again. I noticed in every interview when asked what had inspired her unifying theory she was always a little vague, saying it had come to her in a dream. And perhaps it had. Whenever I thought of that night the memory slipped between my fingers. I could never grasp it – maybe Mrs B had drugged us all. It wouldn't be the first time.

Trevor barked and pulled at my trouser leg as I waved Penny off. 'OK, OK, give me a minute,' I said.

The sun sailed high overhead as Trevor and I left the wood. Before us the long grass danced and swayed and he bounced straight into it, all sign of stiffness now gone.

I took a deep breath of the gorgeous sun-heated air and took in the scent of herbs and flowers and the rich, warm earth. I pictured the world turning and Autumn coming with its fruits and harvest then winter and the beauty of Pagan's Reach in the snow. Then it would be spring.

I would still be here, I thought, opening my eyes and marvelling at the ever-changing beauty of the valley.

I looked around to check if anyone was nearby. There was a huge oak a hundred yards away with thick, well-spaced branches that were easy to climb. The perfect place to start if I wanted to fly across the valley.

THE END

ACKNOWLEDGEMENTS

As ever, a massive THANK YOU for buying and reading this book. I hope you enjoyed it. It's always lovely to hear from readers, so do get in touch on Instagram, Facebook or Twitter as I'm always up for a chat about books, teenagers, and cake.

Thanks to my family for putting up with my constant absence as I disappear into the world of Pagan's Reach. Thanks to Paul for his endless patience and support. He helped me try and understand the Physics books I read and also drew the Feynman diagram on the cover. To my children Joe and Emily for making me laugh and being a constant inspiration. Also, Daisy the labradoodle who brings sunshine to our days and eats all our leftovers.

I couldn't put a book out there without my fantastic gang of beta readers who are so lovely to give up their time to read my (very) rough and ready first drafts.: My Mum and Dad – Penny & Peter Larkman, Helena Lestander, Ruth Muscat, Iga Patel, Jayne Samson, Una 'eagle eye' Willers, and Anna Woolston. Thank you so much – your feedback and support means everything.

I read a lot of physics books when researching Penny – most of which I didn't end up using. But I did get a brilliant email from Jonathan Oppenheim. Professor of Quantum Theory at the Department of Physics and Astronomy at UCL He was kind enough to respond when I wrote to him asking what a physicist would like a wizard to show him:

'I don't know -- depends what the answer is.... Mostly, we would like to see what happens at very small scale, which means the high energy scale, but I think it's also likely that gravity is modified at long distances (low acceleration). So, I'd also like the wizard to take me to the edges of the galaxy, where the acceleration due to gravity is small. Let me know if you know of such a wizard. Best, Jonathan'

For lessons in Physics that were fascinating and I'm sorry I couldn't use more of what I learned - THANK YOU to Laura Mulvey and Mark Orders.

Thanks also to the members of the reddit r/policeuk group for their very helpful answers on police procedure.

And to my mentor, Bill Browning. I couldn't ask for a better one.

The Woman and the Witch Series

Although 'Finding Frieda' can be read as a standalone novel, the characters of Angie and Frieda originally appeared in 'The Woman and the Witch'. You can also read about Frieda's exploits as a very young woman in the short story collection 'Airy Cages and Other Stories', as well as the second in the trilogy – 'Frieda'.

Here is a taster from the opening chapters of 'The Woman and the Witch' out now on Kindle, paperback, hardback and Audible.

Chapter 1: Frieda A Beginning

I knew I'd never die young. Illness, suicide, murder: none could *touch* me. Old age was something I expected. But this old? No. I must be over a century by now. What is a surprise, apart from the obvious horrors of skin swinging from joints and my once fiery eyes disappearing into floury flaps, is that I've mellowed. I'm not quite the evil bitch I used to be. I don't seem to enjoy inflicting the little cruelties that were such a pleasure when I was young. The mean-spirited jabs I'd dole out to people who had upset me are few and far between nowadays.

I still have a good go every now and then - that fool Andy didn't realise it was me who, with a flick of my fingers, forced his toolbox to crash to the floor. Spanners spun, clattering across my flagstones, one smashing into his elbow. A wince squeezed flat the puffed smuggery of his face, and I enjoyed watching him struggle to maintain the facade of the affable handyman. Good old Andy, here to help poor old Mrs B. who lived up the hill. Poor old Mrs B. my backside.

He comes because he's discovered my habit of slipping notes between the pages of books. Since he started working at the house, my Wuthering Heights is £50 lighter, Beloved has lost a twenty and my complete Shakespeare has been picked clean. Greasy fingers, more used to prying apart the pallid thighs of local tarts, have been inserting themselves between the pages of my books and milking them dry.

Firing him would be tedious. Besides, I quite like flexing the old muscles and torturing him, just a little: the sour slime clinging to the edges of the cup of tea I make with a smile, the fragment of glass I spit into his boots so he walks with a grimace. Sadly, I find as I age my powers have more of a cost; they are strong as ever, but inflicting pain leaves me with a hangover, no matter how justified the punishment.

Ha! The irony. It is almost as if a deity in which I don't believe has decided to make me a better person as I grow closer to death - good deeds seem to make my hair curl and my step lighter - bad ones give me indigestion and a headache. A shame, as I always wanted to be the girl from whose mouth toads leap, not the insipid moron who spills forth diamonds and pearls.

ABOUT THE AUTHOR

Amanda Larkman was born in a hospital as it was being bombed during a revolution. The rest of her upbringing, in the countryside of Kent, has been relatively peaceful.

She graduated with an English degree and has taught English for over twenty years. *The Woman and the Witch* was her first novel, and it was followed by a collection called *Airy Cages and Other Stories*. The second in the Woman and the Witch series, *Frieda*, came out in 2022 with *Finding Frieda*, the final novel in the series published in 2023. Amanda Larkman has also published a gripping thriller – *The Bookbinder* in 2021

Hobbies include trying to find the perfect way to make popcorn, watching her mad labradoodle run like a galloping horse, and reading brilliant novels that make her feel bitter and jealous.

She has a husband and two teenage children, all of whom are far nicer than the characters in her books.

Instagram: @Amanda_Larkman
Twitter: @MiddleageWar
Blog: middleagedwarrior.com
Facebook: Amanda Larkman: Middle Aged Warrior

Printed in Great Britain
by Amazon